Show
SERIES
JAMIE
COLLINS

PRETTY
Sensation!

PRETTY SENSATION!

THE SHOW SERIES

JAMIE COLLINS

Pretty Sensation!

(The Show Series Book 1)

by
Jamie Collins

© 2023 Jamie Collins

PREFACE

It is with excitement and gratitude that *Pretty Sensation!* has come to life. The first in the "Show Series", this book is an extension of my "Secrets and Stilettos Series", bringing the ladies of *The Gab* into full view on the talk show.

My fascination with the world of media and entertainment, paired with a passion for writing complex characters, intertwining plots, and redemptive themes, led me to create my first series. Once I invited the characters to present themselves in the process—I was hooked! Their stories poured forth in ink onto the legal pads steadied on my lap (no lie!) in writing sprints conducted on a train ride from a Chicago suburb to Union Station daily on a morning commute. That was a long time ago.

I have written in a turn-of-the-century apartment in Arizona with a view of palm trees and a small kidney-shaped pool outside my window. The very first book in the series came to life there, and it was there, so many years after those prolific train rides, that the first print copy of *Blonde Up!* was delivered to my mailbox. Yes, I cried.

Such is the creative process. The only thing that has since changed is that now I write seated at a desk in my office, on a Mac, with stacks of my books and folders of research surrounding me, forty miles west of Phoenix. I currently look at blooming cacti, desert terrain, and the majestic White Tank Mountains looming in the distance. A multitude of stories are swirling in my orbit, ready to be birthed.

Casey Singer's story as the youngest host has always been a fascinating character to write. She is garishly transparent, yet somewhat complicated in that one never really knows if she can act any way other than as a selfish brat. She comes to us as a fearless, broken, and wild young woman who is her own worst enemy in her quest for stardom—a scarred goal that taunts and eludes her at every turn.

Who is Casey Singer? And why do we care? I'd like to believe that we can learn lessons from her if only by *observing* her destructive behavior. There is freedom in living through the life of a character who is flawed beyond reproach. Casey's antics are large and loud, and she burns down more things than she builds. She is a force unto herself as well as in the lives of the characters she interacts with. Case in point, Bumpy Friedman, who cannot decide if she is an asset or a liability to the talk show.

Still, the public in this glittering world she is immersed in seems to eat it up, and the further she pushes the proverbial boundaries, the higher the ratings soar. Who could ever tame someone so set on barreling through life with such disregard for the rules?

Of course, the fun of it all is watching Casey rise and fall, regain and steady her footing in stilettos that she can't wait to kick off in exchange for cozy slippers. This is a frightened child masquerading as a Lucky Bitch.

Just as the "Secrets and Stilettos" series highlights each woman's unique origin story, the "Show Series" brings them into a common world, the halls, and walls of Global Network as co-hosts of *The Gab*.

For the reader, it will be the first time that all four women are featured together—their storylines converging—when they step into an elevator together for the first time in *Pretty Sensation!*

This is a moment in the book that gave me such a feeling of pride and satisfaction. I think that the moment creates a "payoff" for the reader that only gets better as the story and series progresses.

And yes, there will be three more installments to deliver on the continuing plotlines promised in the previous series for each of the ladies.

This book, *Pretty Sensation!,* is a collaboration thanks to the wonderful people who backed it from its start. My gratitude towards you is immeasurable for supporting authors like myself whose passion for storytelling is as infectious as the excitement of a book that keeps you grinning, gasping, chuckling, and perhaps even shedding a tear. For in such moments, we all win.

Stories move, teach, challenge, and delight us. Thank you with all my heart for contributing to this project and the continuation of this fun, fabulous, and drama-filled world.

Enjoy the ride!

Jamie Collins
Phoenix, AZ
2023

PROLOGUE
FALL 2021

Casey opened her eyes groggily, struggling to make out the strange images coming into focus. There was a nightstand with a clear crystal obelisk base and square lampshade. Tall blackout curtains behind a set of pleated chiffon floor-to-ceiling drapes were letting a stream of bright light shine onto the textured walls. Two matching ottomans and a chaise lounge in the corner were festooned with remnants of last night's clothing—panties, a bra, and one stiletto. She blinked and, swiping her hand across her eyelids, confirmed the sinking realization—she was still wearing last night's fake lashes—and nothing else.

The temperature in the room was blasting cold, and the sumptuous cotton sheets did little to remedy the fact that she was shivering. Her head felt like a bomb had gone off between her ears, and she still tasted the wrath of the Cuervo churning in her stomach. Her crotch was sore in the familiar way that only a night of unabashed banging could produce.

Her companion lay upright; still and silent next to her, bare-chested with the bed sheets in swirls around his hips.

She struggled to release her arm from beneath the billowing sheets and reached awkwardly for a leather-bound menu teetering on the edge of the night table. She squinted to read the gold-embossed letters in the half-light. It read: *The Regency Grand, Las Vegas.*

Then came the stinging realization that caused her to gasp. Drawing her hand up to her face, the gleaming and very large marquee diamond—set in . . . *silver? White gold? Platinum?*—loomed like an augury of doom. She was fucking *hitched!*

CHAPTER 1
ONE WEEK EARLIER

It felt amazing to be back in Los Angeles, if only for the weekend. Casey loved the fall weather, which still felt like a mild summer giving way to cooler nights. She escaped New York as often as she could, returning to the city she loved. She had a rider in her contract that allowed her to fly back and forth at her whim, which was often—so much so that she purchased a townhouse in Newport Beach that was only a four-hour flight away, and once there, in walking distance to the *better* ocean. The stuffy studio apartment in Soho back East did appeal to her Bohemian predilection, but even after several years, it never felt like home. The prospect of sharing her time in between coasts never got dull. In fact, she would fly anywhere at a moment's notice with a passport that never cooled its heels. Berlin, Amsterdam, Italy, Dubai—anywhere a potential job or audition would take her, except for one tiny continent—the UK, which was definitely off-limits. She wasn't due back until the end of next week, as the show was currently running the last of the pre-recorded episodes in advance of fall sweeps.

The past seven years had been a whirlwind. Casey was proud of her accomplishments in spite of the fact that many of the same relentless tribulations still followed her. She had amassed a series of bit parts, commercials, a reality TV stint that lasted only one season, and a brief attempt at teaching acting classes to cocky college liberal arts majors that did little to advance her career quite like she had hoped that it would. Still, in the advent of her thirties, with fine lines beginning to frame her signature blue eyes, she still could not shake the Gen-Y "Brat Moniker" that had become her hardened brand. A cacophony of escapades and bad press always seemed to tarnish her every chance at redemption. Even now. The acting-out and party-girl antics were expected, and regardless of how hard she tried to reel in the demons that seemed to get the best of her, they often arose, sending her spiraling out of control once again. It was a miracle the network continued to renew her contract, year after year. It was the *only* blessing, in her opinion. And it was getting old.

Casey adjusted the rearview mirror and settled in behind the wheel of the retro Mustang convertible. Her shoulder-length hair was pulled into a loose ponytail, protruding from beneath a Dodger's hat with wisps of honey-blonde strands escaping on all sides. The sun was high in the sky, and the road was hers along the beckoning stretch of Pacific Coast Highway. This was her bliss, far more enjoyable than memorizing scripts between talk show airings, flying out to auditions, or dodging paparazzi in the produce section at the local Trader Joe's.

She turned up the radio on the dashboard. The pricey vintage rental did not have satellite. *No matter,* she thought. The local stations would provide the perfect vibe for her Saturday afternoon cruise to Dana Point for the best taco lunch in all of Cali. She skipped across several stations on the dial until she landed on an eighties song that hit the spot. She smiled when she thought about her childhood growing up in a world that was light-years away from an abundance of technology and people germinating inane TikTok-inspired opinions around every corner. *Critics!* She hated them. Everyone was on fire for some cause or against her, it seemed, for just being herself. How could she be anything else? After all, it got her *this* far.

The deejay spoke over the fade-out of Whitney Houston's "How Will I Know?" eager to relay a bombshell of his own. He reported, "In entertainment industry news, music producer Roe Evans of Epic Media announced that he popped the question to his long-term girlfriend, Celeste D'Angelo, an East Coast socialite."

Casey hit the brakes and skidded to a jolting stop on the side of the road. *"What—!"*

She turned up the volume. The deejay had moved on and was now segueing to a George Michael ballad. "Here's one for the lucky newlyweds to be!"

Casey pulled her smartphone from her Chanel bag that had been slumped on the passenger seat. Her heart was racing, the car idling. She swiped away at the social media sites to confirm it. Her voicemail was full. Stacked with calls from Shelly, her best friend in Chicago, who had left no less than twenty texts that went previously unnoticed. Casey had had her phone on silent mode since the night before when she flew in.

Her hands trembled as she scrolled through the messages and the posts on Instagram, Facebook, and Twitter. "Shit!" she screamed, and then, removing her Gucci sunglasses, she buried her head in her hands. The traffic whizzed by, and the sound of the ocean in the background drowned out her screams of rage that went unheeded by passersby as she pounded the steering wheel with her palms, soon exhausting herself, causing her mascara to drip, mixed with the tears of an ugly cry.

Within a minute, she steadied herself and took a few cleansing breaths. Her yoga practice had taught her how to bring herself back to center in an instant. A skill that she needed to employ often, especially when the world was watching for her next move. *What now? What to do!*

She retrieved a wadded tissue from her purse and dabbed her cheeks, sniffing. She donned the Gucci shades and scrolled for a contact on her phone. *I'm coming to see you,* she texted, then tossed the phone back into her purse. She quickly pulled back onto Highway 1, performing a stunt-car-worthy U-Turn. Then, once centered on the pavement, she floored the Mustang back toward LA.

CHAPTER 2

The sun was high in the sky. By the time Casey had haphazardly packed her things, loading her bag down with an ample supply of clothes, accessories, and necessities, it was well into the afternoon. She tossed her Fendi duffle bag and hot-pink Versace vanity case in the backseat and then filled a small cooler with plastic bottles of water and power bars raided from the pantry. Grabbing that last apple from the fruit bowl on the counter, she jumped in the Mustang. Then, she rolled onto East Balboa Boulevard en route to Escondido Freeway. According to her calculations, she would be in Sedona by ten p.m. She set her mind and the cruise control on automatic and settled in for the 260-mile interstate stretch into Arizona.

EIGHT HOURS LATER, Casey pulled up to a ranch house on a triangular lot, bordered by Juniper, Ponderosa Pine, and Spruce trees majestically nestled in the shadows of the red rock mountains. The soft glow of lights emanating from the guest house behind the sprawling ranch home showed that Mona was ready to receive her guest. In fact, she was there, barefoot and beaming, on the terra cotta pavement extending from the house's massive front door.

"You're here!" Mona said, clapping her hands together. "How was the drive?"

Casey turned off the ignition and emerged from the car, which was covered in red mud, and a windshield splattered with all manner of bugs and debris. "Long!" Casey said, reaching her arms upward and planting her white sneakers firmly on the ground for a full-body stretch.

"To what do I owe the honor?" Mona asked. Her sheer floral robe was billowing in the soft night wind. It was quite possible that she was not wearing anything beneath it. Mona was a nudist.

"I just wanted to catch up with my agent and soak in some Sedona vibes." Casey smiled and tilted her head. "Hope that's okay?"

"It's more than okay, sweetie. You are always welcome; you know that. The guest house is yours."

She stepped forward to help Casey with her bags.

"No, I've got them," Casey said. "Why don't I settle in, and we will talk in the morning, okay?"

"Perfect. There's some chili on the stove, and the fridge is stocked. First thing in the morning, then." Mona winked and pulled her robe tight across her chest. "Make yourself at home."

"I will do that!" Casey said, shouldering her duffle bag and large purse, then grabbing the Versace by the handle. She walked around to the back of the house, beneath a covered patio, to the free-standing guest house flanked by a rock garden with water features and perimeter fencing. Mona kept it ready for clients and family who wished to stay in the retro 1980s-style Southwest Ranch that she had gained after the death of her husband, Burton.

Burton Waxman had been a talented artist and a master producer. Many of his modern sculptures festooned the five-acre lot on which the ranch house stood. Mona lived there alone, working from an in-house office where she maintained and operated her agency.

Casey liked the fact that Mona was exceptionally well-connected in the industry, and although she didn't always agree with many of Mona's philosophies and idiosyncrasies, Casey had placed her trust squarely in Mona, at least for her acting career.

Originally from Sante Fé, New Mexico, Mona had left home for California when she was a teen. She joined a commune in the late seventies and, at age twenty, left there to pursue her artistic endeavors. Mona "got lucky," as she often explained it, and on a whim, auditioned at an open call for a part in the TV show *Remington Steele* as a crime victim. They chose her for her extraordinarily long black hair and piercing scream. Mentored by another actress on the set, she was assisted in getting her SAG card. After appearing in a few made-for-TV movies, Mona found representation with a top agency in Los Angeles and landed a part in a rom-com motion picture in the early eighties. When things slowed down in Hollywood, she worked odd jobs to support herself between acting jobs at various talent agencies.

Mona always said, "You will know you've made it when you don't *need* the side hustle."

That took several more years to achieve.

Mona met her future husband, Burton Waxman, at an industry party. At the time, he was a show set producer who also loved to paint and sculpt. The two started a small talent agency of their own in the nineties, out of a small office in Burbank, which they ran together until Burton's fatal heart attack in 2014.

Casey was referred to Mona by an A-List influencer who also juggled the limelight between occasional reality TV appearances and the new opportunities that were blowing up with the onslaught of cable-streaming movies. Mona was plugged in and a whiz with contracts. She could offer her clients infinite ways to capitalize on their artistic content. Of course, Casey wanted more. She wanted to leverage her position with the network and garner acting jobs that would put her on the map, both nationally and internationally. The sad fact was that she was sharing the stage with three other show hosts on The Gab, and her rocket to fame was not taking flight as quickly as she had hoped.

This little visit would have to assure her that Mona had her best interests front and center, or their little love fest would be quickly coming to an end. It was time for Casey to break out into next-level success. Relevancy had an expiration date, and fame had its price. No one understood this more keenly than Casey Singer. *Screw Roe Evans and his misguided choices in life!* Why was she hanging on? What for? It was time, once again, to take matters into her own hands.

And that was precisely what she would do.

CASEY WAS EXHAUSTED. The shallow Formica bathtub held just enough well water to soothe her stiff joints from the drive. What was happening to her? She used to knock out a road trip, shower, and dash out to the nearest nightclub or rave for an evening of unabashed partying. Now, she was content with a lukewarm bubble bath and a cup of homemade chili? The cramps in her uterus that radiated deep into her lower back reminded her that womanhood was not all that it was cracked up to be when your body calls the shots and causes you to cry and bleed at the strangest of times. *Damn fluctuating hormones! Jeez, get it together, girl!*

She stepped from the tub, toweled off, and changed into her sweats and coziest T-shirt, glimpsing the full moon through the rectangular window on the wall across from the sink. Moonbeams danced on the terra cotta tile flooring, reminding her that she was miles away from city lights and beeping horns. This was the life that Mona chose every day. To be here, in the middle of nowhere, beneath the vast desert sky. The thought of it made her feel uneasy, strangely vulnerable in a way that was not calming and restorative. She'd hoped it would be good for her to come here. To take a few deep breaths and just take a beat. Instead, all she could feel was anxiety and dread. She padded to the kitchen in her slippers to see if she could find any weed in the pantry. Wasn't that where Mona said she always stashed it?

Casey heard her phone buzz from her purse. She hurried over to the couch to retrieve it. It was Shelly—her best friend, who had the power to detect whenever Casey was about to go off the rails.

"Hey! Please don't hate me. I saw your messages, but—"

"But nothing, *Chicka*! What is going on?"

"I know—"

"He's kidding, right? That woman he is marrying has burned through every eligible bachelor on the East Coast if you know what I mean!"

"I know."

"Well, girlfriend, if you know, then what are you going to do about it?"

"Nothing. I'm not even home right now. I'm here in Sedona to go over some things with Mona."

"Uh-oh. I see. So, you drove out your feelings with a road trip, then? Right?"

"Yes, but now they are still there. My feelings, I mean. I dunno . . . I'm just so upset over this news. Why? It's been seven years!"

"I am going to go out on a limb and say it's because you never got over him?" Shelly said.

"It doesn't matter. I have no control over the situation. But what I do have control over is my career, and I am going to take it up a notch. The talk show is running smoothly enough, but I will not be content with reading notecards and arguing the issues of the day in between laundry commercials."

"What does Mona say?"

"Nothing yet. I just arrived about an hour ago. We will talk in the morning. I need her to hear me and commit to my career moving forward."

"Or what?"

"Or I'll think of some other way to get there."

"*Chicka*, you know that I love you. I'm seventeen hundred miles away and raising two middle-schoolers, up to my eyeballs in art projects, soccer games, and dirty socks. I would switch lives with you in a heartbeat!"

"Oh, really?"

"No freakin' way! I'm just sayin', though, sometimes things get pretty hectic here in the great Midwest, and a trip to Sedona sounds like a dream! Count your blessings, *Chicka*. You've GOT this."

"I'm desperate here, Shel. My relevance meter is way too low, and I cannot take another hit against my ego. I think I'm just having the worst case of PMS in the world right now."

"Why don't you have Mona read your tarot cards? She's, like, really tuned into the stars and all that stuff, right?"

"Too into it if you ask me. Maybe that's how she's navigating my deals. I'm telling you, if I don't get something with Netflix soon, she's toast! I've suggested five scripts to her that I gained knowledge of—I can't say how I gained a knowledge of them— but she has not put my name in for one."

"Casey, give Mona a chance to explain things to you. She must have a game plan in one of her crystal balls."

Casey laughed. "Oh, right! For sure!"

"Take in the desert, sweetie. The sunshine. The fresh air. All of it. God knows that you have been breathing smog on both coasts for months. Try pulling back instead of pushing forward. It might do you some real good."

"I am sure that you are right, Shel. Thanks."

"Just watch out for snakes and scorpions. When are you back in New York?"

"Five days from tomorrow. I have to be there for the fall promo meeting for the new season. All hands on deck."

"Well, take advantage of the downtime. Listen, I have to go. The twins are back from practice, and I have to feed them. Enjoy your respite, *Chicka*. Send me a postcard of one of those vortexes."

"Ha! Thanks, girlfriend! *Ciao!*"

CHAPTER 3

The next morning, Casey slept in well past the rising of the full-on blazing Arizona sun searing through the windows. She buried her head beneath the pillow and barely heard the faint knock at the bedroom door.

It was Mona.

"Casey, dear. Are you up? I've made coffee, assuming that is your cup of tea."

Casey slid from beneath the comforter and walked barefoot across the cool tile floor. She opened the door.

Mona appeared with two steaming cups of coffee. "This is an organic, indigenously sourced, and healthy brew! No GMOs, shade-grown and sun-dried from Central America."

Casey reached for the hand-thrown mug. It was as heavy as a Volkswagen. "Do you have any sugar?"

Mona blanched. "That poison? Oh, no, dear. Small steps, I suppose. Here, I think there's some that someone left in the cupboard."

They walked into the sunny kitchen. Casey in her silk pajamas, and Mona wearing yoga pants and a cotton tunic. *At least she's wearing a sports bra*, Casey thought.

Mona was willow-thin with sunbaked skin. She had deep

creases around her elbows and across her forehead; her long silver hair was pulled in a ponytail at the nape of her neck. Her arms and neck were crépey and sprinkled with freckles and various constellations of age spots. Despite the obvious, Mona was the picture of health, grace, and calm. Her almost translucent pale-blue eyes suggested a contented soul.

Mona leaned against the sink while Casey pulled the heavy oak chair across the floor and slid onto the hard seat.

"I see you slept in," Mona said, smiling. "You must have needed the rest." She retrieved the sugar bowl from the end cabinet. "I have been up since dawn. I did my yoga salutations, ran a few miles, and then hiked Broken Arrow to cool down before breakfast. Speaking of which, are you hungry?" She retrieved a teaspoon from the drawer next to the sink.

Casey was. She could feel her stomach churn just as the scent of the coffee hit her nostrils. "Yes, wow—that's a lot of physical activity before breakfast," Casey said, stirring the white powder into the black brew.

"Cream?" Mona asked, at the ready.

"No, thank you. It's fine just like this."

"Well, come on over to the main house. I have made some healthy pecan pancakes—gluten-free, of course, and I have some wild-berry jam I've been dying to try in some steel-cut oatmeal. You'll need your energy for today's little workout I planned for us."

Casey remembered that spending the day with Mona was not a day at the spa, which sounded great to her right about now. It was more like boot camp. Mona was always keen to show off her lifestyle, mixing work with pleasure, as she liked to call it. As long as it didn't involve a sweat hut, Casey was game.

"Just let me get changed, and then I'll meet you in the main house."

"Sure thing, sweetie. Have sturdy walking shoes. I could loan you a pair if you didn't bring any."

. . .

MONA'S KITCHEN was contemporary and inviting, thanks to a renovation in 2017. The space was open and glistening, with granite countertops, stainless steel appliances, double ovens, and wide mahogany cabinets with modern hardware. The stone flooring was the same as the tiny guest house, but the ceiling was a light pine that looked like the inside of a sauna, with recessed lighting and a large square center island with a built-in stove.

Mona had outdone herself with a brimming ration of pancake batter in a large mixing bowl on the center counter. A black flat skillet was glistening on the stove, with sunflower oil at the ready.

"What can I help you with?" Casey asked. She wore her best designer athleisure wear, tie-dye leggings, and a matching crop top over a strappy sports bra. She hoped her white Nikes would do as she surveyed the set-up. The aromas in the wide-open kitchen smelled like heaven. She had brought her coffee cup and the sugar bowl from the guesthouse. Mona had arranged two place settings on the massive wood dining table next to the kitchen with its mix-matched wooden chairs and giant antler chandelier light fixture above. There were glass bowls of cut-up melon, bananas, and berries set alongside a pitcher of iced cucumber water and a small carafe of pomegranate juice.

"How many flapjacks would you like?" Mona asked, testing the grill. "I'm good for two. They are a pretty good size with my pour," she said, pointing to the coffeepot. "Help yourself."

Casey refilled her mug and leaned her elbows on the cool granite across from Mona. "This is all so nice, Mona. Thank you for rolling out the red carpet for me."

Mona's smile widened. "Nothing here resembles a red carpet, I'm afraid, Casey. I know it's not your style. But like they say, 'Don't knock it until you're tried it.' I have been trying to get you to come out here for years. Why now? Is Global Network not treating you well?"

"No, it's nothing to do with the show, or the Regina Madison

Agency managing my contract. Regina handles everything on that end, and she's great. *The Gab* has been renewed, and that is amazing. We are going on our seventh season. I guess I'm thinking more now about 'what else,' you know?"

Mona gave a half-nod and tended to the batter, now bubbling into circular cake forms on the skillet. "Be a doll, would you, and get the maple syrup from the pantry? It's the cabinet on the left there. Tell you what. Why don't we enjoy our breakfast and then take a walk? We can talk business then, okay?"

Casey smiled. The smell of the pancakes permeating the air was beckoning. "Sounds good."

She would need to figure out the right way to let Mona know she needed more from her as an agent and that she simply could not keep waiting for the right opportunity to manifest from the "universe." It was time to become aggressive in garnering *her* share of the changing and lucrative entertainment market. She wasn't getting any younger.

Three hours later, the two were high on a rocky ravine, overlooking a breathtaking view of the Airport Mesa overlook, one of Sedona's most splendorous dioramas of pure beauty and wonder. The two stood at the edge of a jagged cliff with a three-hundred-sixty-degree view of the red rocks. The hike was long and, at points, terrifying, with steep drop-offs that made Casey's stomach flip.

"This is one of the most popular spots for photographers and tourists vying for sunset shots over the red rocks."

"I can certainly see why," Casey said, shielding her eyes from the sun and twisting off the cap of her water canteen.

"This is also considered a vortex site. It's an area of concentrated energy that comes from deep in the earth and is believed to give off healing energies to those near it."

"Sounds kind of 'woo-woo,'" Casey said, struggling to

understand the logic behind putting one's hopes into some ether in the air.

"Yes, well, it surely brings in the tourists—thousands a year. People who are searching for something outside of themselves for solutions."

Mona looked thoughtfully at Casey, contemplating the one-and-a-quarter hike down, and said, "Let's make our way back. I know just the place for lunch."

CHAPTER 4

NEW YORK CITY

Executive producer Bumpy Friedman usually got his best ideas on the john. He folded the newspaper, fumbled with unspiraling a generous allowance of toilet paper, did his business, and flushed.

He then padded across the tile, wearing nothing but his boxers and house slippers, to his study to capture the fleeting thoughts he had swirling in his brain. Seven years in, and he was still tweaking and perfecting the show. One year now without his beloved wife of forty-four years by his side. Hylda's untimely death was a tragedy of proportions he had never known. If ever he cared even remotely about himself, his health, or anything else in the world, it all died and was buried with her when the virus invaded their lives and, due to equally invisible complications, snuffed the air right out of her lungs and stopped her heart.

As a result, Bumpy was a shell of a man. Heartbroken and lost in managing his emotions and life outside of work. Producing the show was his only salvation. That, and his indispensable assistant and millennial phoneme, Aubrey Flanagan, willow-thin Irish beauty with flaming-red hair and a bendy Irish brogue that made everything she said sound like music. Aubrey was twenty-seven, which put her squarely at the tail end of the Digital Natives, and her expertise with technology was a godsend. Where Bumpy was inept with 21st-century immersion, Aubrey was a maestro. She kept him on time, on task, and often alive with at-home meal deliveries of healthy fare and maid service on the regular. She took care of him, as he was often "in bits," as she was keen on saying. Her indispensable efficiencies both at work and as his personal assistant, along with cable TV and evening walks by himself in the city, kept him going, breathing at least, and moving forward.

Truth being, little in life interested or enlivened him. Or, perhaps, ever could again. Still, he put everything he had into the show and the network.

What was needed? He'd ponder constantly. What was required to stay on top? To be relevant in a changing world? What should remain the same, and what should go?

He scratched his balding head like a grizzled and eccentric professor in his skivvies, like the genius he was when producing good-quality television. He scribbled some thoughts with his lucky pen, and in large, printed letters, he spelled out one name and underlined it twice: CASEY SINGER.

CHAPTER 5

Mona had chosen the Indian Gardens Market and café in Oak Creek Canyon for its vegan menu and serene open patio. The seating area was quaint and quiet under the shade of beautiful trees that formed a canopy over the scattered iron tables and chairs, many draped with Aztec woven blankets—a bit of an anomaly in the somewhat oppressive southwest heat.

"This is perfect," Casey said, studying the expansive menu above the deli counter. The café also had an adorable little boutique where one could shop before ordering their meal. She and Mona carried their ample lunch plates and Pellegrino waters onto the patio and found a spot in the shade.

Casey had opted for the Hot Ferrari Sandwich with pesto, arugula, and organic tomatoes. Mona ordered a simple broccoli salad with sprouted lentils, radishes, and Brewer's yeast. It was a good time of day, as most of the lunch crowd had since thinned. The setting on the back patio was perfect for uninterrupted conversation under the backdrop of the stunning Sedona Mountains and the late afternoon sun.

"I am so glad that I drove up here," Casey said between bites of her Panini.

"Me too," Mona said, with a slightly exuberant look in her eyes. "I wanted to talk to you about something, and it's perfect that you are here right now. I didn't want to have this conversation over a text or email."

Casey leaned in. She left the other half of her sandwich untouched. *What is happening here?* she wondered.

Mona rubbed her leathered hands together, and a jangle of beads on her bony arms slid down her thin wrists. She appeared nervous.

"What is it, Mona? Just say what you are trying to say."

"I have been doing some soul-searching for some time now. And I have come to a place in my life where I think that if I do not feel like I am adding value to my client's lives, it is best that we part."

"What? Are you dropping me?" Casey was incredulous.

"Well, yes, dear," Mona said. She stopped fidgeting now that it was out and took a generous swallow of her bubbly water.

"Wait. You're firing *me*?" Casey shrieked. Her pulse shot up like a roadside flare.

Mona blinked.

People stared.

"Mona, I came here to tell you I was unhappy with your representation. That I needed you to step it up, or else I would break from *you*!"

This got a rise out of the naturally serene woman. "Well," Mona said, sniffing, "I guess I beat you to it. At least we both agree that this business arrangement has run its course. Casey, dear, I cannot promise you the roles you seek or the happiness you think they might bring. It's just not meant to be."

Not meant to be? Casey took a deep breath of hot desert air. *How dare she turn the tables on me!* She only meant to threaten Mona into working harder for her . . . not cut herself off entirely from the Hollywood pipeline.

"Well, Mona, I really don't know what to say. What exactly do you expect me to do now?"

Mona softened. "Look, I can make a few calls and—"

"Never mind. I have some ideas in mind and a few contacts who have offered their services. I will be fine. No worries."

"I am very sorry, Casey. I am sure that this is the best for you . . . moving forward. You deserve someone who can fight like a bulldog for your career, if that is what your soul truly wants."

Casey smirked. *What does my soul truly want?* All she wanted right now was to get as far away from the heat and the dust and the bullshit that was Mona Waxman. To find a club with an *actual* bar and maybe a band. To sidle up to a bottle of tequila and possibly one of those real-life desert cowboys who didn't just dress the part like the ones in LA. Right now, the only vortex she was interested in filling was the one between her legs. She was DONE. *No one tells Casey Singer what to do or when! Not Mona, not the network, not Roe Evans!* The last time she checked, she was the one who called the shots when it came to her career. Now, she would have to pivot—once again. So be it! She stifled the disappointment that seared deep in her gut.

"You know, Mona, I am going to take an Uber back to the guest house and get my things. I'll find a hotel for tonight."

"If you feel that way about it, dear." Mona's bracelets jingled as she crossed her arms. "Casey, I am really sorry."

Casey nodded, got up from the uncomfortable patio chair, and swiped at her phone for a car, leaving Mona and her bogus crystal-infused apologies behind.

CHAPTER 6

A shower, a wardrobe change, and a quick Google search turned up the Red Rock Ranch. It was rated a five-star, true-grit country experience, with a full restaurant and bar with live bands, state-of-the-art lighting, and a dance floor. Best of all, it was located a few miles from the Hilton Resort, where Casey had booked her room online. She packed the car before slipping into her favorite jeans, an ivory silk camisole, and python boots. Her skin was tan from the hike, and streaks of honey-gold highlights glistened against her shoulders, which had been bleached to perfection by her stylist back in New York. The blonde wisps framing her angular face could give any twenty-something girl a run for her money. Casey *looked* like money, and that didn't hurt.

CASEY CHECKED INTO THE HOTEL, deposited her bags in her room, and slid the key card into her Prada cross-body bag. She jumped into the Mustang, leaving the top down, and headed toward the club, driving right into the setting sun. The picturesque blaze of colors against the red rocks was ethereal and haunting simultaneously.

She pulled up to the Red Rock Ranch with its blinking neon sign, plank board, and hitching post entrance. She made her way to the bar, bypassing the restaurant. She was thirsty, not hungry.

Immediately, she could feel all eyes on her as she sidled up to the center barstool. She was no wallflower. A handsome cowboy from the far end of the bar sauntered over just in time to intercept her order.

"Don Julio. Neat—please," Casey said to the bartender.

"Put it on my tab, Rick," the cowboy said, pausing for effect. He took a long, lingering look at Casey and waited.

He was handsome, ruggedly so. He looked like the real deal, but one could never really know. His boots were not shiny, but his enormous belt buckle was. His fingernails were clean. He wore a black Charlie One Horse hat; he was drinking a premium beer from the bottle and smelled like Drakkar. Old school. It intrigued her.

"Thank you," Casey said. "Would you like to sit?"

His lips snaked into a crooked smile. "Yes, ma'am."

Good teeth, Casey thought and smiled back.

"I'm Casey," she said, licking her lips.

The bartender placed the generous tequila pour on a square paper napkin in front of her.

"Jake Trainer," he said, straddling the stool beside hers. He appeared about six feet tall and had a broad chest and biceps. *This cow-poke lifts weights*, she surmised.

"Hi, Jake," Casey said, extending her hand. She had the feels in all the right places when he gave her an earnest shake.

"Where you from, Miss Casey? Not from around here, I'd reckon."

"You would guess right. I'm sort of from everywhere. My work takes me coast to coast." She was sure that he did not recognize her. The bar light was low, and at that moment, she could be just about any girl from any town.

He took a swig of his beer.

The less talk, the better, as far as Casey was concerned.

The band kicked up a tune, and Jake touched her arm. "Would you like to two-step?"

Casey tipped the brown liquid and drained half the glass. "I thought you'd never ask."

FOUR HOURS and too many-to-count tequilas later, a trail of clothing littered the hotel carpeting where the two barely made it to the bed before stripping each other naked. The foreignness of his powerful hands struggling with her Chanel belt and the tug downward of her jeans nearly caused her to explode, coupled with his hungry rough-style kisses all over her face and bare breasts, sent her senses into oblivion. Casey didn't remember driving back to the hotel, and as it was, Jake the cowboy had to rummage through her Prada clutch for the room key. The two went at it until dawn, much of the event clouded by the tequila and the thoughts of rage and uncertainty that faded with each thrust of passion and carnality. At three a.m., they both finally passed out from sheer exhaustion.

At seven, Casey's eyes opened. She slid from beneath the covers and opened the drapes, letting in the full force of the morning sun.

"Hey, Cowboy! Get up! I am going to need you to go now, babe. It was fun, but I have to head back to LA," Casey said, fishing her panties out of the heap of clothes on the floor, feeling the wrath of her aching pelvis. She found his Calvin Kleins from under the bed and tossed them at him.

He rolled over with hangover eyes and a new grizzle that had sprouted on his chin, glistening in the sunlight.

That explained the rug burn on her face and nether regions.

"I hate to be *that girl*, but I really need to jump in the shower and get going."

"No worries," Jake said, slipping into the briefs. "I'll just get dressed and get out of your hair."

"I had a great time," Casey said, her voice trailing.

"Me too," he said, gathering his Levis and belt. "I'll just get dressed here, and then, if you don't mind, I'd like to call up some room service for you—some avocado toast and coffee, okay? I don't want to duck out without even providing breakfast. It's on me . . . no worries. I'll call it in, and it should be up here once you are out of the shower."

"You don't have to do that, Jake. Thank you, though." Casey just wanted him gone. She was already erasing the night from her mind as he stood there grinning like a bachelor contestant vying for the last rose.

"My pleasure, Miss Casey. Sure was nice meeting you."

"Same," Casey said half-heartedly as she disappeared into the bathroom and clicked the lock.

IT WAS JUST what he had hoped for. A clean opening for him to get to work. He waited to hear the water running, then picked up the hotel phone on the nightstand and hit the dial for room service. He reached for Casey's purse, which lay next to the phone, and rifled through the tiny handbag. Pay dirt—a black American Express Card, and a West Coast bank debit card, wedged in the front compartment. He quickly retrieved his phone from the pocket of his jeans and snapped photos of the front and back of each card, carefully placing them back into the Prada clutch. He then slipped her driver's license out of the second compartment and photographed it too. He stopped when he saw her full name. *No way! Casey* fucking *Singer!* He grinned like a cat that's found the dairy, recognizing her from the television show and salty tabloid stories swirling around about her for years. There was a small wad of cash in the purse that was tempting, but he did not want her to be on to him. He had what he needed.

A voice popped on the end of the line. "Room service, can I help you?"

He ordered the toast and coffee using her account. Then,

humming to himself, he strolled out into the sunshine, headed to his truck, and kicked up the red dirt gravel as he sped away.

CHAPTER 7

Casey tossed her bags into the backseat of the Mustang and snaked around the roundabouts leading to I-17, heading north toward Flagstaff. She had first stopped at a Quick Mart on Route 89A for provisions. Gas, gum, and a tall Styrofoam cup filled with Classic Coke. She estimated it would take just over seven hours to reach the luxury vacation rental she had secured over a hotel app while towel-drying her hair. The mountain-chic penthouse apartment at the Pinnacle Resort in Telluride would be the perfect antidote to the blast furnace hell hole of Sedona, where she hoped Mona would melt to paste along with her tacky Indian jewelry and flimsy wind chimes.

It was clear that "Moonbeam Mona" would not change her mind and ask Casey to come back. She'd rather spend her days talking to crystals or giving herself a sunshine enema, which apparently was a thing, right up there with tantric sex, sweat huts, and goat yoga. All the cactus juice and Lululemon athleisure wear in the world would not cheat the crumbling red-rock dirt of Mona's fading youth, that was for sure. In fact, she was probably giving herself a foreskin facial right at that moment, which she obviously much preferred over humping it for her clients. *Sayonara!* Casey thought. *Good riddance!* Crisper, cooler alpine winds and dancing rows of yellow Aspens were calling. So what if it wasn't ski season yet? The Pinnacle had a bitchin' spa!

ONCE ON THE INTERSTATE, Casey swiped at her phone where it was propped up in the cup holder. No calls except for Shelly, who was checking in, and several text messages from the network reminding her about the promotional meeting on Thursday. There was to be a photo shoot in the morning, followed by discussions with the studio executives and cast. Bumpy Friedman wanted all hands on deck to go over the last of the details for the new fall season. They had been running pre-taped shows all week to accommodate the preparation of the set design for the kick-off of the seven-year anniversary season. She would deal with all that later, leaving the messages in the queue unanswered.

Two and a half hours out of Telluride, Casey stopped at a Walmart. While snow was not in the forecast, the elevation brought brisk winds and cold temps that she was not previously prepared for. She reasoned she would hit the resort boutique when she got there for better apparel, like furry boots and cozy sweaters. The garish superstore was beneath her, with its bright lights and racks of cheap clothing right next to the bins of apples, potatoes, and pints of blueberries. Still, she grabbed a cart with a squeaky wheel and headed for the racks of winter coats displayed in the front section of the store. She loaded up on socks, warm leggings, fleece PJs, a puffy jacket, and a knit hat that came with matching gloves, then went down the candy aisle and grabbed a bag of assorted lollipops. She ripped it open, unwrapped a cherry one, and popped it into her mouth. Then she did a quick lap around to the electronics department, through Office Supplies, and over to the jewelry section. She eyed a pair of sparkly earrings and, without even thinking, she slipped them into her Chanel tote bag. Then she headed for the self-checkout. Minutes later, she was back in the Mustang with the lollipop protruding between her glossy lips. Without a backward glance, she sped away.

THE LUXURY penthouse apartment was picture-perfect. The expansive suite was rustic-chic and had floor-to-ceiling windows, multiple balconies, and killer mountain views. There was a full gourmet kitchen and an ample entertainment area with plush pillowed couches, wool designer area rugs with geometric patterns, and tall, leather-covered stools lined up to a fully stocked granite-top bar. A massive staircase with ironwork railings led to the second-floor bedrooms. Casey rolled her suitcase into a primary suite with a giant king bed with hotel-precision white sheets and pillows, a champagne-colored imitation bear's skin throw at the foot of the bed. The room had a walkout balcony with a stunning view of the San Juan Mountains. She plopped the bulging Walmart bags onto the floor and stepped into the cold mountain air.

The front desk clerk at the check-in had pontificated that the five-star boutique resort offered every luxury and amenity at her disposal. It was perfection. She had full access to the indoor pool, spa, fitness facility, and award-winning restaurants, or she could opt for in-residence dining with a private chef if she desired. This was more her style! Finally, she could breathe. The air was crisp and clean, and she was a world away from her troubles. Ski season was not in full swing, but it didn't matter to Casey. The invigorating air and Alpine beauty were all she needed to feel back on top of the world.

CHAPTER 8
NEW YORK CITY

Bumpy arrived at the office early, as was his routine. He liked the still hours when the halls were dark and empty, and he did not have to close his door to the chatter and bustle rising from the cubicles. He slept little and instead preferred the company of the night crew as they were finishing their shift. He would even make the coffee in the break room, scooping generous amounts of coffee grounds into the paper filter and sending the hazelnut aroma wafting through the executive floor. Aubrey would be at her desk by nine, bounding off of her morning train, either cheerful as a daisy or mad as a wet hen about some such transgression on the streets by some "Bleeding dope" on the subway or in the bagel shop who interfered with her early-morning solace. She was never to be crossed and was always threatening to leave when the assaults of the city got too ugly. "I mean ta get to New Zealand sum day," she would declare. "Somewhere down the road, anyway." As if it could even match in the slightest the hum and the rhythm of the Big Apple, Bumpy would appease himself by concluding. If she wasn't high-tailing it back to Ireland, he reasoned, she wasn't going anywhere. The reality is he would be lost without her.

He noticed the dozen red roses in full bloom that sat prominently on the left side of her desk for the past several days. A gift from one of Aubrey's many admirers who thought he had a chance with the redheaded beauty. Little did they know she was all business and couldn't be bothered with the likes of suitors who might see the built-in advantage of dating someone on the inside of a television network. They were all losers and wannabes mostly. *Schmucks!* With her parents thousands of miles away in Carlingford, Bumpy felt an obligation to look after her. The fact of the matter being, however, she was definitely no shrinking rose. She was one hundred percent as searing as a shot of Irish whiskey.

He unloaded a sack of warm Diet Coke into his desk drawer. A vice that even Aubrey could not get him to relinquish. He had ditched the cigarettes, the stogies, and even the occasional pastrami sandwiches, but the cola was his one saving vice. He couldn't think without the fizz. And without the thinking, there would be no show. No awards. No "next season" to produce. He checked his cell phone for a text, scrolling past an array of messages demanding various aspects of his attention. He had called Casey Singer himself multiple times to secure her commitment for the photo shoot. "One goddamn request!" he fumed. "Just call me back to confirm!" he said to no one.

"Confirm what?" Tom LeMaster, the head of corporate marketing, stood in the doorway with a chocolate doughnut jammed between his capped teeth, holding two paper cups of steaming coffee. He placed one on the desk for Bumpy. "Are you still trying to reach our little 'Darling of Daytime Talk'?"

Bumpy squeezed his now-throbbing temples with his forefinger and thumb. "She's M.I.A.—*again*. I swear, man. This shit is getting old. That one is going to be the death of me! It's like the rules don't apply to Lil Miss Hollywood."

LeMaster chuckled, folded his still-lanky but middle-aging body onto the couch cushions, and crossed his legs. "Yeah, what are you going to do? She keeps the younger demographic tuning in, what with her Instagram and TikTok followings. Have you seen the numbers? It's like we don't even have to run any promo. They can't get enough of her!"

Who was he kidding? LeMaster was right. But the negative drama was wearing him down. It was always threatening to affect the show. That's why he had to draw the line. Casey was bordering on becoming a liability, far more than an asset. Surely there were other relevant female celebrities who cost a lot less, were easier to manage, and who could appeal to the younger set. It was always something—like the time that she dated a rocker, and his hip hop "girlfriend" of two years showed up outside of an LA restaurant in Beverly Hills screaming at both of them at the top of her lungs. Casey punched her in the face with the TMZ cameras running, giving the girl a split lip. Casey was notorious for showing up at the last minute for live shows, hungover, giving Bumpy more gray hairs than he could count. He even had to hire a designated attorney on retainer—just for Casey! He had to pick up the bill for exorbitant charges to the corporate account, multiple no-show appearances, and even had to bail her out of jail once last June for shoplifting a pair of ten-dollar sunglasses from a Walgreens.

"What's the plan, Boss?"

"I suppose we could use still shots of her, but it won't be ideal. Somebody needs to find her. She's got forty-eight hours to walk into this office and show up camera-ready, or it will not be pretty!"

CHAPTER 9

asey slipped off the luxurious, spa-issued robe and sank her naked body into the steamy bubbles of the roaring hot tub. The heat and the vibrations coming from the jets felt heavenly. She closed her eyes and imagined never going back to the fast-paced demands of life. The show. The auditions. The unrelenting pull to be perfect. To be current, trending, and always "on" for anyone who wanted a piece of her. *Wasn't this the aim, though?* Wasn't this what she had wanted? It almost felt counter-intuitive to think otherwise. Had she reached the pinnacle of her dreams and desires? Or was there much more to strive for? To have? She sank lower into the bubbly water and willed her mind to relax along with the muscles that ached in her back and shoulders. She was carrying the weight of the world on herself, as always. Enough was never good enough. It could never be.

Then came the thoughts of Roe. The image of his face, his smile, his laugh. She could see every detail of his face in her mind's eye, a face she missed with a longing so real that it broke her. She thought of the way they met on an icy pavement in 2009 when she had left her going-nowhere job with KTBU and was staying with her best friend, Shelly, and her husband in an apartment in Chicago. She was returning on foot from the market when she slipped on a patch of ice—in moving traffic. Her body slammed against the side of his car, and she went down and blacked out. He was a vision she had seen, only for seconds, through groggy eyes. He had spoken to her briefly, and then he was gone. She had awoken with a searing, broken leg, cursing and despising the stranger who had struck her, causing her to fall, and then fled.

Two weeks later, an apology came as an exquisite arrangement of lavender and mini spray roses, along with a note offering to pay for her medical charges. The gesture was grand and planted a seed that only grew in Casey's mind and heart, causing her to believe that this man, Roe Evans, was special. He had turned out to be as much of an enigma as a sweet, torturous obsession to pursue in a game of cat and mouse that lasted for years in a flirtation and eventual consumption of their desire for one another. Until the worst of choices had to be made. The memories flashed before her eyes. *Damn him! Why can't I just let you go?* She cried, letting one tear slip through and splash into the bubbling water. No one was ever going to love Roe Evans how she could. *No one.* She took a deep breath and climbed out of the hot tub. Dripping wet, she wriggled into the heavy white robe and gel slippers. She padded away from the damp area. Perhaps the dry sauna would help.

She opened the wooden door slowly and stepped into the small, silent cedar-planked room that was spewing oppressive heat, heat that burned your nostrils and penetrated deep within you. The tiny room was empty. She would be blissfully alone. The smell of eucalyptus wafted in the heavy air, and the hot rocks steaming in the stove emitted a soft sizzling sound. She opened her robe and lay prone on one of the hot-planked benches, naked. She closed her cobalt eyes. The glow of the recessed lights calmed her along with the heat, transporting her to another dimension. It felt wonderful on her bare breasts, her stomach, and her thighs, until thoughts of Roe crept into her mind once again.

Shit! She sat upright. The hot rocks were not the only things blazing.

How could he do this? She weighed the facts—not one year ago, he was shacking up with an aging nineties sitcom actress who couldn't act her way out of a paper bag. She was then dropped once Roe got wise to her intentions of using his influence to get her tone-deaf son into Vanderbilt to become the next country-pop star. It had driven Casey crazy, knowing the woman weaseled her way into his life long enough to move in with him. Together, they lived in a large mansion in a suburb outside of Nashville while Roe footed the bills and maintained his transatlantic travel schedule back and forth to see his daughter, Jane, every other weekend. Prior to that, Casey endured a string of incompatible flings paraded on social media that had Roe entangled with everyone from a Louisiana senator's ex-wife to a female sportscaster to a countess with Scottish lineage who was Jane's nanny. Thank God that those relationships came and went! Casey was far too busy or distracted to keep track of her own life, let alone the flavor of the month that Roe was entertaining. But this situation was different. *Marriage? It will amount to nothing,* she convinced herself. It was a mercy marriage, as far as she was concerned. He needed to save face and perhaps find a stepmother for his special needs daughter who was willing to relocate to soggy England. Period. And who *was* this woman? There was nothing in the social media feeds at all. Just the ubiquitous announcement from an inane satellite deejay on a best-of-the-eighties station. Could she even trust it to be real? The heat was getting to her. She felt more like she was suffocating than relaxing. What she needed was a stiff drink.

AN HOUR LATER, she was showered and primped, sitting at the restaurant bar, phone in hand, scrolling mindlessly through her social media feeds. She even checked the online entertainment magazine sites for buzz about Roe Evan's pending nuptials. Nothing! She ordered a veggie burger with a side of sweet potato fries, comfort food as cozy as the pricey Ugg boots she had purchased in the hotel boutique, along with the toasty Burberry cashmere scarf she threw over a long T-shirt paired with her yoga leggings. There was a fire blazing in the lounge nearby, and hotel patrons were flittering in and out of the lodge-style atrium. A band was setting up on the small stage in front of the massive windows that framed the stunning mountain vistas in the background. Casey brightened when she saw heat lamps on the patio and several roaring fire pits. "I'd like to have my dinner out there," she said to the bartender.

"No problem," he said, swiping at his iPad and smiling. "I'll have your server bring it out to you, Miss Singer. Another glass of cabernet?"

"Yes, please."

He disappeared momentarily and returned with a generous pour. "There you go, Ms. Singer. Enjoy your dinner."

She smiled, scooped up the glass, and headed through the sliding doors. She found an open table with a magnificent view of the sprawling golf course. The band started playing just as the server appeared with her burger.

Not fifteen minutes into her meal, she noticed a tall, lean hottie eyeing her from two tables away. He was sitting alone, nursing a brown lager from the bottle. His knee bounced as he listened to the house band play a cover of Green Day. He looked attractive from where Casey was sitting, but it was hard to tell at a distance.

He continued to stare unabashedly right through her dinner, down to the last french fry. She had buried herself in her phone mostly, testing his resolve. As expected, just as the server removed her plate, he stood up and walked over.

"Hi—I don't want to bother you, but I think I know you."

Casey tossed her chin and chuckled. She would make him

guess. "Do you think so?" He had a familiar Midwestern accent that upped his appeal quotient considerably.

"Yes, but I can't place it. I've seen you somewhere . . ."

He bent forward and gazed at her. He had to be at least six-four. She felt like she had seen him somewhere before too. Then it hit her. *Wait. I know this guy!* He was an actor in a movie she had done two years ago for an indie filmmaker. They shared a single scene together, and she'd remembered his height and boyish good looks. He was Ryder McKinley. Chicago-born Ryder McKinley, who hailed from her own hometown and who was now a box office draw since his break-through role in a thriller python flick that brought him front and center. Still tall. Still good-looking. Now worth a fortune as social media's most-viewed bad-boy bachelor.

Just as she was about to solve the mystery, he blurted, "Casey Singer! I know you. We did a film together a while back! What was it . . . ?" He twisted his quirky smile, his trademark move, and snapped his fingers.

They both said in unison, *"Rip Cord!"*

Casey laughed. "Yes, that was it! How are you, Ryder?" She definitely remembered him from back then and the general appeal that came with it—unassuming puppy dog eyes, a deep baritone laugh, and killer dimples. He was said to be friends with Harry Stiles. He looked young, *boyish* even for his age, which she had read somewhere, was shy of thirty. No matter. He looked amazingly tempting and legal from where she was sitting.

"How've you been? Are you here alone?" he said, draining the ale in his beer bottle.

"I'm doing good. I have a permanent gig on the talk show *The Gab.* Perhaps you've seen it?"

"Yeah, I think so. All these women seated at one large table and shootin' the shit."

"Something like that," Casey said. "Guess it's popular. We're about to celebrate our seventh season."

"I've never appeared on your show," he said wryly. "But I've been on *Ellen* twice, I think. So, you guys better step it up!"

"I will tell the producers," Casey said, taking the last drink of her wine.

"Would you like another?" Ryder asked, motioning for the server. "And do you mind if I join you?"

"Sure. That would be great." Casey watched as he folded himself into the lounge chair across from her and got comfortable. He ordered another round. "We'll each have another, and how about a couple of shots? Tequila!" he said. "You okay with that?"

Casey nodded. *More than okay!* She noted he was evidently alone and verifiably single. *Check! And, check!*

The soft glow from the heat lamp, mixing with the bright moon, cast a glow around him she could only hope did the same for her. She ran her fingers through her hair, tossing it into a messy halo. The band launched into a Bryan Adams ballad, and they locked eyes. Something high voltage shot through the air like a circuit.

Casey quickly knew she was in trouble.

CHAPTER 10

NEW YORK CITY

Aubrey was on her cell phone when Bumpy emerged from his office early on Wednesday morning.

"Do you have this morning's numbers?"

The redheaded phenom reached forward, grabbed a folder from her desk, and handed it to him without missing a beat. She was speaking curtly into the phone. "'Twasn't a date the way you're thinkin', and I'm dun telling ya—end of discussion. I have to go. Sure, look—*goodbye!*"

Bumpy frowned. "Your mother?"

"Me mum is obsessed with me love life, or lack thereof," she said slyly, with the most delightful lilt in her voice that made everything she said sound like leprechauns and rainbows.

"She just wants you to be happy. It's her job," he said, checking his Rolex. Bumpy was low-tech. He had a smartwatch at home in a box. It was a gift from the sales team, but he didn't wear it. "Speaking of jobs, have you heard from Casey?" Bumpy asked, fearing the reply. "The promo shots are tomorrow, for God's sake."

"No, I haven't. My guess is that it will be donkey's years before any of us do."

"Why do you say that?"

"Aye. I saw this on me way in." She swiped at her phone and then held up a blurry photo on Instagram of Casey and actor Ryder McKinley alighting from a town car and dodging flashbulbs the night before at a Las Vegas hotel.

"*Christ!*" Bumpy shoved the reports under his beefy arm and headed back to his office, slamming the door so hard that it shook the media awards on the "Wall of Fame" in the adjacent reception area.

He jumped on the phone to conduct damage control. This one was out of control—again! He could feel it. A big, steaming pile of shit was about to explode. His gut was never wrong.

SIX FLOORS BELOW, a flurry of activity ensued like a well-oiled machine. The approximately two hundred people spread over seven floors needed to successfully launch a programming season of highly engaging, smart, funny daytime TV. The cast and crew, both visible and in the trenches behind the scenes, had been working toward the same goal—the upcoming launch of the fall season of *The Gab*. Many meetings, design sessions, and writer collaborations would soon culminate into season seven of the number one-rated talkfest in the eleven a.m. day-part for the network. Global had a lock on the 25-54+ demographic, who found their news and tantalizing talk served smart and sassy with a mid-morning latte or who recorded the show faithfully for later viewing before turning in for the day.

DEANNA CALVIN'S desk phone buzzed. She was just about to dive into an everything bagel before heading over to the graphics department to inspect some proofs for the holiday social media campaigns. It was the boss.

"Hello, Mr. Friedman. To what do I owe this honor?"

It was not customary for Bumpy to phone down unless there

was an issue. Deanna had been at the job long enough to know that the higher in the chain, the bigger the problem.

"Hi, Deanna. I have waited to make this call, but it seems like we might have a bit of an *issue*. The photoshoot that is scheduled for tomorrow. How much wiggle room do we have with the cast photos?"

"Whom are we talking about here?" she asked, knowing full well the answer.

"Casey Singer. She is not responding to our calls. She is potentially not going to show. Do we have a workaround?"

"Yes, I suppose we can go with some previous group shots and some stock clips. It's not the best situation, but we can get by on that if we have to. I just need to have something in place to launch the social media campaigns this weekend. As long as it's still the fabulous four!"

"Thanks, Deanna. Just checking to see what type of damage control is needed. We'll let you know if we will have to improvise."

He was gone with a click, and the not-so-young publicist lifted her eyes to heaven. "That *girl!*" Casey Singer was always the delay, always the reason that budgets got blown and work had to be done and re-done in tight turnarounds. *Skinny girls!* She despised them, especially how they seemed to get away with anything. Especially that one! If they weren't up for another Emmy, she would dust off her resume and take a hard look at gig work. She could promote anyone, anywhere, anytime in a digital world that was fast-abandoning traditional television ad time and buys and jumping ship to streaming and virtual realities. *Real*-reality was not all it was cracked up to be.

CHAPTER 11

LAS VEGAS, NEVADA

The events of the past many hours were like a dream for Casey. She'd remembered how they stumbled from the patio lounge up to Ryder's suite after several rounds of top-shelf tequila and too many U2 tunes to count. They collided on the way up, in the elevator, with hard, probing kisses before the doors slammed shut. Casey peeled off Ryder's clothes, piece by piece, yanking at his belt, letting it strike the floor of the moving elevator like a whip. She giggled as she magnetically found his manhood and latched on as the doors sprang open.

She bit his ear, his lip, and licked the deep crevices of his dimples, causing him to practically explode before reaching the hotel room door.

They tumbled onto the bed, and Casey gasped as Ryder got to work on her boots, undressing her too slowly for her unbridled desires. She was wearing too many layers to make the task easy, so she shimmied off her T-shirt and yoga tights herself when he left momentarily to flip on the stereo in the next room. Soon, the sounds of Lizzo were thumping from the speakers when he returned, and Casey was sprawled out in her lace bra and panties on the bed.

Ryder lowered himself on top of her, caressing her breasts

and running his tongue along her stomach. She arched into him with every electric touch.

They made love for hours, then ordered room service, and talked late into the night before deciding on a very drunk and ludicrous whim to jump a red-eye to Vegas. It was spontaneous and reckless, and every fiber of Casey's body wanted the thrill and adventure that Ryder offered. He was perfect. Hot, sweet, sensitive—and he made everything seem like a free fall into pure bliss. She didn't want it to end. She threw together an overnight bag and slipped into her jeans, a camisole, and a black blazer. She had tossed a pair of Louboutins in the Mustang before she had left LA, which she retrieved from the floorboard behind the driver's seat. She was all set. They popped a bottle of the hotel's finest champs before leaving the rest of their belongings in Telluride, letting the bubbly spill into plastic cups in the Uber on the way to the airport to keep their buzz going.

They couldn't keep their hands off each other. The one-hour-twenty-one-minute flight to Las Vegas offered a dark cabin of only a few passengers and an opportunity that found them upright in the compact restroom, banging away with Casey bent over the tiny toilet with the turbulence only adding to the thrill ride.

She had vague memories now of climbing into an Uber at McCarran airport and driving to the Strip. They partied at several clubs. In the early-morning hours, Ryder had bought two tiny white pills with the letter "X" stamped into them. It wasn't the first time that Casey had tried ecstasy. She threw caution to the wind and downed one pill with her fizzy drink, and the rest of the evening was a multi-colored, dizzying blur.

They inadvertently danced until the bewitching hour; then they ended up booking an on-the-fly Wedding Package experience at Archway Chapel after stopping off at an all-night jeweler. Ryder paid for their rings with his Black American Express Card. She remembered that the Elvis impersonator (old Elvis in the white jumpsuit) performed the nuptials, which went by quickly.

There was more champagne, and an out-of-nowhere paparazzi snapped their photo as they climbed into a waiting car on their way to the hotel.

They were whisked to the honeymoon suite, which Ryder had booked online, sparing no expense. When they arrived at the Regency Hotel, it was pulsing with lights and noisy slot machines in the lobby. They stumbled, exhausted, into a quiet elevator. She was, at that point, oblivious to the details of events of the previous several hours. Casey could see, however, in the mirrored doors, she was wearing a make-do tulle veil that was misshaped and looked ridiculous on her head.

Everything went black after that until she awoke to the Nevada sun—and the truth.

One hour later, after frantically scurrying around the hotel room, gathering their clothes and a quick shower, Casey and Ryder stood silently in the elevator as it swiftly descended to the lobby. They had each channeled their disbelief and shock by quickly planning for an immediate return to their previously already-flawed lives. Ryder had called his assistant to have him arrange a one-way ticket on a flight to Telluride and then an afternoon departure out of Colorado for himself to LAX and back to his Malibu residence. Casey went online to book her flight back to Telluride to pick up her things and her car. She would then drive back to LA, with plans to head back to New York.

"It looks like we are on the same flight," Ryder said as they stepped into the busy lobby. "We have a bit of time. Do you want to get some breakfast?"

Casey nodded, although her stomach was churning. There would be plenty of time later for beating herself up for the obvious and inconceivable lapse in judgment. *What was she thinking?* A sour bile was boring through her throat. For now, that, and the pounding in her head, was enough of a punishment. She darted into the gift shop for a quick minute to purchase a silk scarf, which she tied over her damp hair like a 1950s movie star, and slipped on her Gucci sunglasses. "Now I'm ready," she said as they waded through a throng of tourists to the hotel restaurant, hoping to avoid being noticed.

"Casey, I—"

"Please, Ryder. Say nothing right now," Casey said as they slid across from one another in a booth. Casey was in a state of shock. She was numb from head to toe and was in no position to figure anything out. "Let's just get back to Telluride, collect our things, and check out. You go to your home, and I will go to mine. I have to be back in New York tomorrow morning, and I just don't have the capacity to deal with this right now."

"I hear ya. Me either," he said, folding the papers he had been gripping that officially declared the drunken sham marriage valid into the back pocket of his jeans. "It was a mistake."

"Yes, it was a mistake."

Ryder softened with relief.

The server appeared, and they ordered. Casey could only stomach coffee and toast.

They sat in awkward silence until the food arrived.

"I am calling my lawyer later this afternoon," Ryder said, pouring too much cream into his coffee cup. "You should do the same."

Casey nodded. "Of course."

Great. She thought to herself. *Regina is going to shit when she hears about this!*

CHAPTER 12

"Y ou did *what!?*" Shelly slammed hard on the brakes. She was in the parking lot of the suburban elementary school, inching slowly forward in order to merge into the pickup line that was forming just outside the west gate. The Mercedes SUV was next in line to approach the curb when the irate driver in front of her honked the horn and glared at her in their rearview mirror.

Shelly rendered her palms in apology.

"I said that I got married yesterday," Casey reiterated matter-of-factly. She was cool and unemotional.

Shelly threw the car into park. "What? *Jesús María!*" She had T-Minus seven minutes until the dismissal bell would ring, and her twins would bound into the backseat. Who was she kidding? This was *Casey* she was talking to here! "Spill it, girl. And leave nothing out! Where are you?"

"I'm driving back to LA right now. I was in Telluride, and—"

"Wait, I thought you were in Sedona."

Casey sighed. "Well, I was—but then, I had this urge to drive to this resort. You know, find some crisp, clean air. Anyway, I was only there the one night, and then I met this guy who was checking me out in the lounge. It turned out to be Ryder McKinley and—"

"*Shut-up!* Not the actor?" Shelly was breathless with anticipation.

"Yep. That's the one," Casey said, letting the news sit with her BFF on the other end of the line.

"Go on," Shelly breathed. She knew better than to try to guess the details.

"Well, we started talking, and then shared a few drinks, and then, one thing led to another, and we ended up in Vegas and—"

"Married! You actually got *married*?" Shelly planted her forehead down on the steering wheel, causing the horn to honk. She looked up at the glaring face of the driver in front of her and gave a little wave.

"Apparently so," Casey said. She was, for once, short on explanation.

"Well, are you sure? I mean, do you have any proof?"

"Yeah, he has the papers—a receipt for the rings, as well as the marriage license and the receipt from the chapel. It's legit."

"Holy shit! *Chicka*, this is insane! I mean, did you want this?"

"Shelly, of course I didn't want this! I'm still in shock. Imagine my surprise when I woke up this morning with a blistering hangover and an enormous diamond on my hand."

"How's the ring? I mean, is it nice?" Shelly had to ask.

"It's nice, yes, but it's ridiculous, Shel. This is all ridiculous. We have matching bands as well. Oh my God!"

Shelly could hear that Casey was now unraveling on the other end of the line. "You're not driving, are you, *Chicka*?"

"Yeah. I'm a few hours out of the city. I spent most of the drive in a trance, trying to figure out what to do. I have no idea if any of this has hit social media yet. I mean, there were photos taken, I think . . . I dunno. It's all kind of fuzzy."

Shelly was one step ahead of her, quickly scrolling through her phone's social feeds. She stopped on a clear shot that showed the two exiting a nightclub arm in arm, tumbling into a waiting sedan.

It was too late. It was already happening.

"Don't look at anything. Not until you get back home," Shelly said. "Just get home safely."

"I have to fly out to New York tomorrow. I have obligations with the show," Casey said. "Shel, what am I going to do?"

"Nothing. Do nothing—yet. What does Ryder McKinley think?"

"He agrees it was a mistake."

"Oh, thank God!" Shelly exclaimed. "You two will work this out. It can be undone. The sooner, the better, right?"

"I guess so."

"Get home safely and then call that lawyer of yours. What is her name?"

"Regina Madison. I'll give her a heads-up. Oh, she's going to be pissed," Casey said.

"Hey, think of the upside, girlfriend. She owes you one big fat wedding present, and now she's going to have to actually earn her money!"

Casey let out a yowl of laughter. "Right! Hey, maybe this little faux pas will not turn out all that bad."

Shelly shook her head and smiled. She knew all too well that if anyone could turn a shit storm into a day on the beach, it was Casey.

"Okay, *Mrs. McKinley*, keep me posted. Hey! It has a nice ring to it."

CHAPTER 13

LOS ANGELES, CALIFORNIA

Casey was back home in LA that evening. The thirteen-hour drive was exhausting, and all she wanted to do was collapse into her sumptuous sheets and down pillows and shut out the world. She had already packed her luggage for her departure to New York and placed it at the front door. She was deft at keeping her work wardrobe and sundries separate and at the ready so that she could bounce at a moment's notice to the airport. Unfortunately, she would have only a couple of hours of blissful sleep before heading to LAX to hop on a red-eye to LaGuardia. She would arrive around 8:30 a.m. and, with weekday traffic, walk through the studio doors, hopefully only scantily late.

The alarm on her phone rendered its irritating trill, and she forced her head off the dent of pillows that surrounded her. She slipped into the shower and let the water revive her, although her body felt like it had been three rounds on the game show *Wipeout*, which she had smartly turned down as a promotional gig. *Note to self*, she had thought. While her body still looked good, she was definitely feeling the wear and tear of too much excess and too little sleep. How would she ever get through a stint on *Dancing with the Stars* if they ever came calling? This was the price for pushing oneself beyond the boundaries, for sure.

Casey slipped into a bodycon knit dress, opaque leggings, and combat boots with rhinestones. She grabbed her long wool coat and stuffed her gloves in the pockets. She ran some gleaming eyeshade on each eyelid, applied a few whips of mascara, dabbed on some lip gloss, and pulled her mane taut into a low ponytail.

It would have to do.

On the car ride to the airport, she swiped at her phone for a reality check. There were several texts and calls, some from the Network, two from Shelly, and some unknown numbers that she presumed were reporters. She could not even think of dealing with any of that. Not yet.

Her social media platforms were filled with the usual traffic of inane voice-over videos with trendy sounds and antics, along with endless posts of cats and fashion ads. She tapped on an entertainment app to peruse the headlines—there it was—an alert from *People Magazine* announcing *Music Exec. Roe Evans to wed socialite Celeste D'Angelo.*

Casey's heart sank. There was a collage of photos, including one of Roe and his intended, hand in hand posing at a fundraiser in front of a press wall along a red carpet runner, beaming for the photographers' lenses. Roe was even holding Celeste's cheap little clutch!

Casey swiped through the images, examining every detail, looking for some explanation for the reality. *What does he see in her? What does she have that I don't?* And the searing regret that suggested that she'd had her chance but chose differently. *Why couldn't she have it all?* Why fucking not!

A few swipes more, and there was her answer—a full-on photo of her and Ryder McKinley running out of the little Vegas chapel, all giggles and blurry-eyed, hand in hand—wearing wedding bands. *Pow!* A fan took it. Well, if there were any chance the shit-storm would possibly hold off until she could get Regina, her lawyer, to conduct damage control, it was quickly fading. It was only a matter of time.

Casey bit her lip and steadied her breath. The comments, from what she could see, were pouring in. *"Lovely couple!"*, *"Congratulations Casey and Ryder!"*, *"Why'd he settle for that Ho?!"* and *"Hope these two have prenups!"*

The emojis ranged from infinite rows of pink and red hearts to grimace-face, shrug-face, and ZZZ passive-aggressive digs. A few angry psychos even lobbed death threats on account of their undying obsession with Ryder.

Casey took a deep, centering breath and then ditched her phone deep into her purse.

An hour later, she was lingering in a painfully long security check line. Once she finally got to the gate, she was exhausted from dragging her over-stuffed carry-on and operating on little-to-no sleep from the events of the past seventy-two hours. She would try to get some sleep on the plane.

She found an empty chair near the large airport windows in the waiting area for the flight to LaGuardia. People began arriving. She was next to a family with two sleepy-eyed young boys still wearing their footed pajamas. The mother was ripe with another one on the way, and they were fiddling with the double-barreled stroller. Casey smiled at them. From behind her Gucci shades, they could not see that she was crying. Her heart felt like it was just punctured like a child's balloon, and a gnawing regret seared in her gut. She felt the weight of the ring that encircled her left finger and wondered, *How am I going to play this?* Was she going to be the victim and call foul on her life? Or was she going to spin this so that it looked as if she was doing just what she wanted to do, to own it as if it were her *choice*? At least she beat Roe to it. *She* got to the altar first. That definitely took some of the pain out of it all, didn't it? She would figure it out.

She wiped a tear with a wadded tissue that she found in her purse. Taking a deep breath, she fished further for her phone and then shot a text to Regina Madison—*Call me 9-1-1.*

A voice announced on the intercom that it was time for first-class boarding.

Casey grabbed her carry-on, shouldered her purse, and walked through the jetway.

CHAPTER 14

LOS ANGELES, CALIFORNIA

Regina Madison was nothing if not efficient. Even with the aid of a nanny, she made it a point to spend time with her daughter, Gael, every morning and help with the morning ritual—toast, cereal, and cartoons while Marianna got to work on the morning dishes.

Regina's husband, Bridger, was always awake before the two of them. He had a brisk workout in the home gym, would whip up a protein shake, and was out the door by seven sharp. He had a thirty-eight-minute ride from their home in the Palisades to his studio door in Hollywood.

Having a producer husband was not all it was cracked up to be. Nor was moving to the West Coast to accommodate her husband's career aspirations. Hers were not geographically dependent. Between Bridger's erratic schedule and her relentless stream of whiny and dysfunctional clients—and parenthood—Regina barely had time for herself. They were currently trying for a second, and while it was something they both wanted, it added an extra layer of stress to an already-overflowing to-do list. She had a great husband, two more frozen embryos, a palatial modern Mediterranean, a cook, a maid, and a full-time nanny. Even so, she worried incessantly about her fading looks and keeping her husband happy. In Hollywood, having brains and ambition was nice, but beauty and sexual allure were *everything*. Plus, she constantly felt like a fish out of water, missing her East Coast roots.

She could not buy any more hours in the day, but she could do all she could to keep up with the other "Mrs. Joneses" and not fall back and out of favor in her circles. Women were mean, and that was just the truth of it. She did not trust any of her new gal-pals in their rich ivory towers. She knew better than to trust anyone except herself and her highly desired husband, who registered as a prime "get" for any aspiring blushing young actress or ultra-nipped, tucked, and frequently fucked-up housewife who was bored out of her pretty little mind and looking for a conquest.

Today, Regina wanted nothing to spoil her day. She looked at her daughter, who was now yawning and stretching gleefully in her highchair.

Regina smiled. She could not love her baby girl any more than she did. Little Gael was the perfect blend of her and her husband. Gael had large, only slightly almond-shaped eyes, deep blue like her father's, and soft, sandy curls like his. Not the distinctive Asian features of her mother's heritage, but Gael's face was broad, and her pert nose was the mirror image of Regina's. In disposition, baby Gael shared her mother's bold, capricious Chinese tiger sign and had a set of lungs to match! That was the jackpot from the gene pool that blessed her little girl with a fiery spirit that would serve her well in life.

Regina's day was packed, as per usual. She had a succession of Zoom meetings in the afternoon, followed by a stack of contracts to review and press statements yet to draft. Problems were exploding everywhere, and her job as an entertainment lawyer was to put out the fires. It seemed to come in waves. *What good are the agents who represent the talent in this town?* she wondered. It was their job to keep her clients out of the tabloids and hers to keep them out of jail. More often than not, she had a complete debacle when it finally blew up. Something in her gut told her that a shit-storm was coming. Her intuition was keen, and she prided herself on typically being right in her gut. That was the East Coast blood in her veins.

Her phone buzzed. Little Gael squirmed in her highchair, blowing spit bubbles between bites of her cereal bits.

The screen read, "Casey Singer." It was always something with that one. Like the recent past when Casey had developed an unhealthy addiction to fast cars, DoorDash from the finest restaurants in LA, and an insatiable revolving open account at Nordstrom, Neiman Marcus, and Barney's that kept blowing up her credit cards to sky-scraping limits. Taking on Casey Singer as a client was a favor for her old friend, Baltimore Ramirez. He had said that she was difficult, but she would be worth the efforts in billable hours. Casey was the gift that kept on giving, all right.

She could leave a message.

CHAPTER 15

The flight was uneventful and allowed Casey to catch some shuteye. She was out before the plane even took off. She loved red-eyes for the peace that could usually be assured. Flying in the darkness appealed to her as she transitioned from the West Coast's laidback vibe to the bustle of the East Coast and New York's manic rhythm that commanded a distinct energy. She checked her phone—one more hour, at least until landing.

Casey perused her phone for an article she had saved about a role in an upcoming sci-fi/dystopian film slated for production. She had always dreamed of playing the part of a true action heroine, like Jennifer Lawrence in *Hunger Games*. The movie's working title was *Starbreaker,* and it was cast out of Los Angeles. She was tired of playing the vapid-headed, tragically damaged roommate or psycho ex-girlfriend in *Lifetime* movies. She needed a blockbuster to her credit. It would be the type of exposure that would garner more considerable currency at the box office—on her own merit—not on the coattails of a costar, and certainly not on the back of Ryder McKinley. She had planned to pitch the suggestion to Mona as a last-ditch test of her commitment to Casey and her career, but that was over. So now what?

It was imperative that she find someone to take her on. She knew she needed top-level representation if she was ever going to score a real, respectable role. Casey scrolled through the contacts in her phone until she landed on Spaulding Caine, a lead given to her by the casting director for *The Gab*, Sawyer Landry. Sawyer claimed that Spaulding's projects turned to gold and that he was the best bet for anyone looking to break out— even if one's career path was ten years in the making. As far as Casey was concerned, she had not yet reached her peak, and the best was yet to come.

She composed a quick email to Caine, mentioning the referral from Sawyer, even though she was sure he would be familiar with her work on *The Gab*. She wasn't sure if he was taking on new clients, but what did she have to lose? No gimmicks. No grand gestures. Just an honest ask. *What could it hurt?* She clicked send.

CHAPTER 16

NEW YORK CITY

Casey was touching up her glossy pink lips in the car as it swerved to miss a cyclist on 49th Street. She huffed and looked in the mirror. She looked okay despite the lack of sleep.

"Can you go faster?" she said.

Her smartwatch glared at eight fifty-eight.

"You can leave my bag with the building security desk," she said. "I'm in a hurry to get up there." She tilted her head and surveyed the towering steel building with its gleaming windows and massive chrome-shined doors. GLOBAL STUDIOS loomed in large, sleek metal cutout letters atop a marble and glass atrium. The building stood like a beacon against the bright blue sky. It was not the tallest structure against the behemoths of New York grandeur and infamy, but the network had a prominent place in the concrete jungle that was a testament to the innovation and resilience of media, business, and commerce in a world where people had a myriad of choices and television viewership was getting harder to garner.

The last thing in the world she would need would be the wrath of three irate coworkers who would wait on her, worrying about their precious ratings, there in the conference room with all and sundry production staff responsible for pulling off the live shows every weekday. Well, they could hardly do it without her, so here she was!

Casey stepped out of the car, power-walked her way through the rotating glass doors, past the front desk, and dashed into an open elevator car as if it were waiting just for her. It whisked her up to the executive floor, popped open, and deposited her in front of Aubrey Flanagan.

"You look wrecked, luv," the flaming redhead said, smiling sweetly while clutching an armful of file folders.

"Good morning, Aubrey. Where is the meeting?"

"Conference room B."

Never a kind word from that one. Aubrey had it out for her, and she knew it.

"Great. Can you let them all know that I am here?" Casey said. "I need to find some coffee first."

"Tell them you'self. They're waitin'. There's coffee and gravy rings in the room."

Aubrey disappeared in a cloud of Irish Spring. She surely knew that the sweets in the pink boxes were called *doughnuts*. The woman irritated Casey more than anything with her singsong lilt and condescending demeanor. *Aubrey was so tightly wound that her ass squeaked when she walked,* Casey thought. *Welcome back, all right!*

Casey opened the heavy glass door in a conference room surrounded by glass walls on three sides. One solid wall was covered in gold- and platinum-framed photos of talent and pictures of award-winning moments with Hans Schultz, the station manager, and Bumpy Friedman receiving awards for TV talk show excellence in their day-part time slot six years in a row. Currently, the show was on a six-year winning streak, and no one had any intention of falling behind to any of the competition vying to deny them number seven. Trophies lined the shelves above a mahogany credenza, and the large oval matching confer-ence table gleamed in the center, surrounded by high-backed leather and brushed nickel chairs on dual casters—seating for the holy twelve—the executives, production staff, and talent of the show.

All were in attendance. A folder with Casey's name on it was placed in front of the one vacant chair next to Kathryn Delacorte.

"There she is!" Barry Paige quipped, ever the kiss-ass. "I guess we can get started now."

Casey gave him a tempered smile and slid into the open seat. She plopped her large purse under the massive table on the stiff carpet and folded her hands onto her lap.

THE MEETING ENDED two hours later with a rousing reboot proposition for the team and hierarchical expectations for the new season. The hosts were all primed for another glorious run with contracts sealed, several new sponsors on board, and jazzy artwork for the show logo and set backdrops. *The Gab* was getting a much-needed refresh to go with the push for more entertaining content and segments that would increase audience participation, offer more celebrity chat, cooking segments, and some prize-winning giveaways that would be on par with the competing daytime rivals.

"They'll have us performing TikTok dance moves if it will increase the ratings!" Kathryn quipped as the meeting broke and everyone scattered to their cubicles and offices.

The studio was on the first floor. Casey rode down the elevator with the other hosts.

Hannah laughed at Kathryn's joke. "I don't think that the TikTok crowd is our demographic. Maybe my daughter can show me how to get on there, though. I hear it's all the rage."

La Costa, who looked like a queen in a long, flowing wrap and matching fabric headdress, pushed the elevator button with a lacquered purple nail. "I *got* you, Ms. Hannah—I've been rockin' the platform for months. My oldest, Louis, fixed me up. He's my go-to virtual assistant with the socials."

Casey smiled. The four stood silent and close-shouldered in the elevator car, letting the cables guide their descent. Kathryn smelled like champagne and roses, as always. Hannah eyed Casey from head to toe and smiled. "I love your outfit, Casey. How was the flight?"

"Slept," Casey said, watching the floor numbers count down above the steel doors.

"That's the way to do it," La Costa chimed in. "That is some prime sleep time for sure." La Costa had a beach home on each coast and knew a thing or two about commuting.

"It's good to be back," Hannah said to break the silence that followed. "All of us. Together for another round. Who would have predicted it? We still have the viewers."

"At least for another season," Kathryn said coolly.

The elevator's doors pulled open, and the ladies of *The Gab* stepped in the studio's direction, past their dressing rooms just off the set, their heels clicking across the shiny linoleum floor and out into the lobby.

"I called for an Uber," Hannah said as the four streamed through the revolving door onto the city street.

"The usual?" Kathryn asked, pulling the belt on her exquisite cashmere coat close around her waist.

They all nodded in unison.

Twenty minutes later, they were pulling up to a 19th-century brick building with a Parisian vibe, large blue doors, and floor-to-ceiling windows with spectacular views of Central Park. The mâitre d' ushered the women to a table in the back, where they would have some privacy from the lunchtime diners. It was their favorite lunch spot on days that kept them close to the studio.

The server arrived to take the drink orders. She made no sign that she recognized the esteemed patrons, who were busy checking on the group's preference for daytime libations.

"I'll have a Prosecco," Kathryn said, starting the party.

Hannah followed. "Rosé, please."

La Costa piped in next. "Make mine a Long Island Iced Tea."

Casey was famished. It seemed like an eternity since she had eaten. "Tequila. Neat. Oh, can we get some bread?"

Kathryn shot her a surprised look.

"Yeah, and just put it right here between us two. We are all about the carbs, right, Casey?" La Costa laughed, making her earrings jingle.

It was good to be together again, Casey had to admit. She had missed everyone. It had been a long summer break, and even though she had not accomplished half of what her colleagues did to advance her career, she would get there. She would toast her own next great step forward. In the meantime, she needed to be careful and play her cards right. She could never afford to lose the exposure and opportunities that Global Network and the show afforded. Not at this time, at least.

She had slipped off the ring on the car ride to the restaurant. Why give the others anything to talk about? At least, it wouldn't be at her expense.

The drinks arrived, and Hannah gave a toast to health, happiness, and higher ratings than the year before. They clicked glasses and began the grand discussion about what everyone would be ordering.

"I'm going to use the restroom," Casey said. "Order me the Ahi Tuna salad."

She disappeared into the quiet sanctuary of the restroom with its black-and-white tiled floors, fifty-thousand-watt makeup mirror, and vanity. She was touching up her lip gloss when the door opened, and Kathryn walked in.

"Well, what do you think about the news?" Kathryn said, adjusting her updo in the mirror.

"What news?" Casey replied as matter-of-factly as she could muster. She knew that Kathryn really didn't like her. Deep down, she cared little for her as well. She didn't trust the woman.

"Surely you've heard about Roe Evans and Celeste D'Angelo? It's on all the news outlets. They're engaged. The byline in

Celebrity magazine is touting them as 'the fairytale couple' of the decade. Their love story is clickbait on all the social news feeds." She pulled an exquisite gold compact from her Prada.

Casey was not prepared for this. "Is that so?"

"Apparently, he was one huge catch," Kathryn said, turning to Casey head-on. "Hey, weren't you involved with Roe Evans at one time?"

"Ancient history. We dated on and off back when the show first started, but we broke it off just after that. Separate continents, you know. He has co-custody of a special needs daughter who is with his ex in London."

Kathryn nodded thoughtfully, studying her chignon in the compact. "I've read that Roe and his new bride will live in Connecticut, so I guess the new Mrs. Evans is okay with the transatlantic commute."

Casey yanked on the zipper of her makeup bag.

"We are thinking of doing a feature pictorial in *High Style* of the two of them," Kathryn went on. "You know, an engagement spread with a his and hers clothing line—maybe use that Uptown designer who dresses the do-gooders; I hear Celeste is into several charities. Dolphins or baby sea turtles or something. I am sure my people can come up with something spectacular."

"Well, we should get back out there," Casey said matter-of-factly.

"After you," Kathryn said.

Casey smiled. *Bitch!*

CHAPTER 17

Casey opened the door of her studio loft with its bright, modern furnishings and contemporary framed artwork that hung on the exposed brick walls like a hip gallery. The unfinished ceiling beams from the old Soho garment factory that once was a Sullivan Street mainstay gave a raw, earthy feel to the place. At night, especially, the lights of the city winked and glowed peacefully amid the otherwise chaotic rhythm of the city's heartbeat. It was home—home away from home—as LA was where she felt most content. New York City and the television show were just a means to an end.

She drew a bath and sank into the warm bubbles, looking through the narrow window across from the claw-foot tub at a sky filled with twinkling stars. She slipped on a pair of silk pajama bottoms, pulled on a faded Lakers T-shirt from the bureau, and dashed her feet into the fuzzy slippers lying askew next to her bed, just as she had left them. Living on dual coasts had its benefits and its drawbacks. She had two of everything in her life, from bathrobes to boxes of Band-Aids. It was a lot to manage.

The maid, who came weekly to clean and restock the refrigerator, had gotten the wrong brand of almond milk, and there were slim pickings in the pantry for a quick-and-easy dinner. She settled on a can of tuna over a bed of reasonably crisp lettuce greens and wilted spinach, drizzled with her favorite salad dressing, which she whisked in a bowl herself—olive oil, Dijon mustard, red wine vinegar, and chives. Such was the extent of her culinary feats. Casey was not in the least an excellent cook and could be the poster girl for meal service delivery and takeout.

LATER THAT EVENING, Casey slid into bed and fished around in the sheets for the TV remote. Tomorrow would be a long day of shooting promos for the show. She flipped through the channels on the massive television mounted on the brick wall across from her bed. Nothing interested her.

She eyed her phone and knew better than to torture herself by pursuing the social feeds. As if on cue, her phone *dinged* with a notification. It was a text from Spaulding Craine's office.

She shot straight up and adjusted the pillows behind her. She gave the screen a few taps. The message was from Spaulding's assistant—asking for a virtual call at three p.m. tomorrow. Casey bit her lip and typed her response on the tiny keyboard. Of course, she would be happy to speak with him about representation with his agency. Hell yes! It seemed as if the gods were smiling at her once again! *This* was the next step she would need to get grander projects and, with that, notoriety—the kind that would make all of her sacrifices and struggles worth it.

She sank into the pillows, dreaming of the days to come when she would win her own shiny Emmys, or even Oscars, and write her own ticket to wherever she wanted to go. There would be no stopping her!

With the glow of the TV and sweet dreams drifting in her head, she fell asleep.

. . .

Twenty-three hundred miles away, Jake Trainer was waiting at a back table in a small off-road bar in El Paso with a broken neon light and a jukebox that only played George Strait tunes. He was on time and watched the door.

With each creak of the hinges, he waited. He had been told the contact would be a tall lumberjack type, wearing a plaid shirt, a baseball cap, and boots.

Great! That about describes every dude walking in here, he thought as he nursed another fresh longneck that was as sweaty as his giant palms. This was not his first rodeo, so to speak, but it was definitely out of his standard protocols. He was used to petty theft and such, for sure, but negotiating with a ring that actually *paid* for identity credentials—that was something else altogether. He knew he had hit pay dirt. He had *Casey Singer's* personal information, credit card access, and the keys to her kingdom. Surely this would fetch a great price on the black market. No sense in wussing out now. He was in it deep as dog shit on a shingle.

Jake's childhood buddy, Waylon Wyatt, was an ex-con and knew a guy who knew a guy who had the connections to buy and sell anything. It only took a few well-placed phone calls, and the meeting was arranged. So, here he was, waiting in the dark for some guy named "Tuck." And the dude was fucking late.

Finally, he saw a figure walk in from the dark into the hazy bar lights. The figure eased his way out of the half-light into view. He stood, towering over Jake like a grizzly. He was wearing a baseball cap, and his brick-red flannel shirt was rolled up high on each massive forearm, revealing a myriad of tattoos snaking up toward his enormous biceps. His face was smooth except for a gray, wiry goatee. "Jake Trainer?" he said in a low growl.

"Yes, sir," Jake choked out, half-standing to extend his hand.

The man called Tuck just looked at his open palm and sat down.

"What do you got?" he asked, with no pleasantries.

"Like I told Waylon's contact, I have digital images of the contents of Casey Singer's wallet—a Black AmEx card, bank debit card, and a California Driver's License."

Tuck grunted and squinted into the distance. "Just photos? That's it? Any pics of her naked?"

"No, I didn't know who she was until I lifted the goods from her purse. Didn't record things," Jake said, happy to relay the scenario. "I'm not a perv or anything. I ain't lookin' for trouble. But when trouble finds me . . . well, I'm happy to oblige."

Tuck pulled out his phone. "I'm texting you a number."

A signal dinged on Jake's device, and he looked up at the man. "Okay, so?"

"Show me the pics."

Jake bristled. "And then what? Are you going *to*—?"

"Send you a fucking Venmo?"

Jake looked across the table at the menacing giant stupidly. "No, man. I wasn't implying—"

The giant Cyclops laughed maniacally and rubbed his grizzly cheek. "Hey, relax." He pulled a brown envelope from the back pocket of his Levis and slid it across the table, keeping his hairy paw on top of it.

"Show me. Then you get paid."

Jake stiffened and then fiddled with his phone, hoping that the giant called Tuck could not see his hands shaking.

"Here. It's all here. See?" he said, taking a swig of beer.

Tuck swiped through the three photos. "This is it?" he puzzled.

"Yeah," Jake said.

"Brah, the credit cards could be maxed out for all we know. You don't have the social security digits? Bank passwords?"

Jake shook his head as Tuck returned the crumpled envelope to his giant jeans pocket.

"So why do you need that info? To hack her accounts?" Jake asked.

"What are you, a cop? I sell it to a guy in Philly, who sells it to a guy in Turkey. What he does with it is none of my concern."

"So, you don't actually *use* the info?"

"Naw, I'm just what you call the middleman to the middleman."

Jake broke into a nervous smile. "So, what? This does not interest you?"

"Tell you what, you get the passwords to her bank accounts, investment annuities and shit, plus her social security digits, and then we'll do business."

Tuck stood up and slid away from the table.

Jake sat motionless.

"Lose my number," Tuck said, not making eye contact. "Unless you got something I can get a hard-on for." Then he slipped into the darkness somewhere in the bar's direction.

Jake drained the last of his beer. Then he picked up his phone and dialed his friend Waylon, who lived in LA. "Hey, dude. I need another favor."

CHAPTER 18

NEW YORK CITY

There it was, in bona fide Instagram glory, with a headline that read: *Casey Singer and Ryder McKinley Hitched??* The emphasis being on the two question marks. Kathryn Delacorte nearly spit out her latte when she got the notification on her phone. She was sitting in the stylist's chair, getting glammed up for the promotional shoot that morning.

Hannah, who was sitting in the chair next to her, leaned forward when her phone buzzed from her Birkin. The stylists, Jenn and Alina, each stopped what they were doing to glance at their vibrating phones on the counter.

"What!" Jenn said, backing off from Kathryn's scalp with the curling iron.

"No way!" Kathryn whispered almost inaudibly, scrolling through the post.

"Oh, dear," Hannah said, placing her hand over her mouth.

La Costa burst into the makeup room full barrel. "Holy shit! Our girl Casey is married to *Ryder McKinley!*"

Everyone looked at her with shared shock and disbelief.

"How? When?" Hannah wondered aloud.

"*Why?*" La Costa asked the room, settling into the chair

farthest from the door. She was wearing a paper bib over her stunning satin blouse.

"*Why?*" Kathryn tsked. "Come on, La Costa, why do you *think*? That girl is always up to something to keep her name in the press. But this is truly epic, even for her."

"What do we know about this Ryder McKinley?" Hannah said, smoothing her straight blunt bob that grazed the top of her toned shoulders. The highlights that Jenn had talked her into really brought out the variety in her blue eyes. She slipped on the peacock blue, large-framed glasses that had become her trademark.

"Know about him?" La Costa quipped. "He's a whole lot of handsome, that's what. Plus, he's rollin' in it!"

Alina got to work on La Costa's foundation, throwing in her own two cents, punctuated by her catchphrase, delivered in a broken mix of Polish and English—*Polglish*, as she called it. "Don't be ridiculous! I think Casey is so lucky to find love of any kind at her age, *tak*? So, she likes Hollywood bad boy. I *wish!*"

"Takes one to know one, I suppose," Kathryn said, clipping on a pair of stunning gemstone earrings.

Just then, Casey walked into the room to a deafening silence. She slipped into the middle chair and stared straight into the lighted mirror that told no lies. Her blonde hair was hoisted high atop her head in an elastic band, and her fresh face looked glowing and youthful enough—for being in her mid-thirties. She still held the prize for being the youngest host on the set, yet the fabulous four needed every bit of smoke and mirrors available to get them camera-ready. Lucky for them, they had a crew of talented makeup artists, hair stylists, and dress technicians who transformed them into the faces America loved to chat with mornings at eleven.

Jenn tossed a cape over Casey's floral peasant blouse with a smile that broke the ice. "Welcome back!" Getting to work on Casey with a tube of concealer, she asked, "Anything interesting you want to tell us about?"

Casey knew the gig was up and couldn't delay the inevitable any longer. She slid her left hand from beneath the plastic cape and gave them all what they had been waiting for. "I suppose you are talking about this?"

"Holy shit!" La Costa said with only one brow penciled in. "Girl, you are *kidding* me!"

Hannah peered over with one of her ever-approving placates, "Congratulations, Casey! It's a beautiful ring."

Alina howled, "Are you kidding me? Casey, *jej!* That Ryder McKinley must be a fast worker, for sure! You snagged a hot one, girl!"

Jenn smiled, doe-eyed and sincere. "We are happy for you, Casey. Really. When were you going to tell everyone?"

"Well, it just happened," Casey said. "I'm still working out the rest of it as I go."

The truth of the matter was that she saw the post herself after waking up that morning to a deluge of notifications on her phone from everyone she had ever known or met congratulating her on the questionable nuptials. The comments in her Facebook and Instagram feeds ranged from accolades to accusations of stealing one of Hollywood's most eligible hunks for publicity. In cold fact, public opinion was brutal and true fans were few. Casey would have to own up to it. She just wished that her lawyer, Regina Madison, would get back to her and tell her what to do. She was truly punting in the dark here.

Kathryn was visibly silent. She eyed Casey with cool indifference and then finally brought the hammer down. "What do you think the boss man will think about this? You know how Bumpy can be."

Everyone paused and looked at Casey.

"Controversy is good for ratings, right?" she said matter-of-factly, wondering the same. Bumpy was not one of her biggest fans. She knew very well that she was on thin ice with him most of the time.

"I suppose," Kathryn said, smoothing out her wool blend

sheath dress and checking her reflection in the full-length mirror. "Of course, it's the negative kind you don't need more of, that's for sure. Ryder McKinley is not exactly what one would call *husband* material. You'd better be careful with that one, Casey. That's all I'm saying."

Casey smiled tightly. She didn't expect a wedding shower from her gal pals for sure, but she was not in the mood for a lecture from Lady Delacorte on the rules of social expectations and marital bliss. She was a fine one to talk. Kathryn wore out her spinster card a long time ago!

"Twenty minutes, Ladies!" A voice from the doorway gave the directive.

Jenn patted Casey on the shoulders. "Let's get you ready, Mrs. McKinley! You're all going to look great in this promo!"

"God willing!" La Costa chided. "I'm a few biscuits away from a facelift."

Everyone laughed good-naturedly and smiled, except for Casey.

Secretly, she was fuming.

THE PHOTO SHOOT was a blur of fiery lights and the endless staccato of the camera shutter. The photographer, an over-rated throwback from the *Playboy* era, snapped away, demanding poses of the group in unison. One could only act cheerful and happy for a certain length of time before it became drudgery, and everyone's makeup—and resolve—began wearing thin. Kathryn loved the camera, a by-product, no doubt of her trade as editor for *High Style* magazine. She simply oozed chic and poise. Second was La Costa, who required a nose powdering every twenty minutes. The heat of the stage and spotlights seemed to kick in her hot flashes and halted the session more than once. Hannah remained stoic. Calm in the moment. She required the least coddling or direction, although she claimed never to have gotten used to projecting her image for the masses. She took to knitting in-between takes. It just wasn't in her DNA to sit idle.

Casey thrived under the spotlight and enjoyed the circus of it all more than anyone. She snapped photos for her social feeds, offering behind-the-scenes glimpses into her life both on and off the set, which garnered a robust following that did not hurt the ratings or her personal brand in the least.

After three and a half hours of touch-ups, wardrobe changes, group photos, and headshots, Tom LeMaster, the show's marketing director, gave the directive, "That's a wrap, everyone! Thank you!" A flurry of account executives and PR managers who had overseen the shoot scattered back to their cubicles and desks on the eighth floor.

The network had ordered lunch for the cast and floor crew, which was set up in the green room near the studio.

Casey met up with Kathryn at the deli platter. She checked her dislike for her colleague and instead feigned the camaraderie she had just conveyed on the set. "Can we talk?" Casey asked.

"Sure. Let's take this back to my dressing room," Kathryn said, smiling like a fox.

They both opted for a simple salad and Fuji water, taking the plastic bowls and wrapped utensils back to Kathryn's massive dressing room. She had an actual working office with a table and chairs, vanity, and sitting area that was negotiated into her contract.

Casey barely touched her leafy greens. It was best to just come out with it, she reasoned. What could it hurt to ask?

"I was wondering if you would like first dibs."

"First dibs on *what*?" Kathryn hedged.

"On my story—the complete running-off-to-Vegas-and-getting-hitched-to-Ryder McKinley thing. For your magazine. You know. Maybe we could do a power-couple thing. A segment on unconventional ways to happiness—in gorgeous designer clothes, of course!"

Kathryn did not flinch. "Well, that's not much of a story, seeing as how you two eloped."

"That's the point—people today do not always want the dog and pony show—the whole extravagance of the thing. They sometimes just want to leap!"

"Well, your *leap* has left us scrambling for an explanation to the viewers for that cloudy rock candy diamond on your finger." Kathryn dabbed her mouth with the paper napkin. "Let me ask you this. How long do you think you can avoid telling Bumpy—if he doesn't already know?"

Casey blinked and countered, "La Costa turned up married on the day of the show signing back when we all first started —*and* pregnant. Why didn't that ruffle any executive feathers?"

"Because she was not hiding anything from anyone. Casey, this Elvis-blessed wedding of yours will leak in a hot Hollywood minute."

"I'm just offering you a chance to capitalize on this. It's a win for both of us," Casey countered.

"Hard pass, dear." Kathryn rose and pitched her half-eaten salad bowl in the trash. "If you'll excuse me, I have a meeting."

NOT TWENTY-FOUR HOURS LATER, more photos from the Vegas wedding circulated for the highest bidder. The gossip news show *TMZ* was the first to break the news: *Casey Singer is hitched to Ryder McKinley, with each half of the newlywed lovebirds perched on differing coasts. What does this mean for the plucky party girl and wild-card actress seated on the all-woman talkfest,* The Gab?

Bumpy watched the news clip on the large screen TV from his cushy leather chair in his office. Just before he was about to launch the fall season—great! Of course Casey would pull a stunt like this! *Was she even wearing a wedding ring at the shoot?* He hadn't noticed. All he knew was that the show was going live in a week, and he had little time for damage control.

He pounded the digits on his desk phone for Deanna Calvin in public relations. They would have to spin it.

He yanked open the top desk drawer, revealing an empty bottle of antacids rolling around in the vastness. His shit luck, all right.

CHAPTER 19

The call came in from Spaulding Caine's office at three p.m. sharp. Casey was still in full hair and makeup from the photo shoot earlier. She slid her heels off and stepped into her fuzzy pink slippers that lived there in her dressing room, along with a closet full of sweaters and leggings, a small fridge stocked with Starbucks Iced Coffee drinks, and an unused yoga mat. The star on her door said it all—she was a star with little else on her mind than to do everything she could to elevate her meager celebrity to meteoric heights. Would Spaulding Caine understand that mission? Or would he be like all the rest who only looked to make bank out of the gate? Who was she fooling? Her career was only a dozen years in the making. It was time—high time—that she got her due.

"Hello? Mr. Caine?"

"Please, call me Spaulding. I received your email. Sawyer speaks highly of you."

"He's one of the main reasons for the talk show's success. We've been working together since the beginning."

"How can I help you, Casey?"

Casey sat with her legs tucked beneath her on the large over-stuffed chair across from the makeup vanity, holding the phone out in front of her, now on speaker. "I'm ready for next-level success, Spaulding. I have the time, the energy, and the ambition. Straight up—I want to audition for the part of Amarantha in *Starbreaker*."

He listened, creating a sort of awkward silence on the other end of the line. "Have you read the script?"

"No, actually. Just the hype surrounding the book series. I know that she's a female warrior type. Strong, beautiful, and 'unfading' as her name suggests. She is *me*!"

"Tell me, who previously represented you?"

"Mona Waxman formerly represented me. But we've since parted ways."

"Can I ask why?"

Casey stiffened. "We didn't see eye-to-eye regarding my career. The truth is, I am ready for more, and she could not deliver."

"I see."

"Can I ask, where are you located, Spaulding? Are you in LA?"

"Costa Rica," he said buoyantly. "I travel, actually. Right now, in fact, I am speaking to you from my boat."

"Oh?" Casey hedged. *No address? No physical building?*

"It's a virtual world, right?" Spaulding said from the cell line stretched thin across the miles.

"I suppose so." Casey shifted in the chair, eyeing a copy of *Celebrity* magazine that had mysteriously made its way onto her dressing room coffee table. "Have you checked out my client list? Done any research about me?" he asked.

"I know you represent several young film actresses, girls like myself, if that is what you mean." Could she still call herself young at thirty-four?

"Tell you what. Send me your reel. I will look at it and be back in touch."

"Thank you," she breathed.

"No worries. In the meantime, I suggest you get a copy of the trilogy and start reading. Pay particular attention to the character Oren—see what you think of her part."

"I will. Thank you so much, Spaulding. I will get an email out to you today."

"You're welcome, Casey. I'll be in touch."

That was it. He dropped off the line and went back to drifting, she supposed, on a large boat somewhere on the waters off of the Caribbean, probably with a margarita in hand. Well, it was a powerful hand indeed. Everyone on Spaulding Caine's client list seemed to be gainfully employed and making their own waves in the industry as large-scale projects were coming back with a vengeance, and audiences were ready to fill the theaters and be transported and entertained again.

Casey set her phone on the coffee table. She lifted the magazine that was looming at her, just inches away. *That Kathryn Delacorte!* She had wanted to be sure that Casey had seen the issue. The cover featured the Royal Couple posing for another tell-all feature. She fumbled through the pages quickly, looking for the one feature story buried in the back with a headline that read: *Marriage is Music to Roe Evans's Ears.* There it was, a picture of the happy couple, locked in an embrace in front of a Nantucket beach house. The two were scheduled to be married just after the New Year. Roe was grinning from ear to ear. Celeste was pretty enough to make her stomach flip.

She folded the thin magazine in half and shoved it into her designer bag.

By seven p.m., Casey hit the send button on her laptop from her loft and sent her acting reel and resume into the ether. She secretly prayed to the gods of 5G broadband that her digital delivery would hit Spaulding's inbox and convince him to take her on. All she could do was cross her fingers and wait.

She had stopped off at the bookstore to pick up the *Starbreaker* trilogy, intending to read through the entire series over the weekend. She prided herself on her fast reading ability. It was a needed skill in her business, as entire show segments would require quick recall and follow-through with only a scant few bullet points presented on little blue cards. Each book was a doorstop, around five hundred pages. Much loftier than an average film script.

Her phone buzzed as she was about to crack open the first book. She had just poured a large glass of Cabernet. It was one hundred percent sustainable from South Africa. Things like that mattered to her, although she could never be bothered to recycle the bottles, which proved that, if nothing else, Casey was a contradiction of sorts.

She checked the screen and saw that it was Regina Madison, finally calling back.

"I know—I screwed up," Casey said matter-of-factly, then hit the speaker button.

"Hello to you too, Casey," Regina said flatly.

"I suppose you have heard by now?"

"I have, Casey. And might I ask, is this marriage legal?"

"It is. But we both regret it and will need to have it nullified."

"I can begin working on that, Casey. But hear me; you will need to be very low-key about it. No interviews. No press of any kind. I will intercept the inquiries as much as possible from the media outlets, but you will need to do your part. By the way, what does Mona think about this?"

"Mona is history—a mutual parting. I'm hunting for new representation. Do you know of anyone?"

Regina audibly groaned. "No one who could handle you, I'm afraid."

Casey raked her thin fingers through her blonde mane, gathered it up into loose stands with a snap of the giant hair clip, and gave a little laugh. "Hilarious. What should I do? I mean, about Ryder and me?"

"Well, I think it would be best if you just went with the charade for a bit. Do not perpetuate or create any perceived problem or rift, for example. Appear happy and protective of each other. That is the best course of action. We don't want this to be interpreted as a gimmick or stunt—the public loves a love story."

Casey guffawed this time. "You should have been an agent, Regina. You certainly think like one!"

"It's my job to protect you and your brand. Simple as that. We will do so in a way that does not reflect poorly on you or your employer. Global Network can be fickle. Bumpy Friedman is just looking for a reason to make a change. Don't let it be *your* pretty ass that he thinks he needs to fire."

Casey sighed, rubbing her temples. "Just make this go away, Regina. *Please.*"

"I'll do my best, Casey. In the meantime, stay out of trouble—and, by all means, stay out of Vegas!"

CHAPTER 20

LOS ANGELES, CALIFORNIA

Lucas Morgan was not his best self. A string of bad real estate investments, a lack of initiative, and a raging cocaine habit quickly tanked his career to abysmal lows. His once large-and-loud life was now reduced to a desk and an office chair in a renovated studio apartment of a historical hotel on 8th Street near the Fashion District. His tiny window on the world was right across from a luxury apartment building with a doorman, upscale lobby, amenities—and a bathroom that was not located next to the kitchen stove. He had lost it all—his Los Angeles high-rise office, his luxury apartment, his precious Maserati. All of it went up his nose or down the drain when his life took a plummeting spiral. When one by one, he lost his clients and couldn't be bothered some days to show up, shower, or even get out of bed. He was a wreck, and one hit away from ending it all—more than once.

Somehow, he scraped together enough money to hang a virtual shingle out into the world. He created a platform on a free website and touted himself as a talent agent under the new business name of More Than Talent, Inc. He took on any actor he could find, hungry for representation in a city that slammed doors. Lucas, now calling himself Luke More, shed his former identity and high-dollar clients to con unsuspecting hopefuls into spending money on headshots and agent fees and signing phony contracts that delivered nothing. Lucas created a "talent board" that he posted on his website for prospective clients to peruse. A wall of *losers*, as he called them.

He scoured the beaches to find street performers that he added to his talent database, now a growing file of vagrants, criminals, and wanderlusts. He was, it seemed, in his element. Now and then, he would find an innocent beauty from Milwaukee or Sioux Falls, who would contact him, eager to sign on with More Than Talent, hoping to garner steady work. These, he would send out on published cattle calls after, of course, grooming them for the task. He never met them at his "office," rather, always at a public place close to a by-the-hour motel with a pool because bathing suit shots were mandatory. When not taking the photos himself, he had a photographer at the ready to oblige.

Lucas did not season with age. He fermented in his juices and constantly ruminated about his misfortune in life. His lost chances and the people who wronged him—who stood in the way of his genius. He never forgot, and he never forgave—namely, *Casey Singer*.

So, when he saw the network promo for the seventh season of *The Gab* come across the TV left on in the corner of his tiny shoebox apartment, he stopped what he was doing. He leered at Casey with her fake smile and store-bought tits. She was the perky, quirky one on the panel of four—incessant chatterboxes, each with an axe to grind about something. He hadn't forgotten how he was forced to rebuild his life after Casey's little extortion scheme left him with no clients, no means of income, and no notoriety in the industry. The logo for the talk show zoomed across the screen. He hated the show, and he hated Casey more.

More than life itself.

CHAPTER 21

LONDON, ENGLAND

Roe Evans paid for his usual morning latte and cheese toast at the coffee shop on Kingsway, near to his office. In a city usually bustling with tourists and working-day suits, he enjoyed watching the world from a corner table in a place that smelled like coffee beans and marmalade. It was there that he felt anonymous and ordinary, free from the demands of his high-powered job with the record company and the myriad of demands it imposed on his life.

He eyed his phone, tempted to tap onto the alerts that loomed from familiar and forbidden places—like the headlines that touted his engagement to Celeste: sweet Celeste, who was busy on the East Coast making grand plans for their wedding. It was not the first marriage for either of them and at his age, nearly fifty, it was set to outdo anything he had produced in all his life. And, of course, there, too, were the profiles of Casey Singer on the socials. Viewing them was one of his guilty pleasures.

He tapped the screen, scrolled, and then stopped on an image.

There it was—in full digital proof—Casey and Ryder McKinley, hand in hand, in front of the Vegas chapel, married. There was another shot of the two fist-pumping as they alighted from a limo into the bright neon lights. The deed had been done in less than twenty minutes from start to finish. He could barely believe it. At that moment, he half-envied her and half-regretted the circus of it all. But, then, he thought wistfully, wasn't he accused of the greater charade?

Either way, it saddened him in a place deep in his heart where Casey lived—still.

She was always there, it seemed, even after all the years that had passed. He watched her from afar, always happy for her successes and knowing that he never had the right to deny her any of it. She had made her choice, and he respected that.

He stared at the photos on his phone. The finality of it all made him feel sick. Was it too late to ever have it all? He didn't know.

He hit the heart icon before he could stop himself, sending the sentiment across the miles.

CHAPTER 22

NEW YORK CITY

The entire production team was in full force for the broadcast.

Sawyer Landry, the production manager, who had been overseeing the execution of the technical requirements for the show, now in its seventh year, barked into his headset. "Mitch—how are things on the floor?"

"Ready, Chief," came the reply into his headset. Mitch Bobo, the floor manager, handled all operations of the studio floor.

The camera shots were set, sound checks had been performed, and the prompters were loaded with the day's script.

Barry Paige, the program director, a bit heavier but no less edgy with his now-graying, scraggly ponytail, watched from the booth. His former trademark wire-rimmed glasses had since been replaced with black Tom Fords. It was the first show of the new season, and the staff and crew needed to produce nothing less than a home run out of the gate. The new opening titles would set the tone for a refreshed brand infused with modern graphics, lighting, and a new stage set. Each host would sit in one of four white leather armchairs around a small glass coffee table lounge-style, which was a departure from the previous large center "kitchen table" arrangement. It was executive producer Bumpy Friedman's belief that this would help the panel engage more with the camera—bringing them more front and center. After all, they were beautiful women and deserved to be showcased. The new setting also would highlight their legs more prominently in the shots.

The grand new stage set was also widened in order for the hosts to interact with the guests more freely for hands-on demonstrations, cooking segments, and game and giveaway features. There was even a new signature runway built for Kathryn's fashion segment that extended right into the studio audience.

Everyone from the gaffer, lighting techs, dolly, and key grip operator was poised and at the ready.

The camera operators checked their headsets and re-checked the framing of their shots.

It took a staff of no less than one hundred people, both in front and behind the scenes, to make the show ready for broadcast. When the core group broke from the early-morning production meeting, it was everyone's expectation that this would be the banner year.

Axel Danger, the young showrunner, skidded to a squeak on his sneakers at each of the ladies' dressing room doors.

"Five minutes! Let's go, Ladies! Five minutes!"

One by one, the cast of *The Gab* emerged from their dressing rooms, primped and coiffed for the day's show. The laughter and applause from the studio audience could be heard as the warm-up comic did his job, priming the crowd for the broadcast.

The show's assistant director, assistant producer, and staff writers were seated up front in folding chairs, out of the line of vision.

The cast walked onto the gleaming new stage set to a round of exuberant applause. They needed no introduction as each seasoned beauty took her place. The first chair had always been and remained Kathryn Delacorte, fashion designer and editor-in-chief of *High Style* magazine. Next to her sat Dr. Hannah Courtland Murphy, of radio fame, weekday afternoons with her syndicated talk show. To her left, actress and model Casey Singer waved at the lively crowd, who was hooting and whistling for her. She took her seat wearing polished extensions and side bangs, compliments of her hairstylist, Ericka Naidu, from her personal glam squad. A last-minute pre-dawn call that made Casey ten minutes late for the morning's production meeting. After all, Casey's look was everything. She was every millennial's paragon in her designer mini denim skirt, a tiny T-shirt that read *Girls Rule*, and ankle boots. The wedding ring prominently on her left hand caused a second wave of hoots and applause from the crowd. Seated next to Casey was bestselling romance author La Costa Reed, beaming with first-show bravado.

Back in the booth, Barry Paige was quick with the monitor check.

"—Black online."

The technician swiftly obliged.

"—Roll for record and confirm speed," Barry Paige said, waiting a beat.

"— Speed."

Another beat.

"Ready insert slate . . . *Insert.*"

Five seconds, and then, another command, "Ready lose slate . . . *Lose it.*"

The ladies sat stoic and steady in the hot lights, readying themselves for the broadcast. Their show notes were in hand on stiff blue index cards.

Barry Paige gave the cue, "Have a good show, everyone! Standby!" At the command, all earpieces were silenced except for the key players.

Mitch Bobo signaled to the talent, raising his arm.

Barry Paige's voice was seasoned and calm. "Here we go— Ready, fade up camera two, *fade up music,* . . . in five, four, three, two, one . . . fade all, . . . ready insert title . . . *insert title.*"

The camera faded up in unison with the familiar opening

theme music, now pulsating through the speakers as the opening titles bounced across the screen, ushering in the seventh season of *The Gab* to a round of thunderous applause.

Barry Paige waited a beat. "Fade out music . . . *fade.*"

Then, the directive from the booth, "Ready mic and cue . . . *Mic and cue.*"

Mitch Bobo bounded forward and pointed his finger at Kathryn, who sprang into action.

"Welcome back, everyone!" she said, beaming. "Thank you for joining us this morning! It is year seven of *The Gab*! Can you all believe it? We are so happy to be back, and we have so much to talk about!"

Bumpy Friedman watched from the control booth with a cool stoicism. Not over five minutes in, he hurried back up to the executive floor to watch the rest of the broadcast, ditching his coffee cup outside of the studio door. He had a sack of warm Diet Coke waiting in a desk drawer upstairs.

He instructed Aubrey before disappearing behind his office door, "Have Casey see me after the show."

"Aye, sir," she said, shoving her phone back into her purse. There was a riot, for sure, on the social feeds. She didn't have to ask why. But the good of it was that the show was trending like crazy.

In a remote town outside of Phoenix, Jake Trainer sat in a furnished studio rental with a pay-by-the-month exit strategy if he needed it. He sat at a Formica kitchen table with his laptop propped up on an ancient phone book. He had several websites open, and his hands shook when he typed in the digits from Casey's Black American Express Card to purchase some apparel, a new hat, and a belt buckle. He would use the apartment number of a neighbor one floor above him, marking the purchase as a "gift," and retrieve it before the tenant came home. He knew the old man's schedule, as Jake had been observing his comings and goings for nearly three weeks.

If the transaction worked, it would not register as a red flag on Casey's account. He would start small, keep the purchases reasonable, and see if he could actually get away with it. Why not? He had the images of the stolen cards on his phone, just sitting there. Why let Tuck's guy have all the fun? He filled in Casey's billing address from her license and clicked send. It couldn't have been easier. Casey would be none the wiser.

He smirked and closed the laptop.

This deserved a cold one from the fridge.

CHAPTER 23

The show broke, and the cast headed down the hall to their dressing rooms, chatting about the outcome.

"One down," Hannah said, ripping the blue note cards in half.

"Only fifty-one more for the season!" La Costa joked, checking her smartwatch. "Oh, and I only need five thousand more steps for the day."

Hannah was on her phone and out of her stilettos before she even hit the door to her dressing room.

Casey unclipped her mic and handed it over to one of the floor crew.

Axel slid up behind them and announced, "Production meeting for tomorrow's show. Here's the agenda." He handed each one a copy and disappeared.

"What a waste of paper!" Kathryn moaned. "Couldn't they just email us the notes?"

Each host hurried off into her respective dressing room, and the doors closed in a staccato symphony.

As soon as Casey fired up her laptop, there was a call on the landline. It was Aubrey.

"The show today was class, Casey. Well done!"

"Thanks. I'm sure that you didn't call just to tell me that," Casey said, checking herself in the mirror.

"Aye—Mr. Friedman wants to see you, stat."

Shit! Casey flinched. "Okay, tell him I'm on my way up."

"Sure."

Casey hung up the receiver and took a deep breath. It was *happening*.

BUMPY WAS PREDICTABLY AGITATED when she arrived at his door.

"Sit down, Casey," he said curtly.

She entered the room and was surprised to see that Deanna Calvin was also there, seated on the leather couch across from Bumpy's desk.

Casey took the chair next to the couch. "I'm sure that you have seen the news."

"We have, and while your business is your business, there is still a concern as to how it reflects on the network," Bumpy said.

A knock at the door signaled that yet another suit was invited to the inquisition. It was Tom LeMaster, head of corporate marketing.

Tom slid in next to Deanna, looking uncomfortable as usual.

"Should I have my lawyer, Regina, patched into this meeting?" Casey said, reaching for her phone.

"I have spoken with Regina Madison already, and we have come to an agreement," Bumpy said. "We just want to ensure everyone is on the same page with this . . . recent development."

Casey swung her head from side to side. "I don't think I fully understand. This is about my personal decision to marry someone?"

Deanna chimed in. "Honey, you certainly can have a life outside of *The Gab*. What we are concerned about is how it might affect our efforts to keep a wholesome image of the show in the foreground. The buzz going around is painting you as a head-line, a wild-child party girl who ran off to Vegas to marry bad-boy actor Ryder McKinley. While that brings publicity—it's the *wrong* kind for the show."

"Not that we shy away from controversy, and we love the press. But right now . . . the timing is not ideal," LeMaster added. "We're rolling out the new season and need the attention to be on the show for the *right* reasons."

Bumpy folded his pudgy fingers into a vise grip on his ancient desk blotter and sighed. "I'm an old man, Casey. Old school all the way. Still, I pride myself on the vision I had years ago for the show—one that I sold to the network and that took a chance on a young girl who had her share of, let's say, *issues.*"

Casey bristled. *Why did she constantly have to prove herself? Half of their viewers would bail if she weren't in the third chair!*

"This is not an inquisition, Casey," Deanna said. "We just need to agree on a path moving forward."

Bumpy cleared his throat. "I've spoken with Regina, and she assures me she is running interference with the media outlets as best she can."

Casey tensed. Her lifeline—her job—was riding on this. "Yes. We—Ryder and I—are aware that the whole thing was a rash decision and have agreed to a clean divorce."

LeMaster slapped his forehead and audibly moaned. "Great! Anything else you want to tell us?"

Bumpy nodded like a kindly grandfather. "Casey, the divorce will be public, and the buzz will reignite the story back to the forefront." Then, turning to Deanna, he said, "Can we spin this in a way to maybe benefit us?"

Casey's nerves prickled.

"The question is, do we bring it up on the show? Perhaps Casey can explain to the viewers about the *misjudgment,*" LeMaster said, surveying the room.

"Do you mean like a public *apology*?" Deanna asked.

Digging her nails into her palms, it was all Casey could do to hold her tongue.

"Regina will handle the divorce. That will be the end,"

Bumpy said. Turning to Casey, he added, "Get your divorce, and we cross that bridge when we get there. In the meantime, we'll keep things tight-lipped on our end. No need to make an issue out of it for now."

Everyone nodded in agreement.

Everyone except for Casey.

She was flatly humiliated. How dare they call her to the carpet! The only carpet she aspired to was the red carpet, and damn if she was going to blow her chance at achieving that! The talk show was only a stepping stone to the dream. *Her* dream on her terms!

"Apologies to everyone for what I've caused. Bumpy, I will make this right," she said in her sincerest team-player platitude. It was Oscar-worthy on all fronts. Inside, she was broiling.

"Thank you, Casey. I am sure you will," Bumpy said, rising from his chair, indicating that the meeting was over.

Everyone rose and cleared the room.

Casey passed Aubrey's desk on her way out, detecting a slight smirk from the auburn beauty.

"Did you get an earful, Aubrey?" Casey said, not waiting for a reply.

"I haven't a badly notion of what you're talking about," Aubrey said without looking up.

BACK IN HER DRESSING ROOM, Casey kicked her stilettos clear across the room and shoved her feet into the waiting slippers. She checked her phone, eager to drown the day's unpleasantries with a dose of dopamine, cat videos—anything to take her mind off the dangerous charade she was being asked to play. She tapped the screen, and there it was—a tiny heart emoji from Roe Evans—there on a photo she had posted from the day of the photo shoot. A heart! She knew it meant more than a cursory gesture. It was a *sign*, a message that he was reaching out to her! Her own beating heart raced, and she felt dizzy with adrenaline.

Then, she looked down at her hand and the sparkling ring Global Studios wanted to leverage to *their* advantage. Everything inside her told her to be patient and to play her cards carefully.

She wanted to reply. To let Roe know that she, too, was thinking of him. But she would wait.

She could only trust her gut. It had gotten her this far.

CHAPTER 24

Three weeks later, an eternity, Casey was a mess. Her sweetest torture was camping out on her couch, logging onto social media, and following both Roe and Celeste's profiles as plans for their wedding progress were unfolding in public view. This was a dark place from which she could not extract her twisted focus. It didn't matter if she was on the East Coast or the West Coast. It was an all-consuming obsession—scrolling through her social feeds and binging on Tab, Cool Ranch Doritos, and Netflix. Everything was laid out there for the world to see in all the celebrity magazines—the engagement announcement, the pre-wedding photos, and the heart-to-heart interview of the loving couple on *E-News Tonight*.

In addition, Casey's feeds were blowing up, with fans and foes jumping on the bandwagon of her and Ryder's nuptials. Still, she was not about to let a little thing like a sham marriage get in her way. Let the social media frenzy do what they were going to do! The buzz about her and Ryder was incessant. The chatter, the speculation, the fascination about their lives, the wedding, the plans for their future. It was all good for her, as far as she was concerned. It was publicity all the same. She was even receiving offers from Hollywood agents and production companies every day—the heightened exposure was waking up sleeping giants and wannabes.

Regina and Ryder's lawyer were hammering out the paperwork for the divorce, she presumed. She couldn't be bothered by the details. Besides, she had learned that Ryder was out of the country, filming in the UK. At least that's what his social feeds were saying.

Waiting for the phone to ring and hearing from Spaulding Caine about representation was an exercise in patience and trust —two virtues she sorely lacked. She was just about to shoot Spaulding a third text when his name popped up on her phone.

"Hello?"

"Hello—it's Spaulding Caine. Have I caught you at a good time?"

Casey ditched the Doritos and turned down the TV. She would stand when she received the news, moving away from her Italian sectional to pace the cool loft floor.

"Yes, Spaulding. Are you calling with good news?"

"I am, Casey. We want to take you on, if you are still a free agent and interested."

Casey fist-pumped the air and bent forward like a marathon runner after a race. Her body was surging with adrenaline. "Yes, Spaulding! Thank you. I would love to sign on."

"Terrific. Listen, I am in my Miami office right now. Could you meet with me here to sign the contract and discuss the next steps?"

"I can fly out on Friday afternoon. Will that work?"

"I have a private plane out of Teterboro in New Jersey that can pick you up. I'll have my virtual assistant make the arrangements. Her name is Mia Rhone."

"Thank you so much, Spaulding. I look forward to meeting you."

"See you on Friday then. Mia will be in touch. *Ciao!*"

"Bye!" Casey hung up and danced around like a manic ballerina. "Ouch!" Her bad leg reminded her why she did not make it as a dancer, or exercise more. It was going to be all right. Her star-shine was coming back with full force. She would find her way forward—again. And this time, there would be nothing to stop her.

CHAPTER 25
MIAMI, FLORIDA

Casey arrived at Miami International. The oppressive heat hit her like an old friend. It had been many years since she had been back in Florida. The memories, mixed with the oppressive humidity, brought back a flood of memories. The flight was wonderful. She had the entire plane to herself. It made her feel like the VIP she knew herself to be. *Now this is how you treat a star!* she thought as she descended from the small jet onto the wobbly stairs stretching down to the tarmac.

A driver wearing a turban and holding a sign that said "Singer" stood in the vestibule just as she passed through the glass doors into the cool terminal.

"Welcome to Miami!" the jovial driver said, helping her with her carry-on. "You'll get used to the heat."

Casey smiled, peeling off the blazer she was wearing over a sleeveless lace camisole. It was now sticking to her like a wet Kleenex. She slid into the backseat of the car and turned her face toward the vents, basking in the cool, forced air-conditioning. A cold bottle of water was waiting on the armrest, along with a bucket of ice near an impressive bar with decanters of brown liquor, clear rum, and sliced limes.

"Would you like to go to your hotel first, miss?" the man asked. "I can wait and then take you to Mr. Spaulding's office."

"That would be great," Casey said, sinking into the cool leather seat and the deliciousness of it all.

AT THREE P.M., and right on time, Casey arrived at Spaulding's building. It was a simple structure of office suites near the cruise ship ports close to Dodge Island. The main entrance was a small lobby with no reception desk and two banks of elevators.

She hit the button for the fourth floor—the top of the quaint, salmon-colored building with matching stone balconies. She felt like she was on a 1970s movie set of a taping of *Columbo*. She was half-expecting to see a throwback actor appearing from behind the glass doors of Spaulding Caine's office suite, fleeing for the parking lot after just having executed the perfect murder. *Had she been watching too much vintage TV?*

She walked into the tiny waiting area. There was no receptionist behind the sizeable green desk, and two empty chairs flanked a low rattan coffee table with outdated magazines. The walls were lined with framed photos of every actor from the 1930s to the present day. A photo of Ronald Regan beamed at her, strangely juxtaposed with a photo of Ryan Reynolds.

Casey was taken aback. Just then, a voice filtered in from the back room. "Casey? Is that you? Come on in!" It was Spaulding.

He was sitting at a large oak desk covered with stacks of papers, file folders, and scripts. He was on his phone, chatting good-naturedly with a client.

"Okay, let me know how it goes. I think they are going to be wowed by the project. Tell them there are several interests on the buy. I'll be in touch.

"Well, there she is!" he said, rising from his eco-conscious black mesh chair—the only modern amenity in the place.

He wore Bermuda shorts, a Hawaiian shirt, and loafers—*sans* socks.

He was just what she had expected. His sun-tanned arms were smooth and muscular, and with his receding hairline, broad nose, and five-o'clock permanent stubble, he was definitely a hottie in a Ralph Fiennes kind of way.

She had done her homework. Caine was originally from North Dakota. Moved to LA after college, where he studied theater to pursue an acting career. He did his own stunts, which garnered him more action film work than he could handle. He started to rep stunt talent by virtue of his connections and became an agent. He earned a business degree while booking talent for production companies in and out of Hollywood. He had all the ins and was reputable. He earned his way to the top of his game. From the high-adventure photos surrounding him and the little Italian import parked at the entrance, it was clear that Caine loved fast cars and lived on the edge.

Casey didn't mind the testosterone that oozed from his pores. Honestly, she *preferred* her agents to have real balls, and this guy more than filled out his briefs. He was the complete package, all right.

"How was the flight?"

"It was perfect, thank you. I appreciate the red-carpet treatment. The limo, the hotel, and everything. You really get me, Spaulding."

"Good! Off to a great start, then. Well, Mia faxed over a mountain of paperwork for you to look over and sign. I have it here," he said, handing her a crisp new manila folder. "You're official once all that is done."

Casey reached for the folder.

"Take a seat," Spaulding said, scrolling through his phone. "Give me just a sec."

Casey smiled and looked around the massive room. It was sparsely furnished, but it was clean except for the explosion of sorts that made his desk look like Bourbon Street after a Mardi Gras parade. The sliding glass doors behind him revealed an incredible view of the ocean stretching out between towering palm trees.

"What a spectacular view you have!" Casey said, rising from the rattan chair. "Can I take a better look?"

Spaulding stood up and unlatched the door. He slid it wide open, and the sounds of the surf and the street rushed to the fourth floor.

"This is incredible!" Casey said.

"Yep. Could have had any swanky high-rise tower on Brickell Avenue. But nothin' trumps this view. I love being so close to the beach. I've got seawater in my veins, that's all."

"Are you here, in your office, very often?"

"A couple of days a quarter. Most of the time, I'm either here, in LA, or on my boat."

"Do you have an office in LA?"

"No, Mia books me a room in town when I need to be there for an extended period. Most days I meet with producers and directors on their turf, or in steak houses. Sounds so cliché, but it's true. That's how deals get done. If ever I need more space, say to entertain, I book an Airbnb."

"I see," Casey said. "Nothing like juggling between two coasts—I wouldn't recommend it. Unless you have a sixty-five-foot sport yacht, a hot rod, and a bitchin' private plane like you do!"

Spaulding laughed. "Casey Singer, I think that you and I are going to get along just fine."

THE TRIP WAS A SUCCESS. Casey arrived home the next day a bit sunburned on her nose and shoulders from a three-hour lunch at a restaurant on a pier two blocks from Spaulding's office. The papers were signed, and she was officially on his roster. She left him with a current headshot, a better understanding of who she was, and a copy of the script to *Starbreaker* on its way to her inbox.

Spaulding had convinced her she would be perfect for the part of Oren. After having read the trilogy, she agreed. If she got it, it would be the biggest part of her acting career.

"I'm certain that you can do this, Casey. You've never been given a chance to show your versatility," he had said over the lunch of fresh crab legs, Cabernet, and a killer chowder. "You'd be amazed at how things are done these days. Have you ever worked with CGI?"

"Does working a green screen as a weather girl in a two-bit minor market count?"

Spaulding laughed. It was a good-natured, kind laugh that totally disarmed any fear that she could have about stepping into the unknown. He reminded her of an Indiana Jones-type—sweet and vulnerable on the inside, but a person who, when put to the test, could do the impossible.

He would have to be able to, she'd thought.

Because she was about to go there.

CHAPTER 26
NEW YORK CITY

"Welcome back!" Kathryn brightened once the floor manager threw up the cue. The audience provided enthusiastic applause in response to the flashing lighted sign hung from a suspended ceiling.

The director called for a close shot of Kathryn and then a wide angle of the entire set. The hosts were all present, sitting at a shiny, curved counter behind their signature coffee mugs, with the show notes on blue cards in front of them. From this angle, their legs were clearly visible, spray-tanned and glistening in the stage lights, each wearing decisively towering stilettos, as was the signature protocol.

They had been discussing a hot topic in the previous segment that Barry Paige was happy to continue. Hannah was about to chime in prior to the previous break. It was about family, marriage, and kids, concerning a news story out of Rhode Island in which a custody battle ensued regarding frozen embryos.

"One has to determine the ramifications of this situation, especially when 'who owns what rights' comes into play," Hannah said with austere authority.

"It's a dangerous and slippery slope," La Costa added. "And something to be considered when rich folk start hoarding frozen embryos like an everyday commodity to be used against a previous partner in custody cases."

The topic was top of mind with the recent battle raging between a divorcing celebrity couple in the news who were currently making headlines in a hotly contested battle over four unused embryos.

Casey waited a beat to chime in. "It comes down to so many issues, like who should really call the shots here? Do women have the last word regarding fertility and their own bodies, or not?"

Kathryn was happy, as always, to play the devil's advocate. "At the expense of unborn children? I don't think so!"

"See, this is the real problem," La Costa countered, shifting in her chair and pointing a lacquered dagger nail at Casey. "What's next? Designer genetics? Ain't nothing good is going to come out of messing with Mother Nature."

The audience applauded. Cheers were heard from the back row. "You *Go, Girl!*"

Barry shifted his weight from sneaker to sneaker in the control room. It was anybody's guess what would happen when La Costa got agitated. He was ready for the toss to the next topic should things get out of hand.

"I'm with Casey on this one. It should be the woman's right to decide whether to have the embryos implanted," La Costa said.

Hannah frowned. "Remember, though, there is a father present, and he is half of the equation."

"I don't know," Kathryn said. "It seems to me to be an impossible choice. Thank goodness this gets hashed out in front of a judge. We could never all agree on one course of action."

They all nodded and agreed to disagree.

Mitch Bobo heeded the directive from his headphones and was ready for the break. He tossed the cue to Casey.

"Well, next, we are going to take a look at a new trend for

skin care. We have Dr. Ava Anderson here to wake up tired skin with a new product that will amaze you!"

La Costa piped in, "Oh, I need that, girl! Bring it on!"

"We'll be right back!" Kathryn said, leaning into Hannah's ear and whispering something that made her nod.

The audience kicked into applause, and the control room faded into a commercial break.

Casey's mind was anywhere except in the present. She had to struggle to feign interest, but that was the job. The insane banter that ensued some days on the set was unbearable. Kathryn constantly vying for the last word. Hannah droning on about the moral implications of everything from love affairs to choosing eco-friendly household products. La Costa was the only one who seemed to have a carefree and non-opposing outlook on things. Casey wondered how La Costa managed to embrace everything so happily and in the moment. She would often say, "Honey, you can't sweat the small stuff." What was the small stuff, anyway? What mattered to one person certainly was not the same for everyone.

Casey had big dreams for herself, but rather than seeing the show as a success in her life, she was looking for the next goal-post to break through. It never quite felt as if she had "arrived." Casey was a basket case with her whirring mind, anxieties, and plans for the future. Getting a feature role in a major film might just bring her the satisfaction she craved. Here on set, she felt stilted and objectified for being who she was. They were an interesting lot, for sure. It was a good thing, though, that for the present being, the audience still tuned in for more. She much preferred to hide behind the role of a noble character written for a script. Was she changing? Losing her edge?

The ratings said no. LeMaster had boasted in the quarterly review meeting. "Casey is holding strong as the host of choice for women in the 18-34 demographic."

The data confirmed that having a younger, more rebellious perspective drew and held viewers—at least for now.

Still, Casey was not content with leaving her fate in the hands of the fickle Zoomers, self-absorbed millennials, and vapid thirty-something soccer moms who watched the show while crafting and homeschooling their children. She wanted more.

That's why she had to ace this audition.

Jake Trainer had nearly used all his chits in this and any former lives—four times over. Like the time that he pissed off a bull so badly that it not only threw him into the stands, but it took a crap just after it did so, breathing fire. It took four men to corral the beast back into the stall.

He survived a motorbike accident on a county road playing chicken with a tractor; he gave himself food poisoning after eating a tuna salad sandwich left out in the sun all day; and perhaps most treacherous of all, he got his cock bit by an irate girlfriend who lured him to bed after learning that he had banged her sister.

He wasn't proud of these accomplishments so much as of his ability to bounce back from trouble, like Stretch Armstrong. Either that or he was truly bat-shit crazy. Bedding drunken women lured to bed from a bar and robbing them blind before the dawn only made him a petty thief. But selling off Casey Singer's bank and credit card information—and using them himself—was another thing altogether.

Jake climbed the crooked stone steps, taking them two-by-two until he arrived on the landing in front of apartment 10B. The box was there, propped between the front and screen door. He swung his head in all directions and then quickly picked up the parcel and carried it down to his unit. If anyone had tried to stop him, he would say that he was just helping old Mr. Miller out by taking in a package from the blistering sun.

He ran a blade over the taped seam and opened the brown box. Inside, he removed the wadded craft paper and Styrofoam peanuts and lifted a second, more exquisite box. Opening it, he held his breath. *Pow!* There it was, an exquisite vintage Rolex, a Stainless-Steel GMT-Master II. He had gotten it for a steal at eight thousand dollars. It even came with authentication papers. He couldn't resist it when he saw it online. Once he started spending Casey's money, he couldn't stop. He just kept on pushing his luck. His obsession for small, sundry purchases that would hopefully go unnoticed soon gave way to more extravagant items that came with more risk. He was always careful not to return to a previous website or to make the purchases too close together. He wasn't an idiot, after all.

It had been nearly two months, and Casey Singer did not seem to notice the uptick in her debit withdrawals or the mounting charges on her credit card. How lucky could he get? The watch was beautiful, but why stop there? Surely, he could push his luck just a bit further. So, when he heard from his old buddy Waylon, who agreed to meet up at a taco stand on Venice Beach, Jake was ready to listen to what he had to say.

"Hey, man. Your guy in El Paso was a colossal waste of time," Jake said, curling his beefy fingers around a giant burrito. "He wanted more than just a shopping spree."

Waylon cracked a crooked grin. "Yeah, I reckon those big boys don't play in the kiddy sandbox. They want the keys to the whole fucking Sahara!"

"I've been doing all right using the bank and credit card myself," Jake said, swiping his chin with the back of his hand. "Unless, do you think there is any way that she can link any of this to me?"

"Shit, man," Waylon said, tossing a curly fry onto the pavement for a squabble of seagulls to dive bomb. "She could have had her information lifted by a server in a restaurant or a clerk at a hoity-toity hotel," Waylon said, gazing out toward the beach. "You can't be traced, but watch your step. Hey, have you seen the headlines?"

"What headlines?"

Waylon slurped the last of his Mountain Dew. "I've done a

little fact-checking like you asked me to. It's all over the news and the supermarket rags—*Casey Singer and Ryder McKinley: Newly Married."*

"So? What's the angle?"

"Dude, their bank accounts are merging as we speak! Who's looking at the coffers? I say, strike while the wedding bells are hot!"

"Ryder McKinley, you say? Holy shit!" Jake said, warming to the prospects.

"That's what I'm telling you. Pay dirt, my friend, right there." As if money even meant anything to Waylon. He was a drifter, a free spirit, a con only when he needed the dough to get him by.

Jake grinned. "Do you still have that contact at the Porsche dealer in Newport Beach?"

"Sure do, my man," he said, pulling out his burner phone. *"And* he owes me a favor!"

CHAPTER 27

Casey was on a flight to LA that Friday with the *Starbreaker* script in hand. She had left the studio just after the show, practically rolling her carry-on right off the set and into the waiting car. Spaulding Caine had called one week after their meeting in Miami to deliver the news that she had a reading with director Alto Vuoria with Siren Studios at their West Coast office. Casey was elated. She would audition on her own turf. The film company that Alto Vuoria owned was primarily based in Bristol, with an office in Los Angeles as well. The innovative production company specialized in drama for film and television and had won acclaim more than once at Cannes for outstanding, groundbreaking work. Vuoria's current project was the *Starbreaker* trilogy, and Casey was about to read for the part of Oren.

She gazed out of the tiny window at her glittering city coming into view as the plane made its descent into LAX. How could she be so lucky? She was on the precipice of her dreams. It all hinged on everything falling into place at the right time. How many chances would she be given? How many more? She looked on dreamingly as the plane floated through the clouds until it faded to white, reminding her it could all be taken away just as easily as it came. That was the game. She clutched the script that she knew forward and backward to her chest. She was ready. Truly ready to show the world what she could do.

The car ride to Siren Studios afforded additional time for Casey to transform into the character of Oren. For her to become the outspoken, slighted sister of Amarantha, who leaves their home planet and family to seek a post-apocalyptic Earth several years after the re-colonization of the globe. The fearless and rebellious Oren stows away on the starship in order to join her unsuspecting sister, each with no sure means for return. It was a plum role, one in which Casey would have every opportunity to show her acting range. For the audition, Casey had braided her hair into two neat plaits that gave her a younger vibe, which she hoped would convey Oren's youthful but rebellious spirit. Casey removed most of her makeup and changed into a conservative button-down blouse right there in the backseat, making the driver wait, not caring what he could see in the rear-view mirror. She was already wearing dark jeans and swapped her heels for suede flats. She hoped the transformation would present a more natural, earthy version of herself. When it came down to it, there was nothing she wouldn't do to make it happen.

The driver deposited her and her luggage on La Cienega Boulevard in West Hollywood in front of the unassuming warehouse building with one entrance door with a sign that read: No Solicitors. She took a deep breath and walked in. Just as she did so, an alert on her phone buzzed but went unnoticed because she had switched it to silent mode for the audition.

It was her bank.

CHAPTER 28

The waif-like girl behind the reception desk looked Casey up and down with cool indifference. Her heavily lined eyelids were extreme, with the exaggerated cat eye flourish and metallic silver shadow high to her brows. She looked like she had just stepped out of a horror movie with her penciled matte lips the color of dried blood.

"I have a meeting for a reading with Alto Vuoria at four p.m.," Casey said, holding her own in front of the peculiar girl whose droll personality matched her black head-to-toe attire. Her blood-red acrylic coffin nails tapped across the keyboard with a mysterious precision. She had stakes and studs of piercings everywhere—one stud above the Cupid's bow of her lip looked painfully situated.

In a single moment, Casey felt the sweep of pride. She never wore her angst and sorrows for the world to see like the twenty-somethings of today did—even if it were the case, there was nothing authentic about this creature. She existed in a costume instead of her own skin.

"I will inform Alto that you are here," the girl said flatly. "Have a seat, Ms. Singer."

At least Morticia gets points for being polite, Casey thought.

A few brief minutes passed. Casey studied the script even though she knew every line forward and backward. She took a few deep, cleansing breaths. *You've got this, girl! It's just like every other audition.* Only it wasn't. How would it look if she blew a reading right out of the box? What would Spaulding think? She had to be better than that. Better than ever before.

Alto bounded in from an adjacent doorway, motioning for her to join him. "Come on in, Casey. We are ready for you!"

She entered a bright room set up with a video camera, tripod lighting trees, and a single chair in front of a plain white scrim.

Four other people were in the room, plus Alto. Each took their position behind a six-foot rectangular table. There was a technician present who motioned for Casey to take a seat in the empty chair under the swath of hot lights.

Casey was hoping to have a conversation with Alto, one-on-one, before the audition. She realized at this point it would not happen. From a look at the stacks of papers in front of the producers, Casey could see that she was not the only person who auditioned that day.

"So, whenever you are ready, Casey, if you would . . . slate for the camera, and then you may begin," the skinny, plain-faced woman said. Her rat-nest hair was tied in a messy bun, and she wore Birkenstocks and a T-shirt beneath a plaid blazer that read, "I Did Not Come From Your Rib."

She seemed tired, which only bothered Casey for a moment. She perused the other people seated at the table—three men and Alto. The men appeared to be in their mid-thirties, all jean-clad and stoic, with identical flat expressions and trendy, well-groomed facial hair. Alto was the most animated, with his frizzy white mop of hair and Robert Graham shirt rolled up at the wrists, revealing the contrast paisley print. He wore slacks and an Italian leather belt with Loro Piana moccasins that were as expensive as sin.

Someone was wearing Sauvage cologne by Dior. It hung in the air with the heat.

"Whenever you're ready," the technician said from behind the camera.

Casey looked directly into the lens at the red glowing light. "Casey Singer. Spaulding Caine Talent Agency."

The woman with the bun began reading the part of Amarantha flatly, and Casey easily slipped into Oren's skin like a pro.

When the reading was finished, Casey quickly scanned the room for a reaction, smiling widely.

"Thank you, Casey," the woman said. "We will be in touch."

Casey stood. "Thank you, everyone, for the opportunity. Please let me know if you need anything further from me." No one blinked.

She walked back to the reception area to retrieve her carry-on that the ghoulish girl had been watching for her.

"How'd it go?" the girl asked, interested. "Nice bag."

"Thanks." Casey showed no emotion other than to shrug. "Oh, you know. Hard to tell." Then she pushed her luck. "Do you know when they are going to make their decision on the callbacks?"

The girl batted her spider-leg lashes. "There's a few more reads after you. But my guess is that it won't be long. The callbacks won't be until the New Year, though. And they will be in the UK.

"Thank you," Casey said and then pulled her luggage behind her, out onto the street.

"All in a day's work!" She sighed and promptly tapped her screen to order a car.

TEN MINUTES later she slid into the back seat of a gray Sportage, checking to confirm that the driver matched the tiny digital photo on the screen.

Just then, her phone buzzed—it was Shelly.

"Girl!" Her beautiful smile popped onto the screen via

FaceTime.

"Oh, don't *Girl me*," Shelly said. "You've got some explaining to do, *Chicka*! I haven't heard from you in ages. I need my fix, girlfriend . . . What's going on with your hair?"

Casey mugged for the screen in her braids and minimal makeup.

"Holy Jesus! Did somebody kidnap you?"

Casey howled. She finally felt a sense of relief. The last forty-eight hours had been a constant obsession over the script—how she would interpret the character—how she would embody the part. With Shelly, there were no dangerous moves or boundaries. Shelly was her best friend in the world, and only a best friend could understand. "I just got out of an audition for a part in the *Starbreaker* trilogy. I am telling you, Shel, this would be such an opportunity for me to get this role."

"I have all the faith in the world in you, *Chicka*. And with those braids, how could they say no?"

"Right?"

"How did you land this?" Shelly asked.

"I just signed on with Spaulding Caine. He's a one-man agency, but he has incredible status in the business. I just have to trust him."

Shelly smiled good-naturedly, which was her way. She could defuse Casey's fears with a word, even through a tiny screen. "Listen, if it's meant to be, it will be. What I want to know is what is going on with your hubby situation."

Casey rolled her eyes. "Well, it's a wonderful marriage because there is no fighting, no bickering—"

"—and no sex, right?"

"Girl, I haven't seen the guy since Vegas."

"Right. There are no photos of the two of you together except for the Vegas shots. Still, social media seems to be eating it up! What are you planning on doing? About the marriage, I mean?"

"Regina is working on the divorce papers, I presume, as is Ryder's lawyer. That's only going to add to the frenzy."

"I'll say, girlfriend." Shelly was sitting on a sectional sofa. A sleepy brown Chihuahua folded itself onto her lap. She tilted the phone down to show Casey. "Nacho is happy for you! You know, people are making bets on how long the marriage will last. It's a freakin' feeding frenzy. I'm sure you're loving all the PR, though, right?"

"Well, it's not exactly rainbows and unicorns for the network. Bumpy has already called me to the carpet and informed me that if it tarnishes the show's image, there will be repercussions. I'm taking heat from the ladies and starting to wonder how smart this decision was."

"Just *now*, you're wondering about this, *Chicka*? That ship has sailed! You will make the most of it. I know you will. Let it play out."

"I suppose you're right," Casey said, already feeling better.

"Listen, I have a bit of good news. It looks like our little holiday family vacation is going to be in your neck of the woods. I convinced Hal that we should take the kids to Disneyland before they age out. It's the happiest place in the entire world, right? I figure that if he takes them for one day on his own, I will have a full day of bliss of *my* own. Are you up for that?"

"Hell yeah!" Casey said. "When are you planning this?"

"In a couple of weeks, over the kids' Thanksgiving break. We will stay at the theme park, but I'll break away so that we can have some gal-pal time. I'm booking the spa appointments as soon as we hang up!"

"I'm in!" Casey rallied. "Shoot me the dates."

"Girl, I can't wait!"

The two blew each other air kisses like secret sorority sisters and signed off.

Shelly was the closest thing to a sister Casey ever had, and she loved her like one. A day away from the media frenzy and circus that was becoming her life sounded just like heaven!

Casey leaned back and closed her eyes. She felt like she could sleep for days.

CHAPTER 29

Casey's phone buzzed.

She had just stretched out on the chaise lounge and gotten into position with the sun high and bright above her in the California sky. She had a paperback in hand and a cool iced tea in a koozie on the low glass table there on her tiny patio.

It was Ryder.

"Hello, husband!" she said when she picked up the line, trying to sound playful and casual.

Ryder laughed hesitantly. "Hello, wife! How are things?"

"Great," Casey said, feeling that the conversation would be a bit stilted after the pleasantries had been exchanged.

She was right.

Silence.

Then she said, "Where are you?"

"I'm at the Alnwick Castle location in Northumberland. It's epic—they made some Harry Potter films here."

Of course that would appeal to him, she thought. He was a boy-child. She tried hard to picture him in a fur pelt loincloth or a Scottish kilt.

"The *Downton Abbey* location?"

"Yeah, I think this is the same place. We've been going at it all day and into the night. I have a late call for a night scene in the woodland. Apparently, the moonlight is in our favor for filming. How are things in sunny Cali?"

"Oh, you know," Casey said. "The usual. Actually, I am waiting for a callback right now on an Alto Vuoria film."

"Really?" he said, interested. "For the *Starbreaker* movie?"

"Yes," Casey said smugly. "You are not the only one in the family who can act!"

They both laughed because it was actually funny.

"When will you hear?" Ryder's voice sounded shrill across the miles, like he was straining over high wind gusts.

"Hopefully soon. It's all I can do to keep myself occupied while I wait," Casey said, then shifted the tone. "Have you heard any news from your lawyer yet? About the divorce, I mean?"

"Yeah, he just needs our signatures. That's what I'm calling about. We need to find a place and time to do this."

"How long will you be in Europe?" Casey asked.

"No telling. Hopefully, I will be back before the holidays if I'm lucky," Ryder said. "I have back-to-back projects."

"Wow," Casey said. "Keep me posted. I will meet you wherever you like."

"Cool. Well, I guess I ought to go back. They're calling for me."

Casey hesitated and then relented. "Okay, Ryder. Thanks for the information. Contact me when you get back into town."

And the line went dead.

Opening her texts, she scrolled to Roe's name and typed, *Hope you are well. Miss you!*

She hit send and let the reality settle in. What was she doing? She was non-apologetic. Not in the least. It was *Roe*, and there were no rules with him. He wasn't married—*yet*, and she was about to become a free woman once again.

CHAPTER 30

It wasn't until the following day that Casey noticed the text. In fact, it was the second one from her bank. She had just finished a yoga session in the spare bedroom that she had decorated with candles, pillows, and crystals to create a serene workout studio and meditation room. She walked onto the patio with her phone in one hand and a green drink in the other.

"*What the—?*" She scrolled through the email with mounting distress. "Did I approve of a purchase for—*what?*"

Ten minutes later, after listening to on-hold Muzak from the seventies, a representative for the bank was on the line.

"Ms. Singer. We are checking to see if you have authorized a purchase on your card for a Porsche dealer on Pacific Coast Highway yesterday afternoon for two hundred eleven thousand, three hundred eighty dollars."

"What! No—I certainly did not."

"Someone used your account to do so, Ms. Singer. Did you want to dispute the charge?"

Casey felt faint. *Who would do such a thing?* She racked her brain as the representative droned on.

"Yes, please. I did not authorize the purchase."

Just as she hung up with the bank, a call came in from her accountant, Chantelle Grafton.

"Chantelle—?"

"Hi, Casey . . . we have a minor problem with the books."

JAKE TRAINER DROVE like a bat out of hell in the Porsche he had bought on Casey's dime.

Clueless Bitch! He chuckled.

He was on the run. He couldn't have gotten out onto the interstate any faster if he had nuclear energy in the tank. He was heading east toward El Paso and then onto the border. He would take his game to the warm waters and beautiful beaches of a resort town in Mexico, somewhere he could shed his cowboy boots for flip-flops and a year-round tan. Hell, if it worked for the likes of Jimmy Buffet, it could work for him too! He turned up the Sirius XM station and began belting "Margaritaville" at the top of his lungs.

And, if he was smart, he could finance his early retirement off the backs of unsuspecting tourists.

Women! They were only good for two things: *money and sex.* And nothing was sexier than money!

With his looks and charm, he couldn't afford *not* to cash in on both.

CHAPTER 31

Casey met Chantelle at a quiet restaurant in Newport Beach that was free of tourists and had killer mimosas. She figured she would need both when Chantelle indicated with her text that there was definitely a 9-1-1 situation with the books.

Chantelle was waiting at a table in the back, near a window overlooking the public marina. "Casey! Over here!" She was waving good-naturedly, looking stunning in her expensive chiffon blouse, crepe-cropped pants, and kitten heels. *I'm definitely paying this woman too much*, Casey thought. The truth is, she wasn't Chantelle's only high-profile client, and she was definitely known as a rock star regarding all things financial. If Chantelle said that there was trouble brewing, Casey was all ears. Chantelle would fix it. She would earn that Versace purse propped on the chair beside her.

"Hi. I hope this will not be too horrific," Casey said, sliding into the chair across from her. She was still in her yoga leggings and gym shoes. "It's not too early to drink, is it?"

"Hell, no. It's brunch time!" Chantelle brightened.

The server appeared and took their orders for two mimosas and two coffees.

When the drinks arrived, Chantelle raised her glass. "Cheers, first of all, to the nuptials."

Casey smiled wryly. "That's a discussion for another time. I'm sure you've seen the Vegas charges?"

Chantelle nodded. "Yes, and the social posts. You've been busy, girl!" Her calm demeanor was always comforting. She looked to Casey like a modern-day Nefertiti, with her alabaster skin and regal features. She was a beautiful mix of Jamaican and European genetics. And she was an outspoken lesbian. She could have been a model with her tall, slender frame. Instead, she was a wiz with numbers, and that was about to serve Casey richly.

They clinked glasses, and Casey drained half of the flute of orange fizz before even touching her coffee. "How bad is it?"

Chantelle delivered it to her straight. "Tell me. Have you been doing a considerable amount of retail therapy? I mean, *more* than usual?"

Casey puzzled. "No, not any more than usual. You know about my travel expenses in Sedona . . . Telluride . . . and Vegas."

"Yes, I'm not referring to that."

She opened her laptop and clicked her mouse around a series of spreadsheets. Then, turning the screen toward Casey, she said, "I've highlighted these debits. Do you recognize any of these purchases?"

Casey perused the spreadsheets. "No. What is all this? Charges for *men's western wear*? *Cowboy boots*? A vintage *watch*?"

"And, of course, the latest." Chantelle touched the screen with slender fingers, enlarging the image. Up popped the charge just the day before for a Porsche.

"Yeah, I've already spoken with the bank. None of this is mine," Casey said. "Now what? What do we do?"

"I took the liberty this morning of contacting your bank and the American Express account. It looks like the charges were all made from the Southwest and West regions. They are using both accounts. I have alerted both entities to your accounts' suspicious activity and disputed the charges on your behalf. You will, however, have to talk to them yourself to officially close the accounts. I'm just the messenger here, but I have to ask, have you been at all reckless with your information? Have you left yourself vulnerable in any way? That's how these assholes get into your banking."

Casey shook her head. She was more annoyed with the freeze on her wallet that this was sure to cause until the whole thing could be straightened out.

Chantelle read her mind. "You cannot withdraw any funds from your bank for a while. You will be issued a new account number. The Black Amex card is currently suspended and will be closed. I suggest you change over all your other bank cards, just in case. I can help you with that. In the meantime, I have withdrawn some cash to tide you over. From now until further notice, you are on a cash-only basis."

She handed Casey a thick envelope with hundreds and twenties.

"Oh my God, Chantelle, I can't believe this!"

"Believe it, honey. It happens. You should just be grateful that we caught it when we did. This should be the end, at least for the checking account. Credit charges can lag for thirty days. We really don't know how bad it is."

"Thirty days! I have to wait thirty days to see if these jerkwads make any more purchases on Amazon?"

"It could be worse, Casey. Trust me. We caught it."

"Yeah, I hope they're enjoying their new fucking car —on *me*!"

"That issue is going to be a bit more difficult to resolve. Once you make the appeal to your bank, they will reverse the charges. Then, it will be in the hands of the police. They can often find these deadbeats and shut them down. Maybe we'll be lucky."

"This is unbelievable," Casey said, shoving the envelope of money—her only lifeline now—into her Gucci.

"Don't worry, we're going to get you solvent again,"

Chantelle said, placing her hand on Casey's. "Care to order something to eat? I'm buying."

Casey nodded. The thought burned in her brain like a hot branding iron—like the image at the Red Rock Ranch in Sedona, where she met the slick and charming cowboy she left *unattended* in a hotel room after a night of lust and too much tequila. Yeah, she had gotten screwed, all right.

Royally screwed!

CHAPTER 32

"You've got to be more careful, *Chicka!*" Shelly said from behind an avocado and seaweed mask. She and Casey were on Rodeo Drive having twin facials at a posh day spa the day before Thanksgiving. It was Casey's treat, and she couldn't be happier to have her bestie by her side and the full use of a brand-spanking-new Amex Card to make everything right again. There even was a nip of autumn in the air as they sipped their chai teas in their fluffy bathrobes by the pool as the masks set. They had one glorious day to catch up, bond, and tackle all of life's absurdities and trials. Although, all the spa treatments, champagne and caviar lunches, and *Pretty Woman* shopping sprees could not match the treasure of Shelly's friendship. Casey relished it like an elixir and knew that nothing good —or bad—ever happened to her until she shared the experience with Shelly.

"I know. I'm an idiot, right? How could I be so reckless? That's the last time I will put myself in that position again," Casey said, sipping the spicy brew. Her hair was nestled in a white towel turban, and her toenails were still drying from the lacquer.

"Is that all that we learned from this?" Shelly said smugly.

Casey lifted a cucumber slice from her eyelid. "Excuse me? I said never again. No more *Cowboys*! I'm saying this to you with produce on my face!"

The two laughed so hard that their green masks peeled away and fell in chunks onto their spa robes.

"You kill me, *Chicka!* What in the world were you doing, anyway? Stop cutting yourself short. Here you are, married to the hot, badass Hollywood hunk Ryder McKinley, and you are not even fully cashing in on *that commodity*. I don't get it. I think you're losing your touch, girl."

"Far from it," Casey said, sitting up and ditching both cucumbers. "The sham marriage was the best thing that has happened to me since—I don't know when. Social media is still having a heyday with it all. I retained *the* Spaulding Caine for representation, and I got to read for the part of a lifetime with Siren Studios. Do you think all of that would have happened if I were just plugging away on a little talk show, competing with three other divas for the spotlight? It's all good, right?"

"I guess so, but—"

"But what?"

"You tell me, girlfriend. I think there is still a problem. You should lean into this more."

Casey paused. Then averted her eyes.

"*Jesús María.* You're still in love with Roe Evans, aren't you?

Casey's blue eyes softened.

"*Mi amore*, he's getting *married* in, like, two months! You have to accept that fact and move on with your own life. Seriously, *Chicka*, get that divorce and start your new year on the right stiletto! Get your glamour on and go to some of those industry holiday parties. Show the world that you are not shrinking. Instead, you're slaying it!"

Casey knew Shelly was right. She was always right. She would see Ryder soon, sign the divorce papers, put an end to the charade, and carve a path for herself, even if it meant being alone in the end, again.

"You're right. I'll take care of it."

"Good, then," Shelly said. "Besides, I never got you two a wedding present. I'm not still on the hook for one, right?"

Casey laughed. She untied her spa robe and jumped stark naked into the peaceful swimming pool that glistened near their chaise lounges.

Shelly squealed, doing the same, causing a slight tidal wave when she cannonballed in. The two splashed like children in the blue water, their facemasks dissolving into a green mess.

CHAPTER 33
DECEMBER 2021

The holidays were approaching with a vengeance. It was nearly Christmas Eve. Despite the amped-up show segments centering on gift-giving, holiday meals, and surviving the stress of parties, crazy relatives, and calorie-packed baked goods, Casey had little time to catch her breath. Still, in the quiet moments, as when she returned to her town-home in LA for the holiday break, it was all Casey could do not to think about Roe's upcoming nuptials and her failure to make the right choices in her own life. One thing was for sure; she would have to begin making smart decisions about her career—starting with the *Starbreaker* film. It would be her only wish and focus moving forward.

She would get the part. She already felt that it was hers. She would manifest it into existence no matter what. It was time for the industry to stand up and take notice of her in a way that mattered. She was not a screw-up. She was a fucking boss babe, and the bad choices in her life would not define her!

She purchased one of the last Douglas firs from a lot down-town and managed to get it back home after strapping it to the top of her new Audi SUV with blankets and bungee cords. The tree was on the smaller side, so it slid nicely into the nook of her living room, just in front of the bookcase.

A quick trip to a hobby shop yielded all of the items she would need to anchor and deck out the tree in high style. She went with a gold and red motif—plenty of glitz and glitter to convince even the sourest skeptic that she was on board with the holiday and sending good vibes into the Universe. She poured herself a generous glass of cabernet, put on a Harry Connick Jr. Christmas album, and settled in on the couch to admire her work. One solitary stocking hung from the mantle of her electric fireplace.

No matter, she thought. The coming year was going to be different.

It would bring only good things her way. Saying goodbye to 2021 would be her supreme pleasure.

She turned up the tunes and took some photos of herself in front of her beautiful tree that twinkled with magic and promise.

CASEY DECIDED that New Year's Eve would be far less low-key. She was eager to step out of the reclusive cocoon of her holiday festive townhome in LA, back to New York, and into the pulsing lights of Sprocket, one of Manhattan's most exclusive clubs. It was the hottest ticket in town save for the Times Square crowd who braved the weather of freezing temps to watch the ball drop to usher in the new year. Celebrity was the price of entry from behind the velvet rope stanchions into the vibrant, laser-bathed nightclub, wall-to-wall with movers and shakers from all realms of film, music, and media.

A swarm of paparazzi descended on the car as it pulled up to the curb.

"Where's Ryder? Casey! Over here! Where is your man?"

"He's on set filming in the UK!" She smiled, tossing them a coquettish glance. "I'm stag tonight!"

Once past the door, she recognized film actress Brantley

Simone, who waved her over. The two had met on the set of *The Gab* two weeks earlier. It was Brantley's suggestion that Casey join her and her crew at the exclusive soirée.

"You made it!" Brantley shouted above the music, delivering two hot pink lipstick kiss marks onto each of Casey's cheeks. "Right! Let's get you a drink!"

It was a small price to pay for the publicity of being seen out and about, even if it was without her famed other half. With Ryder still on location in London, the appetite for them as a couple still flourished. Any publicity at this point was welcome as far as Casey was concerned.

She checked her phone. It was nearly eleven, and she would only have to endure things until the stroke of midnight. Then, like a fated Cinderella, she would slip into a waiting Uber alone and be whisked away to her Soho loft.

No, she wasn't losing her edge. She would keep them guessing, as always, in Casey Singer's signature style.

She would soon slip into her silk pajamas, sink into the pricey sheets, and close her eyes as the turn of the calendar and the New Year ahead would hopefully bring with the morning, all of her hopes and dreams.

CHAPTER 34
JANUARY 2022

Roe and Celeste's New Year's wedding had been tantamount to the Royal Wedding in size and scope of its own. Celeste's gaudy East Coast family demanded pomp and circumstance that would no less put their otherwise aging daughter into the spotlight and onto the society pages, embedding her even more into the fabric of their fake and appalling causes.

Casey flipped through the social feeds until she thought her fingers would callous, just as her heart continued to break with each brutal swipe. "That's it. It's done. They're married."

"You're going to drive yourself crazy doing that," Kathryn said, peering over Casey's shoulder behind her makeup chair. "Seriously, it was a match made in the Hamptons."

Casey sniffed, putting down the phone. All the concealer in the world would not erase the pain in her eyes.

Alina, the makeup artist, bounded in. Kathryn shot her a look, and she retreated from the doorway. "I'll give you a few minutes," she said, closing the door behind her.

Casey let a tear slip from her eye, hating herself for appearing vulnerable in front of Kathryn, of all people. She readied herself for the blow, but Kathryn lifted Casey's chin from behind her in the chair and spoke to her reflection in the mirror.

"This is a mercy marriage. Celeste was a senator's wife before she found her husband dick-deep into Frederick, his personal assistant. She quickly divorced with a gag order not to pen a book for half of the bastard's pension, 401-K, and house in Rhode Island. The marriage had been childless because Celeste cannot have children."

Casey's eyes widened with each word.

"That's right. Barren as the Sahara. She had a hysterectomy in college, the poor thing. So, after the very public divorce years later, she began parading around with Roe Evans. Hanging on the arm of a high-profile music executive could help her regain her standing with the in-crowd, as she played concerned step-mother to Roe's disabled daughter, Jane."

"How do you know all this?" Casey was aghast that Kathryn even knew about Roe's daughter. She felt the chair move as Kathryn slowly turned it until she and Casey were eye-level, and Kathryn was facing her dead-on.

"Because my people did their homework. We looked into Celeste's story fully before considering the piece for the maga-zine. Lots of dirty laundry in that one's closet, for sure!"

Casey finally blinked. She did not know if it was the news or Kathryn's unusual act of kindness comforting her with her beau-tifully manicured, slender fingers resting squarely on her shoulders.

"You're going to be okay, Casey. It's not worth the tears. People do things to advance their careers, the perception of their lives—you know this. People make their choices. This is not yours to carry."

Casey was frozen to the chair. Kathryn had never spoken to her like this. No one ever had. Her voice felt like it came from somewhere small and broken.

"What do I do now?"

Kathryn removed her hands from Casey's shoulders and

handed her a tissue. "I always say that there is more than one way to make your mark in this world. Regardless of what you cannot control, you can always write your *own* fairy tale, if that's what you want."

Casey managed a half-smile. "Are you going to do the exposé on Roe and Celeste?"

"Hard pass. I don't wish to give them any steam."

Casey was touched beyond words. *Did Kathryn actually do her a solid?*

"I hope I can find my happy ending," Casey said, spinning around in the chair to face the lighted mirrors.

"Women like you do not wait for happy endings," Kathryn said to Casey's reflection. "You fucking make them *happen*."

CHAPTER 35
ONE MONTH LATER

Casey yawned. Suffering through post-show production meetings was not her idea of a good time. She exchanged a painful glance with La Costa, who was mindlessly doodling on a pad of paper in front of her, drawing butterflies and flowers, coloring them in with blue ink. That's what Casey loved about her. La Costa always had a sunny heart and disposition, no matter the circumstance. Team meetings notwithstanding.

Hannah listened intently; eyes fixated on Bumpy as he ran down the quarterly numbers for their day-part. They were still neck and neck with another network that had a big-name host in the afternoon competing time slot.

"We've got the ability to push the lead," Bumpy said. "What have we got?" he asked no one in particular.

This did not faze Tom LeMaster, who was biting his cuticles with his capped teeth, avoiding eye contact and the question.

Barry Paige cleared his throat, the little kiss-ass that he was, and commended Bumpy unabashedly. "Well, Boss, it looks like we have the perfect formula with our cast, and the addition of the new features has really made a difference. The viewers are eating it up. I think we could double down on this."

Everyone nodded in unison, feigning agreement.

Casey fidgeted. *More mindless drivel,* she thought.

Kathryn crossed her legs and went in for the pitch. "If anyone is interested, I have a suggestion that would ratchet this up another notch."

"Of course," Bumpy said. "What have you got in mind?"

"Well," Kathryn said, "since celebrity news is all the rage and ever-changing, I think we should have Casey run a segment that is a real-time take on the latest gossip, like a trending tabloid piece. Lord knows she is no stranger to the concept."

Casey snapped out of her reverie.

Barry Paige chimed, "Maybe commenting on social media posts that come in live. A sort of real-time interaction segment."

Bumpy scribbled on his notepad. "I like it."

Casey rolled her eyes. Sure, put *her* in the hot seat with viral Gen-Zers who have absolutely zero to offer the world!

Kathryn continued, "And, of course, I could continue to deliver on all things fashion and high style. That's my wheelhouse. Maybe we should offer a way to showcase new designers and connect viewers to the merchandise sites in order to buy the looks featured on the show—our clothes as well. I get emails all the time asking me who I'm wearing and where to get it."

Bumpy exchanged glances with Barry Paige. Both men nodded and jotted on their legal pads.

"It's being done already. We just have to figure out how to do it better," Barry said to no one in particular.

Deanna Calvin was next. "Hannah is rockin' it with her Q&A segment. But I wonder if we could pull in some of her more popular podcast features onto the show."

"Why not?" Hannah brightened. "I think that would be a wonderful addition. I could call it 'Gratitude and Graces'? Maybe a Tuesday feature?"

The pitch went into the machine that was Bumpy's keen mind. He nodded. "I like it. It's a fresh take on things."

Casey raised a perfect brow. *A podcast!* Maybe that was the missing link in her burgeoning career. *Why not?* Everyone who was anyone was doing one these days. She could increase her following substantially by hosting one of her own. She made a mental note to look into it further.

The idea-fest continued.

"That leaves us with La Costa," Deanna said. "She is the perfect choice for a book club feature. Everyone has one. Reece Witherspoon, Drew Barrymore, Kelly Clarkson—we should follow suit."

A collective series of nods circled the table.

"And I've got a new release right around the corner!" La Costa said. "Doesn't hurt book sales when you give me the airtime!"

Everyone laughed good-naturedly. Isn't that what it was all about? They each had their own agendas and were always angling for new ways to increase their net worth, with the relevancy factor looming. No one was keener to this than Casey.

Bumpy clapped and rubbed his hands together. "Barry, can you work up the specs on all this?"

He nodded dutifully.

"We can do some fifteen-second promos that can be worked into the media packages," LeMaster piped in.

"I think we have something workable here with these ideas," Bumpy said, scratching his bristly chin. "Let's make it happen!" Then, he checked his Rolex. "Have a great weekend, everyone!" he said, ending the meeting.

CASEY MADE a beeline for her dressing room. She had a flight in less than two hours to Chicago, and according to her phone, her Uber was waiting at the curb. She was going to meet up with Ryder. He had finally called her a few days prior to see if she could meet him.

"I'm heading home for a much-needed break," he had said

on the call. "Do you think you could fly out? I've got the paper-work for you to sign."

Casey was hoping to make light of it all despite the situation. A shopping jaunt on Michigan Avenue, some deep-dish pizza, and the stunning Chicago skyline over the lake surely could do her some good, right?

Or not.

She hadn't been back to her Windy City hometown in many years. In fact, not since she left at eighteen to pursue a career in journalism and broadcasting. Right after—after everything in her life had changed with her mother's mental breakdown and two shots of a handgun.

Chicago did not hold the same allure for her as it surely did for Ryder. She had wondered if meeting with him there would be a good idea. Was it time? Time to go back and face some demons she had left behind? She had decided she would go. If nothing else, there was the chance to erase the sham Vegas marriage and cut herself free once again.

The flight was crowded as usual, but Casey did her best to take it all in stride. It would be a short flight to O'Hare.

A handsome gentleman helped her with her carry-on, placing it in the overhead bin while smiling at her good-naturedly.

A promising sign, she thought. *Chivalry is not dead!* She slipped into the window seat, oblivious to the several rows of passengers who had recognized her and were unabashedly raising their phones to get a shot of her from the aisle.

Casey hunkered down in her seat, pulling a sequin-studded cap down across her forehead, and stared out of the plastic window. She ignored the intrusion, never welcoming it in a confined space. She wouldn't put it past the paparazzi to go to great lengths to snap her picture at the most inopportune times.

She let her mind drift as the engines whirred to full force. She would spend the weekend in Chicago, meet with Ryder, and try to catch her breath.

It had been a whirlwind month. There had been good news.

Siren Studios had since called for a second audition—this one would be in Bristol. It was less than two weeks away now, and she would have to arrange for someone to cover her seat for the talk show. She knew the network would choose someone who was not as controversial but could draw fresh eyes. She could only hope that it would not boost the ratings in her absence. It was the chance she would take for calling out. *No matter,* Casey thought. *Anyone can substitute for a show host once or twice. It takes someone with longevity to keep the seat warm and deliver what they expect to the viewers.*

It was a miracle that Bumpy approved the time off just as viewership was ramping up.

"I'm going to Chicago to end things between me and Ryder," she had said to Bumpy on an elevator ride down to the studio earlier that week. "I just need to sign the papers, and that will be the end of it."

Bumpy grunted. "Okay, then. Go take care of it. I'll have someone stand in your place. Two days, Casey—that's all you get."

What harm could be done in two days?

Now, opening her laptop propped on the tray table, she could see the answer to the question. There was an email from Aubrey, Bumpy's assistant. The network had chosen Kimber Hunt, a vapid-headed Instagram influencer-turned-reality show star. She was about a set of lashes short of a Kardashian car wreck. *This is who they are replacing me with?* Casey thought. *Jeez!*

Nothing to worry about, she assured herself. Shows you what they know. She could just as easily make the frightfully anorexic little Gen-Zer her first guest on the podcast she dreamed up. She made a mental note of it—and to book her flight to London. There were simply too many things to do in one day, and too many details to manage! She closed her laptop, shut her eyes, and tried to catch a few winks before landing.

CHAPTER 36
CHICAGO, ILLINOIS

Casey arrived at the terminal and wheeled her carry-on down through baggage claim and out onto the bustling chaos of taxis, shuttle buses, and cars picking up tired and harried waiting passengers. The rush of city fumes and the brisk wind hit her face like an old friend. It was there—the sweet, earthy smell of the Midwest that only existed for her in that one big, beautiful, unpredictable city.

She jumped into a taxi, which took her toward downtown. In the late night, the city lights in the distance on the Kennedy came into view, causing her heart to race. There was nothing like it, the Chicago skyline at night! She would put it up against New York's best skyscrapers, bridges, and burrows—hands down.

Her hotel towered high above Michigan Avenue with a view of Grant Park that was not visible in the shroud of night. But the stars and full moon high above the city made up for what the streetlights could not illuminate. She spent a good amount of time just staring out of the windows down at the bustling street at the endless car lights and pedestrian traffic that swirled around the avenue, streets, and thoroughfares near the museum. The expansive lake was only blackness in the dim stretch of space, with the occasional boat lights twinkling beneath a cold, black sky, void of any clouds or starlight. It was overcast, typical for Chicago on the prelude of winter.

She was home, yet she was a stranger there, treading lightly on the memories that came back in a flood as soon as her Prada boots hit the pavement. Her childhood in a home that only knew chronic anger and dysfunction. She became a rebellious teen, trying to break away at every turn. And then there were her two brothers, orphaned at a young age, that she had to leave behind to find her own way forward. They were both young men now, living their lives at East Coast colleges, earning their degrees. She rarely heard from either of them, receiving only the occasional email.

It was all there, brimming to the surface. She could see it in the vast darkness from the high vantage point of time and distance. Nothing ever stayed the same. How could it? Still, she berated herself for not staying in better touch with the boys. They were her blood; in many ways, she had left pieces of her heart where she once thought she had no right. *I can't erase the past,* she thought. How did she ever survive some of those choices? Her choices? How did she ever survive *herself*?

She did not know.

THE NEXT MORNING, she donned her wool peacoat over a chunky bright sweater and slipped on leather gloves to greet the morning. The wind was already whipping from the lake, and the crisp air felt glorious on her face. She had forgotten to bring a scarf, so she was on the hunt to remedy that. She grabbed an Uber to Water Tower Place, the towering mega retail mall in the sky. The smell of department store perfume hit her hard when she entered the glass-and-chrome atrium. The sleek tower on the Magnificent Mile had sky-high escalators and all-glass elevators and created a bustling city of its own. Many of the stores were not yet open, so she opted for a coffee shop and a corner table looking out onto the marble mall.

She swiped at her phone and bypassed the slew of notifications on the screen. She had one mission: connect with Ryder and get this thing over with.

She opened a text and typed: *I'm here! Where are we meeting?*

Next, she scrolled to the website *Finders, Inc.*, which connected entertainers, producers, and writers with industry news, resources, and job listings. She clicked on a job posting board and searched the listings for suitable candidates for a personal assistant. Most were freelancers who were savvy in managing social media accounts, purchasing advertising, and running promotions, media, and general publicity functions.

Casey sighed. Finding the right individual from a sea of eager candidates would not be easy. With the gig economy in full swing, this was the way it was done. Business and commerce had gone the way of online dating services, and if you wanted the best results, you would have to pay. She entered all the pertinent information and clicked send. Immediately, all access to the gleaming profiles opened, and she could pursue each one to her heart's content. She "favored" as many candidates as possible, planning to research them later. Maybe it wouldn't be as difficult as she had thought.

The time passed quickly, and the stores and shops began to open. Just as she had made a purchase from one of the pricy boutiques, her phone dinged.

It was Ryder. *I'm flying in this afternoon. Pick a place for lunch at around one o'clock.*

Casey texted back: *Lou Malnati's on Wells?*

Ryder volleyed back with a pizza emoji and three thumbs up.

Casey smiled. He was a bit of a nerd. She liked that about him. And the fact that he, too, loved the deep-dish delicacy that only Chicago could produce.

Too bad fate wasn't as easy to order up.

She snapped a selfie of her mugging for the camera in her new red cashmere scarf tied around her blunt blonde bob, making a goofy face like a forties starlet. *Be there!* she typed, adding her own emoji signature—camera with a flash, star-eyes, and the flame.

A FEW HOURS LATER, Casey plopped into a tall leather booth by the window, looking out onto the street. The restaurant smelled like heaven—oregano, basil, and garlic swirling in the air, perfumed by the pizza ovens that emitted their intoxicating potions. She was surprised by her feelings of anticipation of seeing Ryder again.

In a strange way, he reminded her of her first love, back when she was young and dumb, for sure, giving her heart to a boy in a leather jacket whose kisses tasted like Jim Beam and Marlboros. It was all so thrilling back then, when everything was in place . . . her dysfunctional family, her future, her dreams. It wasn't perfect, but she had everything one could hope for. And then, in an instant, it was gone.

She scolded herself for feeling nostalgic—again. The memories just wouldn't stop since she had touched down at O'Hare. She had to remind herself that she was slaying dragons that she could never have dreamed of when she was eighteen and naïve.

Such were not the usual thoughts of one sitting in a pizza parlor on the brink of yet another life-changing event. It was, for Casey, just another chapter that was her life story.

The door opened, letting in a gust of winter wind. Ryder bounded to the table on long, stilt-like legs. *Was he that tall?* she wondered, not having remembered him to be so.

"Hi!" he hedged, and bent over to give her a light kiss on the cheek.

"Not awkward," Casey said, smiling.

He slid into the booth across from her. "Here we are."

Casey folded her arms and nodded.

Silence.

He was wearing Dior Homme, with base notes of leather and patchouli that took her right back to that night in Telluride.

The server appeared with menus and another glass of iced water.

"Do you guys need a minute?"

Ryder looked at Casey. "You do the honors."

She remembered he was a vegan but gave no heed to the details. "A medium deep dish, butter crust, with sausage and pepperoni."

Then she smiled. "What are you having?"

Ryder ordered two house salads and a beer.

"I'll have a Sangria," Casey said, surprising even herself. "It's five o'clock somewhere, right?"

The two clicked glasses when the drinks arrived. Ryder joked, "This got us in trouble in the first place, right?"

Casey laughed. "We're a couple thousand miles away from Vegas, so I think we're safe."

More silence.

Finally, Ryder said, "I have the paperwork in my suitcase back at the hotel. Take the time to look it over before signing today or tomorrow. I have to be back on the set in two days."

"Where are you staying?" Casey had never been good at small talk.

"At the Four Seasons. My assistant books these things. I just go where he tells me to go."

"So, you have a male assistant?"

"Yeah, only he's called a lifestyle manager. His name is Tristen. He keeps me sane."

"Wow—I could sure use one of those! I'm looking right now for a virtual assistant."

"Don't go on the internet to find one. You need to get a referral from someone you trust. My agent found Tristen. He's fire."

She made a mental note of it. And another on how Ryder talked in short spurts and then silence. He was wearing tight jeans and a faded Pink Floyd T-shirt. His shoes were high-dollar loafers, and he wasn't wearing socks even though it was near freezing temps. This was a fish out of water. Even though his roots were from the Midwest, he now had West Coast vibes all over him.

"You grew up here too, right?" he said as the salads arrived.

"I did. We lived in Lake Forest when I was young, and then after my parents' divorce, I stayed with my dad in a condo on Michigan Avenue. I went to Columbia for journalism."

"Cool!" he said, tearing into a forkful of radicchio. "We were in Buffalo Grove."

It occurred to Casey that the boy sitting across the table from her—her husband, knew little to nothing about her. She knew little about him other than they shared the same hometown with vastly different childhoods and formative years. Yet, somehow, they both ended up colliding into a mirage marriage, held together with spit and duct tape.

He grinned when she made a joke about the irony of it all, charming her in a way that was absolutely kryptonite.

He had a grin that made something flip inside her that she knew better than to heed.

That would not happen *ever* again, she reproached, as she felt herself being pulled like a moth to a flame.

Despite her resolve, by the time the pizza arrived, hot out of the oven, it was Casey who was burning with a fire of another kind.

CHAPTER 37

The two embarked on a joyride around the city to reconnect with their childhood haunts in a rented Camaro. They did it all. Lincoln Park Zoo, the aquarium, and a long walk along the lakefront. Casey was fine with skipping the shopping circuit for a boat ride on the Chicago River, selfies in front of the Wrigley Field sign, and eventually ending up in a neighborhood brownstone tavern, four pints into a sea of Guinness. It was like one long glorious date between two lovers who were not celebrities or fodder for the Tabloids—until someone got a tip that the two were sharing fro-yo in Old Town, busting their cover.

A quick dash into a costume shop produced a long, dark wig for Casey, which she wore with a beret. A hippie wig and glasses for Ryder completed their disguises. From that point on, they slipped unnoticed into the eclectic mosaic of Chicagoans running through their daily paces.

The bar was called McKloosly's, and it anchored the corner of a quaint residential block with its large oak door and broken cement stoop. Stools set along the large glass window looked out onto the quiet street, lined with oak trees, barren of their fall foliage. It was perfection in every way—the perfect ending to the perfect day.

Eli McKloosly, the gray-bearded barkeep, ran a modest Airbnb by converting one large apartment above the tavern into three separate suites to rent. Enterprising as he was, he also featured a live Irish band on weekends, local stand-up comics on weekdays, and hosted the occasional bridal or baby shower when the occasion arose. He was prominently a fixture behind the bar and ran everything from A to Z.

Despite their efforts to resist one another, Ryder and Casey soon found the warmth and joviality of the pub and the day's adventures an aphrodisiac to their libidos. They were strangers in disguise, far away from the flashbulbs, the hectic pace of Hollywood, New York, and the unabating demands of their lives. An afternoon of day drinking, now into the night, brought with it a sweet bliss of excitement and reverie that quieted all the noise in Casey's head. It was her go-to reflex to be reckless in the face of reason.

They booked all three suites for total privacy. *What did it matter?* Casey reassured herself. If two married people do what married people do, what could it hurt? Only, it did not feel like a typical tryst—it was far more exciting and forbidden. *One last romp for old times' sake,* she told herself as his boyish grin pulled her into a kiss that threatened to lock them together far beyond eternity.

They were free to do what they pleased—no apology required.

"No regrets," Casey breathed in between deep, penetrating kisses.

"No regrets!" Ryder repeated as he seized her shoulders and traced her neck and breasts with soft, teasing kisses.

The result was an explosion of pure ecstasy.

And when the morning came, because of a well-timed call made at the service of Eli and his establishment that could use the surge of publicity, several photographers were there, waiting on the wet grass to capture the two emerging, arm in arm, into the daylight.

CHAPTER 38

Lucas was the slimeball who scoured the dark internet for his daily news. He was an opportunist. On the prowl, constantly, for any type of information or lead that could advance his desires. It didn't take long. The pictures of Casey and Ryder emerging from the Chicago tavern, arm in arm, were racking up the views. The press had been hungry for any information about the two so-called lovebirds and their whereabouts. Lucas licked his lips. Surely, there was an angle here that he could exploit.

He just had to figure out what it was.

Lucas arrived at the photo shoot in San Carlos, having driven the seven hundred fifty miles in a rented minivan filled with photography equipment that was also rented. He would take the photographs of several young women whom he had promised to help put together their modeling composites. He used seed money he had won on the fifth race at Del Mar one month prior. This would be enough to pull off the photo shoot to "add" the girls to his client roster. It would also earn him a getaway to an island paradise seven hundred miles from Los Angeles.

He arrived a day early in order to get the lay of the land. The girls were expected to find their own way to the Sea of Cortez Resort for the shoot and to shack up together in one of the pricey suites. In exchange, he would oversee the production of their photo shoots. He often worked on a barter system with his clients, who were desperate for inroads into the modeling world. The younger, the better, as they were gullible and easily manipulated.

Lucas would charge inflated costs for the printed composites, even though digital headshots were now acceptable for potential work.

He found a lounge chair near the edge of the resort pool and planted himself squarely on it while balancing a margarita in one hand and a cell phone in the other. His skin was pale. The sun's brutal rays would have him burned to a crisp within a half hour. He closed his eyes behind his dollar store shades and leaned back, enjoying the heat of the sun on his face. He smiled contentedly, thinking about which of the five luscious beauties he would deflower first. Who was he kidding? They would all put out willingly and were far from innocent. And, if he played his cards right, maybe he could score two or three of them at once.

Just as he settled in, a burly, cowboy-type walked up in his flip-flops and surf shorts, shirtless, tan, and gleaming in the sun.

"This chair available, brah?" he asked, pointing to the chaise lounge next to Lucas.

"It's all yours," Lucas said, avoiding eye contact, which was his way.

The man was medium height but had a build that could only be bought by spending hours on end in a gym. He had earbuds dangling around his neck and an iPod strapped to his bulging bicep. He pulled the chair forward and placed a hotel towel on it.

"Man, it's hot as hell out here!" he said with a distinctive Southern drawl. "Ain't it beautiful, though?" He was talking to no one in particular. He was wearing a Texas Longhorns cap. "I'm going to enjoy me some George Strait right here," he said, putting the earbuds in place and lying back on the chaise like a man with no cares in the world.

Because Jake Trainer had none.

CHAPTER 39

Casey was not proud about what happened between her and Ryder—*again*. It was like a fond farewell. She had come to Chicago to sign the papers, and regardless of what transpired, she had to do so and be on a flight by eleven a.m. back to LA.

They met at a restaurant near O'Hare, typical of their blighted fate. Meeting the moment, cold and sober in the early morning, across from a couple of coffees and some scrambled eggs.

Ryder laid the large manila envelope between them on the sticky Formica. Casey paused, and then opened it and slid out the documents, fanning them out on the table. She removed a pen from her purse that, ironically, was one she had taken from the Vegas hotel. It read: *The Regency Grand, Las Vegas.*

She signed all the pages that were marked with little yellow Post-it notes, then gathered all the papers together, slipped them back into the envelope, and handed it back to Ryder.

"You're officially free," she said with a smile.

He half-smiled and looked down pensively at his coffee. "For all it's worth, Case, I enjoyed the ride."

"It was okay being married to you," she said, feeling like she needed to say something. "You took me to a place that I thought I'd never go, and I am grateful to you for that. This could have been so much more of a disaster."

She was thanking him in her own way and hoped that he understood.

"What's next?" he asked, attempting to make more conversation.

"I'm heading to London," she said and brightened. "I've got a second reading for a part that I'm pretty sure I'm going to get, and I couldn't be more excited."

"Yeah, I've heard that Alto Vuoria does amazing work. And I think, Case, this part will really help you make your mark."

"It's the one I've been waiting for," she said. "I have a wonderful feeling about it."

"That's dope." He smiled. "I'm on my way to Atlanta after this one wraps. Apparently, there is a romantic comedy with my name on it that begins shooting in a few weeks."

"Well, I'll be waiting for the time when we can do one together," Casey said.

"That would be amazing!"

It really would be, Casey thought as the two stood up at the same time to leave. She reached for her wallet.

"I've got you," Ryder said, grabbing the check.

"Thanks," Casey said, glancing at her phone. "My Uber is a minute away. Ryder, I really wish nothing but the best for you."

"You too," he said, walking her out.

Then, reaching in for a hug, he pulled her close, the zipper on his leather jacket digging into her cheek. She inhaled his cologne one more time.

"See ya around!" she said, as the car pulled up. She climbed into the backseat like a bachelorette without a rose. "Stay weird!"

He laughed, hands in his pockets and sporting that boyish grin.

Casey waved through the glass. It was time to go home.

CHAPTER 40

NEW YORK CITY

"It's finally done," Casey said, popping her head into Bumpy's office, much to Aubrey's displeasure.

The harried assistant quickly closed in behind her to shoo her off. "Christ on a bike! You can't just barge in there!"

Bumpy was deep into staff reviews, with his shirtsleeves rolled up past his elbows. Looking up from his desk and peering over his wire-rimmed magnifiers, he said gruffly, "I've signed off on your leave, Casey. Good luck with the project in London. I count against your paid time off."

Casey smiled and pushed her luck. "Thanks for that. But do you have a minute? I wanted to talk to you about an idea I have."

He sat back, removed the specs, and rubbed his eyes with a beefy forefinger and thumb. "Sure, come in and have a seat." He signaled to Aubrey that the intrusion was okay, and she slithered back to her lair. Casey gave her a smug side-glance and crossed the sacred threshold into Bumpy's domain.

Casey took a seat across from his massive desk, feeling like a wayward granddaughter, small and remorseful in front of him, about to get his permission for her next crazy scheme. Truth being, he was actually the closest thing to a father that she had known for some time. She respected him and felt the two of them were finally beginning to connect on a very special level.

It was best not to waste his time. She knew that much.

"I want to start a podcast. Is that okay with the network?"

He tilted his head as if to process the idea. "I could check with legal. What kind of podcast?"

"Something like empowering women my age. You know, all the typical beauty, fashion, and relationship tips."

His face grew animated. "*You* talking about relationships?"

"Well, you know. Everyone has their difficulties. The most important thing is how we come out—shining and on top. I think I would be relatable to my audience. Young girls need to hear a message about being their best selves and what that means today."

He leaned forward and nodded. "Yeah, I think that a podcast would be a great idea for you, Casey. It would be a way to grow your following and give you a bigger platform. I don't think it would hurt the ratings one bit. We'll look at your contract and see if there is a work-in for the network. We'll draw something up, and then you can have Regina look at it."

"It should help women of any age to realize that you are never too young or too old to Blonde Up!" Casey said, quite proud of the idea.

"That's what you should call it—'Blonde Up! With Casey Singer!' It has a ring to it," he said, chuckling.

"I like it!" She beamed.

"Knowing you, Casey, it won't be long before you have sponsorships. This could be a wonderful springboard for you. I'm sure that Rick in audio would be happy to get you set up. Where are you thinking about broadcasting from? Here? Or in LA?"

"I'd like to have dual setups to make things easier for weekly episodes."

"Weekly!" his eyes widened. "Let Hannah know that you are giving her a run for her money."

Casey smiled and stood up. She wanted to hug him, but

instead, she settled for a firm handshake and made sure to look squarely into his eyes.

"I appreciate the faith you have in me, Bumpy."

He grunted. "Go! I've got work to do. Get back out there. The show notes are ready for tomorrow."

"I'll make you proud, Bumpy. You'll see!" she said, bounding out the door.

Aubrey sniffed when Casey walked by the assistant's desk just off of Bumpy's office.

"Top of the mornin' to you!" Casey said gaily. *Why was it always war with that one?* she wondered. She had Bumpy's ear *and* his heart. Wasn't it obvious? Aubrey was just his handmaid.

She laughed at her own joke and hit the elevator button.

It didn't take long for Jake Trainer to start up a conversation with Lucas once he noticed the bevy of bikini-clad beauties— young ones—prancing around the beach and stopping several times to chat with Lucas.

"Damn, man. What's up with the harem? Are you all vacationing here together?"

Lucas languished in keeping the dumbbell in suspense.

"Yeah, I'm like ole Hefner here with my den of bunnies."

Jake cocked his thick neck, ignoring the sarcasm. "C'mon, dude. What's up with that? It's like they are working for you or something."

"Sort of," Lucas said, keeping his gaze through his imitation Ray Bans on the Cortez water splashing on the shore. "I'm a talent agent. Doing a little photo shoot this afternoon with the girls. They are all clients of mine."

Jake raised an eyebrow. "*Clients?* Well, ain't that interesting." He swung his bronze tree-trunk legs over the chaise, planted his feet on the hot sand, and looked around. "I don't see no production crew. Where are you setting up?"

Lucas, now annoyed with the questions, removed his

sunglasses and stared Jake in the eyes. "I am the photographer, and all my equipment is back in my van. I'm waitin' for the perfect lighting. Going to shoot down by the rocks."

Jake nodded and then took a shot in the dark. "Hey, man, do you need a hand? I was once a roadie for the Zach Brown Band back in the day. I'm mighty handy on a set."

Lucas guffawed. "I don't work with nobody else. Don't have the dough for an assistant. Doin' it this way is saving bank, if you get my drift." *This dude was easy. He would be willing to give his left nut for a chance to muscle in,* Lucas thought.

"I think I do," Jake said. "Well, let's call it a good deed for sins unnamed. I ain't got nothin' going on this afternoon, anyway. I'm happy to help."

Lucas was no fool. What did he care, though, if he picked up free labor on the beach? It beat paying a local whom he wouldn't trust with the rented equipment. Hell, the girls would have no way of knowing that he had just met the guy.

"I'm Jake," the tan cowboy said, extending his hand to Lucas.

"Luke More," Lucas said, sealing the deal with a sweaty shake. "What's say we get a couple of cold ones and then offload the equipment? I want to get set up when the sun is optimum."

"You got it, Hoss." Jake grinned, slipping into his beach shoes.

The two kicked up the sand padding toward the Tiki bar.

CHAPTER 41
BRISTOL, ENGLAND

Casey arrived at the Bristol airport in the late afternoon and asked the driver to take her directly to the studio, even though her second audition would not be for another two days. She had built in extra time to learn the lay of the land and to rehearse. The production company was inconspicuously housed in a 17th-century brick building on King Street that was once everything from a hospital to a monastery and, later, a multi-flat workman's residence in the late eighteen hundreds. It was eventually converted into commercial offices in the late 1970s and now housed Siren Studios' esteemed headquarters in South West England. The thriving and eclectic arts scene was a mix of legacy and modern production companies, of which Alto Vuoria had hung his shingle for the past decade. It was a vastly different feel from the ritzy five-diamond Marriott Hotel that the studio had arranged for Casey's stay.

She eyed the stoic brick building without getting out of the car. It looked like it had endured a thousand misfortunes and held the promise of a turning point in her career—her *story*. She would check into her hotel room at the Marriott and get to work, going over the script and keeping her focus on the prize.

She was, according to Kathryn, in charge of her destiny.

But who was she fooling? Roe Evans's number was still the first entry on her "favorites" in her phone.

And he was now only a two-hour drive away.

What if destiny was asking her to choose—*again*?

The thought of it both frightened and revived her.

She typed out the words before she could talk herself out of it. *Hey—I am in London for work. Would love to see you.* She added a cup of coffee emoji to infer that a casual meeting would do.

Then she sent it with a bracing exhale.

CHAPTER 42

The photo shoot was set up near a rocky ravine at the shore. Lucas had instructed the girls to wear bikinis, which they accessorized with conch shell necklaces, macramé bracelets, and oversized hoop earrings. They had busied themselves all morning getting ready for the shoot. There was no stylist on hand, so it was up to them. The girls had a collection of props, including colorful beach balls, striped towels, and even an old surfboard they found near a piling. Each waded in the water and knelt provocatively in the sand, running their hands through their gleaming hair.

Jake, touted as Lucas's set assistant, happily applied suntan oil liberally to each girl's arms, legs, and back. If the girls thought it unorthodox, they did not show it or seem to care. They seemed eager as ever to be given a chance at their shot at fame, posing seductively for Lucas's clapping shutter.

He took several shots of each girl and then a few more of them together. "For my website!" he told them as they fell into place, arms linked, giggling giddily in the midday sun, kicking up sand and mugging for the camera.

"Looking good, girls!" he would say, as they moved through their poses.

Jake stood in the background, watching with hungry eyes like a wolf overseeing the lambs' den.

Lucas had several cameras that Jake assisted him with throughout the shoot. Changing lenses and adjusting the reflector screen to catch the sunlight as it set on the beach.

One girl, named Dixie, eyed Jake with flirty glances and fluttering eyelashes. She had a Hello Kitty tattoo on her left shoulder blade. She listed her birthdate on the modeling application as twenty-one, but she didn't look a day over seventeen.

All the girls responded to Lucas and seemed eager to please.

"Man," Jake said, "these beauties are really something. You gonna get them all work from these photos, ya think?"

Lucas shrugged. "You never know. It depends. Might lead to gigs at department store perfume counters or trade shows next to shiny sports cars as hood decorations."

"That's Hollywood for ya," Jake said as if he were knowledgeable. "It's all *T and A*—still. Especially today. I guess sex sells."

When they had finished the shoot, the girls scurried off to their room to shower and get ready for dinner. Lucas had agreed to appear at the bar and buy everyone the first round. This was the extent of his schmoozing, and he was sure that by then, one of the girls would be more than happy to accompany him back to his room.

"This was sure fun," Jake said as they broke down the last of the equipment and huffed it in the sand back toward the parking lot. "Mind if I ask Dixie out to dinner tonight?"

"You don't have to ask my permission, man," Lucas said, shoving a couple of large duffle bags into the back of the van. Then he slammed the doors shut. "I ain't their pimp," he said slyly. "I'm surprised, though, that you would be interested. My guess is that she is not exactly your *type*."

Jake looked at him, scratching his bristly goatee—something he was trying out, but it garnered more scratch than snatch as of late. "I don't follow, man."

Lucas had a hunch, and his gut was rarely wrong. "It's just that when we were having drinks earlier, I saw more than one older woman pass by you with a smile or a glance that suggested that she knew you. It's quite obvious to me you got a little thing going here. Tell me—am I wrong, or am I right?"

Jake grinned like a kid with his hand in the cookie jar.

"It's no wonder that you are looking for some young tail, dude! Hey, I'm not judging!" Lucas said, throwing up his hands and landing them deep into his cargo shorts' pockets.

Jake chuckled. "Well, a guy's gotta make a living, you know?"

Now Jake was singing Lucas's tune. They were more like-minded than Lucas had initially thought. Suddenly realizing that his pockets were empty, Lucas clapped his hands together. "Dude. Got any weed?"

Jake, happy to oblige, slapped Lucas on his sunburned shoulder and smiled. "Yeah, Gringo, I can hook us up. I know all the connections on this island. What's your pleasure?"

AN HOUR LATER, the two were sitting in a bar away from the resort in an off-the-beaten-track fishing town where the locals went to drink tequila and drown their woes.

"You won't find a tourist here—ever," Jake said proudly. He was setting up several shots along the bar along with tall, cool bottles of *cervezas*.

"Let me get this straight," Lucas said as the warmth of tequila loosened his tongue but not his knife-edged mind. "You live on the resort, right?"

"Correct," Jake said. "I have a bungalow there."

"So, what's the con?"

Jake leaned forward and delivered like a babbling idiot. "I service wealthy women who are looking for companionship. Tourists are very thirsty, if you know what I mean. Especially the senior ladies. Their husbands are off playing golf or whatever the fuck. After the spa services and the poolside martinis, they are hot and ready for action."

Lucas nodded approvingly. "Very nice, man. I gotta give you props. I don't know if I could do that sort of thing."

"Well, it's not all hags and bags. I've had my share of bedding many women who are more than happy to offer me full access to their cash, checkbooks, and credit cards—when they are in the shower."

Lucas raised a sun-bleached eyebrow. "Tell!"

"Yeah." Jake puffed with bravado. "Been running that scam for the past five years. You'd be surprised at how easy it is. Once you bed them, they go for that shower—and *Bam!* That's my window to score!"

"So, you just, what? Rip them off and that's it?"

"I lie low for a while. Stay out of sight. They think I skipped town, and they are not inclined to report it to anyone for obvious reasons. Hell, most of them see it as fair payment for services rendered. Sometimes I sell the digits to a third party through an acquaintance. Other times it's a shopping spree for me. Man, when you have the gold card, it's Christmas every fucking day!"

Lucas lifted his shot glass and clinked it against Jake's. "Wow, man. So that's how you survive?"

"Yeah," Jake went on. "I even scored myself a big fish not that long ago. Casey Singer, from the talk show *Women Who Never Stop Gabbing* or some shit."

Lucas nearly choked on his beer.

"What?" he said, the color draining from his face.

The loud music in the bar might have distorted what he had heard.

Jake repeated, "You know, *Casey Singer*—the actress. Got into her panties and then into her Prada. It was a pretty big payday for me, let me tell ya!"

Lucas could hardly believe what he was hearing. He played it cool in every way.

"Good for you, man," he said and then paused. "Did you rip

her off—a lot? I mean, wipe her out in any way?" He was hopeful.

Jake shook his head. "Naw, but I got a badass car out of it that got me here—traded it in for a Jeep. It fits my style a bit more now that I'm an island gigolo! One in flip-flops!" He belly-laughed at his own joke. "Did a lot of shopping on Ms. Singer's dime, though, I'd have to say."

Lucas could not stop thinking about the conversation that he had with Jake earlier as he lay in bed with Amber, the tall one with the dark brown hair. She was fast asleep, while his mind was whirring with his thoughts ruminating in his head. *What are the chances?* He couldn't believe that Jake from the beach had swindled Casey! It was impressive, but it got him thinking that if she could be so easily fooled, she didn't have her shit together, that's for sure. The keys to her castle were unguarded, meaning said castle could be *breached*.

Amber sighed and turned over, slipping her slender leg over his as she nuzzled into the pillow. An idea popped into his very pickled brain. Casey needed an assistant for sure, and she could be convinced to hire one if the right candidate came along— someone who knew what she would need to keep her life on track. To look after her affairs and manage her everyday life, finances, etc. That would be the in! That would be the way he could get to her.

And he knew just the right person for the job.

Nudging the beautiful young woman next to him, he said, "Amber! Get up! We have work to do."

"Wait! *What?*" she said groggily.

"You're an actress, right? You want an acting gig? I've got just the part for you!"

CHAPTER 43
LONDON, ENGLAND

Roe had not noticed at first that his phone had dinged. He was at the sink shaving when he glanced at the screen. Celeste was brushing her teeth beside him and going on about the massive task of still having to complete the list of "thank yous" that needed to go out post-wedding, some four weeks past.

"I think I should have the last of them addressed and in the post by this afternoon," she said over the running water.

Roe flinched as he nipped his chin with the blade, and then reached to flip his phone over, screen down. "Sounds great!" He then reached for a square of toilet paper to dab the blood pooling on his chin.

"Oh, darling! What did you do? You need to be more careful. You don't want to mar that handsome face, do you?" She blew him a little air kiss and then disappeared into the massive walk-in closet.

Roe snuck a peek at the message, certain that she was out of eyeshot as her muffled voice droned on from the other room.

It was Casey Singer! She was in town and wanted to meet up with him. His pulse quickened, and he had forgotten how to work his fingers for a quick reply.

He simply hit the smile emoji and one loaded word—*Yes!*

The Berners Tavern was an upmarket, modern restaurant in a London hotel on Berners Street. It was both posh and eclectic and had a great vibe. Stunning framed portraits covered every inch of the walls, and ornate friezes created a Greek palladium feel amidst a contemporary, posh backdrop. Every table was filled with a lunch crowd of eager business executives, the kind that relished in the old-school martini lunch deals. It did nicely to conceal the clandestine meeting of two former lovers who hadn't laid eyes on one another in over seven years.

Casey's heart raced as she approached the maître d' stand, knowing that Roe was already there waiting. He had texted so after confirming the meeting the day before, giving Casey the biggest dose of nerves she had ever felt when the text came over her phone: *I can meet you for lunch at Berners Tavern. Does twelve thirty work for you?*

The room was a jungle of patrons and servers busying about. The solemn young man who looked like a groom escorted her to a back table for two, where Roe was waiting. Her heart leaped when she saw him.

Slowly, he rose from the chair and looked lingeringly at her from head to toe. Finally, he reached out his arms, and the two locked in an embrace. It was awkward and over in a quick minute. Casey just wanted to sit and steady herself from the moment. It was a reunion that was about to test her resolve, to try the passing of time, during which nothing existed from that point on except for those bright, penetrating eyes and Roe's boyish grin. It was still there—all of it, right across from her.

"I hope you're hungry," Roe said, reaching for his napkin.

Eat? Who could eat? She was reeling from the electricity of the room . . . and the reality of the moment. He had a magnetic effect on her that calmed and excited her all at the same time. She remembered it all . . . the late-night phone calls, the waiting and the wanting for his attention; the gala in Washington, D.C., and the night in the park; the stolen kisses when he had to leave again and again. Was this really happening? And then, the cold reality that hung between them—the truth of how things were.

"So, congratulations on your marriage," she said as the server filled her glass with sparkling water and a bobbing lemon wedge.

"Thank you," Roe replied in a matter-of-fact tone, as if the weight of the words didn't fit the sentiment.

Casey smiled nervously, berating herself for showing her vulnerability.

"You look amazing," he said, staring.

"Well, a lot more work goes into being 'me' these days," she joked. "Time marches on, that's for sure. You too. You look great yourself."

He knew that time had made its mark, as a few creases had etched their way onto his forehead and around his deep-set eyes. His hair was holding strong, though, with just a hint of gray at the temples. Although he benefitted from a daily jaunt on the treadmill, he still had his vices—a love of bourbon and the occasional cigar. That, and too many industry meals, however, made it impossible to ditch the extra twenty pounds he carried mostly around his midsection.

The two loosened up once the drinks arrived. Casey had a designer martini and Roe his usual, two fingers of Maker's Mark.

For the most part, the lunch was a blur of light conversation and Roe's gentle interrogation of her life on the set of *The Gab*.

"It's okay, really. I enjoy working with my cohosts for the most part. The network is always pushing for more, of course. We live and die by the ratings."

"I see that you've held the top spot in the daytime lineup for the many years. That is truly an accomplishment."

"It takes a small army of people to make every episode happen, though. Our part is the most visible, but we have our own lives to consider. That's why I am out here working my butt off to break away from the box that Global Network has put me in. I have so much more to show the world."

Roe smiled widely. There she was. The Casey Singer who took no prisoners and never stopped going for the gold. "It looks like you've got it all figured out."

She shrugged. "Looks like. I can't tell you how nervous I am about this second audition. Everything is pending on it. I am reading for the supporting role of Oren, the protagonist's tenacious sister who stows away on a starship flight. It's science fiction. A bit out of my wheelhouse."

"You got the callback, though?"

"Right." Casey drew in a deep breath. "That's why I'm here. I just would feel better if I ran this by somebody."

"I've got an idea," Roe said, signing the tab and returning a garishly expensive fountain pen into his inside coat pocket. "I can get you a perfect set up to record your audition and play it back for critique."

"Really? That would be great! Where is it?"

"Here's the address . . . I am texting it to you now." He tapped on his phone and then retrieved his key fob. He removed a single key from it and slid it across the white tablecloth. "Take it. Let yourself in. It's my flat in SoHo."

Casey blinked. "You have a flat in SoHo? What for?"

"I stay there sometimes when I am working late in town. No worries. Please take it. It will provide all the privacy you could ask for. I'll break away later this evening and join you—to see your progress. I'll be your mentor!"

Casey stared at the key and then back at Roe. What did she have to lose? It was a kind gesture, and rehearsing in a new environment might be just the thing to jolt her performance. "Okay, I'll do it."

Roe smiled. "Great! You can record yourself on your phone.

There is a tripod in the front closet. Oh—shall I bring Chinese? Do you still fancy spicy shrimp?"

"*Fancy?*" Casey giggled. "You definitely need a shot of Yankee to bring you back to your roots. Better make that some hot dogs and apple pie!"

CHAPTER 44

LOS ANGELES, CALIFORNIA

"So, let's go over this again. Who are you?"

"Selena Rapp."

"Age?"

"Twenty-three."

"Native?"

"Born in Orange County."

"School?"

"ASU. Communications major."

"Skills?"

"Versed in all social media, marketing platforms, and public relations protocols. A wiz with Instagram, TikTok, etc."

"Experience?"

"Former assistant to two recording artists, a relationship coach, and one reality star."

"Perfect. Why are you reaching out to her?"

"Because I admire her and want to learn from the best, how to be the best, Yada, Yada, Yada."

"You're ready," Lucas said, handing her a fake I.D. and phony credit cards embossed with the name Selena Rapp. He even had a monogrammed designer keychain for her purse.

He clapped his hands and rubbed them like he was

summoning a genie. He was. He knew that his little protégée, Amber Herrera, could play the role like a pro. She was a native of the area, knew the business, and she had a take-no-prisoners way about her that would impress Casey and convince her that what she needed was a hot-shot millennial assistant who was smart, connected, and competent.

Casey was about to meet Miss Selena Rapp—and come to *need* her. The perfect setup for Lucas to get closer to Casey than ever—and everything she held dear.

It would start with an introduction email and then several follow-up emails to see if Casey was receptive to a meeting with Selena. Lucas wrote the correspondence. It was unlikely that Amber could produce anything slick enough to lure the likes of Casey Singer into a conversation. Lucas knew how Casey's mind worked. To her, fan mail and accolades were catnip. She loved to be loved and admired, but one had to be careful not to assault her with stalker vibes.

So, when Lucas sent Amber in to "bump into" Casey, it would have to appear casual and natural.

After several attempts to catch her at her favorite coffee shop near her townhouse, Lucas retreated, wondering, *Where the fuck are you, Casey?*

CHAPTER 45

LONDON, ENGLAND

Casey let herself into Roe's flat with tentative caution, feeling as if she were intruding on his private life. Even though she had his permission and the key, she tiptoed gingerly across the large area rug to the center of the sunny apartment.

It was nicely appointed. The open floor plan made it easy to size up the place—an ample kitchen with modern appliances, a medium-sized living room with sectionals, a retro low coffee table, and wide original windows with Roman shades. She peered into the dark hall just off the living room that led to two bedrooms. One had a large king-size bed with a stylish duvet and tufted headboard; the other was a converted office with an electronic keyboard, a computer, and a few file cabinets. A leather sofa was set along the longest wall. The bathroom was between the two bedrooms. It smelled dusky, with just a hint of Roe's aftershave.

Not a sign of a female or the influence of a woman anywhere. This was indeed a man's dwelling.

She returned to the living room and set down her Gucci bag. It felt strangely forbidden to be privy to Roe's little pied-à-terre, which, clearly, it was.

She was thirsty. She walked around the raised counter onto the diagonally tiled floor into the little bistro-influenced kitchen, complete with gourmet pots and lids stacked on the stove and an array of spices arranged in racks along the backsplash. She smiled. *Did he like to cook?* She could not remember.

Suddenly, she felt certain that she really did not know him very well at all. Most of her memories of Roe were her imagined fantasies about what life would be like with him. And as of late, never to be with him.

She opened the stainless-steel refrigerator and chuckled. It was empty except for a Brita pitcher filled with sparkling clean tap water.

"Perfect!" she said. Then, she started searching for a glass.

Just then, her phone buzzed. It was Shelly.

"Hey, girlfriend!" Casey burst, realizing that it had been ages since the two had talked.

"Are you in exciting London, *Chicka*?"

"I am," Casey said, pouring a full glass from the pitcher. "In fact, you will never guess *where* in London I am."

"No telling with you," Shelly said.

"Would you believe I am in Roe Evans's hideaway apartment in SoHo?"

"*Christ!* What? No way . . . !"

"Wait. It's not like that. We just met this afternoon for lunch, and then he offered his place to me to rehearse. I'm going to record myself doing my scene. He wanted to help ease my mind about the audition tomorrow. That's all."

Shelly was silent for a few beats. Finally, she spoke. "*Chicka,* you are playing with fire here. What is he to think of the fact you accepted his apartment for your rehearsal? Why does he even have a separate place from his home?"

"Exactly," Casey said, moving to the couch near the windows like she now owned the place. "It's Roe, though. So, one never knows why he does what he does."

"Sounds like he is a player, for sure. I am sorry, girlfriend. I'm just begging you to be careful. Remember, he's a married man, plus his wife has connections if you know what I mean."

"Shelly, you are watching too many Netflix movies! Don't worry. I will get through this and walk away with a plum part in a great new film . . . and will have restored my friendship with Roe."

"That's the thing, *Chicka.* You cannot—and should not—be friends with a married man. Especially not Roe Evans." A crashing sound came over the line. "*Jesús María!* Look, Casey, I have to go. My sons are attempting to clean up the garage. I have to protect my potted flowers. You listen to me. Just rehearse and then get out of there. Okay?"

"Okay, Shelly. Go! I'll catch up with you later. *Ciao, Bella!*"

With that, the line went dead.

THREE HOURS LATER, the daylight had turned into a gray hue, casting shadows on the living room, causing Casey to have to turn on every lamp to illuminate her recording session. She had found an adjustable tripod in the front closet that fit her iPhone perfectly. She could pair the Bluetooth function with her phone, using the remote that was taped to the base. This did nicely to give her lead time before starting the recording from various positions in the room. She ran over her lines, standing, sitting, and even off-camera, to see if she could achieve the exact delivery she intended. What Alto Vuoria would look for was anyone's guess. All she knew was that she would need to nail the reading in any light, setting, or position that he would find brilliant.

By six-thirty p.m., she had gone over the scene nearly fifty times, and she was exhausted.

The door cracked open just as she had collapsed onto the suede couch. It was Roe—and he was packing Chinese takeout and a smile. "Hi there! Who wants spicy shrimp?"

The two shared a casual dinner at the low coffee table, eating right out of the takeout cartons with real utensils from the kitchen drawer. Jamie Cullum's smooth jazz sound was streaming from expensive speakers, hidden out of sight. Roe had opened the aged Chianti he had in a wine fridge beneath the counter. "I'd say that reuniting after all of this time is as good a reason as any to pop the cork on this." He poured them each a generous glass and then settled in for a walk down memory lane, reminiscing about their unusual way of meeting that made Casey laugh until she felt her sides would split. "To think that I pinned you beneath the wheel of my car, there on the pavement, with your groceries rolling down the curb!"

Casey slapped her hand over her eyes. "I know! *Not* one of my finer moments!"

"I thought I had killed you—you can imagine my relief when I saw you lying there, staring up at the paramedics."

Casey wiped a tear from her eye. "Yeah, and then you split, leaving me there in my pee-soaked jeans to try to regain my dignity."

"I sent you flowers," Roe said in his defense.

"Yes, you did. And then several boxes of CDs from the record company. You arranged two tickets to a Garth Brooks concert, was it?"

"Ah, yes. Apology by singing Cowboy. That's *definitely* my style!"

"I loved it, Roe. All of it. That was the beginning of our *friendship*." She said the word as if it was not indicative of the feelings that she had developed for him over the many months and years that followed. He could never know that she had carried a torch for him ever since—not if it caused her to second-guess every choice that she had made that day behind Global Studios, waiting in the running car, and finally, choosing to walk through the door, a decision that changed her life forever. She knew then that what he needed was not something she could give or become.

Roe sighed heavily and then hoisted himself up from the

floor and onto the couch. "Let's see these clips that you have made. I promise I will be brutally honest."

Casey set her wine on the table and picked up her phone. "Hold it away from your face to get the full effect."

He smiled, watching each video with rapt attention. He particularly liked the ones at close range. "I think you need to read this standing very close to the other actor. When whoever is reading the part of Joshua, he should be right there in front of you."

"How do you mean?" Casey asked, looking up at Roe with innocence and vulnerability that she did not shy away from. Their faces drifted inches apart.

"Like this," he said, inching closer. "Yes. Just like that! Wait, let me turn this thing on."

He affixed the phone to the tripod and fished for the remote on the table beneath a greasy napkin. "On three . . . let's go. Do it again."

Casey looked squarely at Roe and read the lines with sincerity and depth. She let herself get lost in his eyes and let the words make wonderful shapes and pauses that conveyed more than simple syntax and sound. She was breathing life into the words, and in turn, not resisting the magnetic pull that was over-powering each of them in the least.

They collided into a deep, forbidden kiss that felt like home, drawing forth a passion that could not be explained.

And hopefully, could be forgiven.

She was helpless in his embrace, and he, the same.

The two were locked in an unbridled passion with no turning back and no regrets. He dropped the remote onto the carpet—as the phone's camera captured every frame.

CHAPTER 46

The flight home would be a blur. All she could think of was the feelings of intense lust, love, and desire that she and Roe exchanged until he had to pull himself away and leave her, alone and dejected, in the bedsheets.

"You understand that I have to go," he had said in the darkness, unable to remain a moment more. "A late night at the office was all I could buy."

What was the point of having a second apartment if it didn't even afford them a bit more of each other until the dawn?

Casey had kissed him one last time and accepted the reality that fate would never allow them to fully realize the soul connection that she was so certain they shared.

She made it to the audition, prepped and ready for anything. She knew her lines forward and backward, and when it came time, she nailed the part of Oren. Alto Vuoria called her himself in her hotel room right before she had checked out for the airport.

"Expect to have a busy schedule, *amore mio*. We start preliminary shooting in LA in a couple of months."

Casey gasped with disbelief and was, for once, at a loss for words.

"You can make the shooting schedules, correct?" he had asked her.

To which she promptly replied, "Yes, Alto! I will make it happen. Thank you so much for this opportunity. I won't let you down!"

She drifted to the airport as if on a cloud, her mind whirring from the emotional highs and lows of the past forty-eight hours. She texted Spaulding to let him know the outcome.

Next, she owed three words at least to Roe for all that he had done to help her.

She simply typed: *I got it!*

FINALLY, it happened. One week later, Amber caught sight of Casey alighting from her racy new Audi SUV, which she had just parked in a loading zone. She was definitely in a hurry to get somewhere, so Amber had to think and act fast.

"Excuse me. Are you Casey Singer? The talk show host?" Amber sidled in next to her as the two walked through the glass doorway into the cafe. The smell of deep roast hung above the din of chattering patrons and lone souls hunched over the glow of their laptops pounding out screenplays and emails.

"Yes, I am. Do you watch the show?" It was Casey's standard question to suss out the value of the intrusion. What would it take? A photo? An autograph? She was ready for the bane reality that rubbing elbows with the locals demanded.

"I do! In fact, I have followed your career for some time."

Casey stopped cold and gave an incredulous look. *Where was security when you needed them? Five alarm alert!*

"Oh, no." Amber laughed. "Not in that way. In fact, I think I might help you, Miss Singer. I am a qualified personal assistant." She flashed a glossy business card—thick white stock with bold black letters: *Selena Rapp—I've got your back!* There was also a website address and a phone number. "I'm betting that staving off stalkers and coffee run errands have you neglecting the things that you really would rather take care of. Am I right?"

Casey was stunned. She still didn't know how to take the girl's pitch. *Was this a nutcase, or was she for real?*

The two approached the counter at the same time. "Let me buy you a cup of Joe," Amber said, smiling sweetly. She was wearing a cotton summer dress, wedges, and had a purse in the shape of a lemon. A designer-inspired backpack was slung over one bare shoulder. She was sun-kissed and appeared to be all of about one hundred pounds, soaking wet. Her chestnut-brown hair was flowing in cascades down around her shoulders. Casey pegged the Latin girl for being only twenty.

"Okay, sure. If you'd like."

"Two of whatever she's having," Amber said, pulling a twenty from the lemon purse and laying it on the counter.

Casey reached for the hot latte and headed for a high counter seat near one of the large windows. "I have five minutes. Make it worthwhile."

Amber followed and joined her on a high stool. "I'm on the market and come highly recommended."

"References?" Casey asked, blowing on the steamy brew.

"Of course. Anything that you would need. I am reliable, trustworthy, and competent. I am proficient in all computer plat-forms, great with numbers, have stylist/cosmetology credentials, and am a wiz with all the socials. I can schedule and keep you on time for your meetings and auditions. I do light housework and can cook. I have no current boyfriend, kids, or obligations to distract me from providing you with top-rate service. Oh, and it looks like you better move your car before it gets towed. There's a curb cop out there."

Casey jumped up from the stool. Then, she asked the girl for her phone. Casey punched in her personal email address in the contacts. "Send me your references. Then, we'll talk again. Okay, Serina?"

"Oh, it's *Selena*. Selena Rapp."

Casey smiled and waved her off. "Gotta run. Thanks for the latte—email me! Bye!"

Amber smiled. She was as good as in.

CHAPTER 47

MARCH 2022

Casey knew she was in over her head, but what could she do? She would need to somehow juggle the live shows, segment tapings, and eventually, the *Starbreaker* shooting schedule—plus a weekly podcast! It would all be so simple if she could only clone herself, she thought.

The technician, Rick, from the studio had set her up nicely in a spare office on the eleventh floor of Global Studios. A small plywood recording booth was built and positioned in the corner with padded walls, a small desk, and a Blue Yeti microphone. A small cut-out in the shape of a circle afforded her a submarine view of the New York skyline from the tiny swivel chair in front of the screen. It was remote, for certain, and would afford a quiet place for her to record her broadcasts. Twenty-minute segments at first, she thought. Just to ease into the pool. If things went well and she could build listenership, she would then consider setting up a similar studio in her Los Angeles townhome.

She would record on Thursdays, after the show, when she could expound on the most newsworthy segments—hers, primarily, with commentary and the occasional guest interview. It would not be difficult to contact show guests ahead of time to persuade them to agree to stay on after *The Gab* and to pop up to the eleventh floor for a quick appearance on the podcast, *Blonde Up!* with Casey Singer. And if she played her cards right, the exquisite and outspoken Mandy Fisher of reality show fame would be her first bonafide guest. They had hit it off in the past, and Casey knew that Mandy was slated for next week's show. Of course, this involved planning, time, and commitment—three things that Casey was short on.

The post-show production meeting couldn't come at a worse time. Casey was psyched to head up to the eleventh floor to record her first solo podcast. The general gestalt of the moment called for someone with a keen eye who could break through all the noise swirling around on social media and in the ether on topics of most interest to the younger set. Casey was poised and ready to pitch her show—herself—to the world. She would promise to road test and opine on everything from the newest mascara to the trendy subscription services, streaming shows, and celebrity gossip. This would be her weekly platform, free of censorship or scripted notecards. She could not wait to launch her first episode to the world. *Let the F-bombs fly!*

Instead, she was sitting in a hot conference room with her show mates, producers, and showrunners, awaiting some big announcement.

She tapped her Giuseppe Zanotti pump, cross-legged, as she swiped at her phone, checking her show notes.

"Hi, everyone—I'll keep this brief," Barry said just as Bumpy Friedman walked in, Diet Coke in hand, and plopped into the chair closest to the door.

"We are going to do a remote broadcast for the spring ratings —in Miami!"

Everyone nodded, and a few even produced a little "Woot!"

"Who wouldn't like to get out of freezing New York City for the sandy beaches of this global metropolis?" he added.

Remote broadcasts were a beast of their own. Everyone knew it. A challenge that the production team relished and thrived on.

"We are partnering with a huge resort and will tie in the guest spots with the local feel. We'll capitalize on the trendy vibe and pulse of the city," said LeMaster, who was all-in on the idea.

Kathryn seemed pleased, already calculating how she could parlay the time on location to her best advantage.

Hannah smiled and rendered her support.

La Costa riffed in her put-on diva bravado. "Snap! Cue the fabulous! I can get my Miami on!"

Casey considered the implications. Now she had to be available for at least five days, live on the set in Miami, *and* somehow available for the forthcoming shooting for *Starbreaker* in LA? And what about her podcast? She could definitely do that remotely, but how would she manage the demands of being everywhere at once?

When the meeting broke, Casey hurried to her dressing room and closed the door. Reaching into her purse, she riffled through it for the business card that she had gotten from the coffee shop girl who had been leaving her incessant voicemails for weeks. Who listens to voicemails anymore? *What was her name? Lena? Dena? Selena! That was it!* She found the crumpled business card and swiped at her phone.

It was time to dial up some H-E-L-P.

SELENA HAD to be roused from a deep nap when her phone buzzed from the back pocket of her denim cut-offs.

"Hey, you got a call!" Lucas said from the kitchen table. He was working on obtaining bookings for his eclectic client list while giving Amber a place to crash in his dismal apartment, which also doubled as his office. It wasn't ideal, but it worked.

Amber mumbled and barely moved.

"Hey! It's her! It's Casey Singer." He could see the name on the screen as he grabbed Amber's phone from her shorts, giving her arm a hard yank. "Get it together. Answer it!"

"Uh, hello?" Amber said, almost unintelligibly.

"Hi. Is this Serena Rapp?"

Amber sat up at attention and slipped right into character. "Yes! Casey—hello. Thanks for calling me back."

"Are you still looking for a position as a Personal Assistant? I would like to meet with you, if possible. The sooner, the better."

"I am. That would be great. Let's say . . . "

Lucas scribbled on a notepad from across the room: *her place.*

"Would we be able to meet at your residence? It might be the most private."

"Sure," Casey said. "I will text you my address. I'm not back in LA until Friday night. How about Saturday at ten a.m.?"

"Perfect! I'll be there."

"Okay. Oh—I never received your references. Might have gone to spam, so be sure to bring them. See you then," Casey said, ending the call.

Amber returned the phone to her back pocket and blinked. "We're all set, but she wants references."

Lucas nodded. "No problem. I can come up with something that will work." He knew more than one voiceover actor who could pose as anyone convincing for a price. "Just to be sure, you will need to be ready—we start going over some runs tonight."

"Okay," Amber said, yawning. Then she lay back on the couch and rolled over.

CHAPTER 48

Amber arrived on Casey's doorstep, as summoned, at ten o'clock sharp. She was juggling two hot Starbucks drinks in a cardboard coffee holder in one hand, and an iPad in the other.

Casey answered the door wearing leggings and an oversized tie-dyed T-shirt. Her hair was twisted into a large clip.

"Good morning!" Amber said, extending the coffee. "I remembered your order—a soy latte with no foam."

"That was very nice of you," Casey said, thinking that this one was on the right track all right.

The two sat in the living room, which was tidy and modern. Casey folded herself onto the pricey Danish import chair that set her back as much as a Kia Rio.

Amber, aka *Selena*, set the coffee tray on a magazine on the low profile coffee table. "Is this okay?" she asked.

"Sure," Casey said casually. "It's just a *High Style*. I only have it because my cast mate is the editor."

"Kathryn Delacorte, right?"

Casey smiled. Selena had definitely done her homework. "Yes, there are four of us, and we have been at it for a very long time. Do you watch the show?"

"I do," Selena said, taking a draft of the hot brew. "I think you are great—all of you. It's really a must-see for morning viewing."

"*Mid*-morning viewing," Casey corrected.

Selena nodded and then opened her iPad. "I have the references here that you requested. I also emailed another copy to you, so you have it."

Casey lifted her phone and swiped at the screen. "Yes, I see it here. Tell me, what do you know about Gen-Zers?"

Amber stalled. That was not something that she and Lucas had gone over. She did have a younger sister and knew a thing or two about what made her tick. "I know they are very tech-savvy and very influenced by bloggers and internet celebrities. Oh, and that they are very locked into sustainability and social issues."

"What do you mean, exactly?" Casey was taking mental notes.

"I mean, they only like to wear products that come with a cause. For example, my sister wears a line of athleisure wear that is made of recycled water bottles or something. I guess that environment-friendly clothing is all the rage with them."

Interesting, Casey thought. "Can I ask you how old you are?"

"Twenty-five," Amber said, which was the truth.

She looked younger, for sure, but Casey was glad to know she was seasoned and dialed in to the Gen X through Z demographics. Casey knew she had to appeal to them as well as to the millennial progressives who were looking to make a positive impact on the world.

"The next question, Selena Rapp, is can you keep me freed up from daily tasks to enable me to travel and work without having to sweat the small stuff? That's key."

"I can," Amber said with conviction. "I promise I will be indispensable to you."

Casey paused. She liked the sound of that. But there was trust. It was the one thing she needed from her, which could not be granted too quickly. Maybe she could just try the girl's services out for a while and see how things went. So far, she was sold.

The two chatted for over an hour, and Casey found herself more than impressed with Selena's sharp mind, efficiency, and professional demeanor. She didn't need a best friend, just a competent personal assistant.

Three days later, after having called the three names on Selena's reference list, Casey was certain.

"You've got the position, *on spec*," she told Selena on a call from the back of an Uber on her way to the studio. "Let's give this a try."

WITHIN A WEEK, Amber had the keys to Casey's condo, the passwords to her laptop, the PC in her home office, and her Netflix account. With Lucas's help in the background, she had created a digital schedule for Casey that mapped out her every meeting, move, and commitment. *Selena* and Casey communicated via a text chain Amber shared with Lucas daily. He was looking for anything that he could use for his purposes. At present, Casey's intercoastal travel plans, private yogi, Door-Dash dining services, and Beverly Hills esthetician appointments did not interest him.

"She's going to be traveling even more once she starts filming the movie," Amber told Lucas, bare feet propped up on a thrift shop coffee table in the center of his rat-hole apartment, scrolling through TikTok. They had been spending way too much money on "work outfits" and lattes for Amber to keep her looking the part. Lucas also took half of her earnings as a PA to "offset living costs."

"It's a lot, Lucas. She works me like a dog. I'm constantly booking her travel, whipping up smoothies when she's here in LA, schlepping her dry cleaning, and cold-calling potential guests for her podcast. She thinks I'm more connected than I am, dude. I'm going to need more compensation for this. You promised me an *actual* screen test. When is that going to happen?"

Lucas popped the tab of a cheap beer. "Soon. Like I said. Bring me something juicy on her, and we can end this charade."

Amber huffed. Like something "juicy" would drop from the sky! The only thing that Casey ever did was work her ass off, return online purchases, and drink way too much wine. What was he looking for?

CHAPTER 49

asey arrived back in LA to an airport filled with throngs of harried travelers. She jockeyed past a slew of foreigners wearing shorts and sandals—oblivious to the climate. She checked her phone. No messages from Selena or anyone else. On some level, she had hoped for an email or text from Roe, but after so many weeks gone by, it was best that neither of them indulged in a hopeless fantasy.

It was just better this way.

Earlier that day, she had placed a call to a fresh get, a Gen Z designer who only worked with sustainable fabrics, creating "wearable" art that packed a strong social message. Casey's podcast listenership was climbing, and she would soon be able to take on a sponsor or two. Things were definitely looking up. Her little side hustle was a thrill in every way, but like most everything else, it was a lot of extra work.

She was happy to finally be back home and was looking forward to some time off before flying out to Miami. The show would run the "best of" *The Gab* segments for the next week, giving the cast and most of the crew a well-deserved break. Everyone would have to be in place two days before the remote broadcast and ready to go.

Almost as soon as Casey retrieved her bags, her thoughts of work faded. She found her car in the lot and jumped in. She swiped at her phone to call up her latest podcast episode to listen to on the drive. It was automatic. She critiqued her work constantly—always looking for ways to improve her performance.

Just as she backed up, she hit the brakes, bringing the Audi to a stop. Someone was standing next to her door and peering in.

She squinted in disbelief. *Lucas?*

It was him, all right. Standing there, waving like a dumb baboon.

She lowered the window, much to her disgust. *What in the world—!*

"Hi, Casey," he said, grinning. His hands were in the pockets of his track pants, and he wore a gray Dodgers hoodie. "Long time no see."

"What do you want?" she said coolly, shifting the car into park.

"I thought it was you. I am here to meet a client who is flying in from Philly. I wanted to congratulate you on the success of the show—and on the new podcast."

"You listen to my podcast, Lucas?" She found that to be as incredulous as him standing there in the flesh. It bordered on stalking.

"Yep! Actually, my niece does . . . she mentioned your show one day, so I checked it out."

"Great. Well, I gotta run." Casey was feeling uncomfortable. He looked like shit, and she could see that he appeared strung out and jumpy. If it weren't so predictable, it would be sad.

She raised the window and pushed the gear into reverse.

Lucas did not move. In fact, he stepped forward and gave the window a punch with his fist. "Hey, bitch!"

There it was! She pressed the gas pedal and spun the wheels hard, quickly pulling out of the stall. Rolling over Lucas's foot in the process did nothing to make her slow down.

CHAPTER 50

"Hi, Xennials and Z'ers—it's Casey Singer here with another installment of my show, *Blonde Up!* I hope you are all feeling beautiful today and loving life! The struggle is real, y'all, and we are here to spill the tea. And hey—what's going on with Emilia Clarkes's caterpillar eyebrows? Girl, get those things tamed! What can I say? A good brow grooming is everything!"

Casey was crouched down on the floor of her walk-in closet, wearing her PJs, headphones, and fuzzy mules. Her laptop and microphone were balanced atop an overturned Amazon box, and she was sitting on a beanbag. This was her remote LA recording room for her podcast. The space was ideal for the job, as the racks of clothing, shoes, and lack of windows afforded a cushy and silent atelier in which to work. She had pulled the double French doors closed and hung a sign on the door handle that read, "RECORDING IN PROCESS," just in case Selena or the housekeeper would chance by.

She packed all that she could into the twenty-minute segment, with plans to expand once she could secure regular weekly guests. Doing social celeb interviews took time and required that she would be available to tape the segments on their schedule. This meant sometimes conducting the Zoom calls late at night. Casey didn't mind, though. She loved being relevant and sharing her ideas with the world, even if it was the younger set, which appeared to be her core audience.

She had thought to reach out to Ryder to gain access to his current co-star, Londyn Kenzie, for a guest spot. She was all the rage with her pixie coif and Euro-punk style. Her listeners would eat it up if she could get the two of them, Londyn and Ryder, to agree to a duo interview. The wheels of progress were always turning with Casey.

And what was the deal with Lucas? she wondered as she packed up her portable setup and emerged from the closet. She hadn't stopped thinking about the incident since she ran over his foot in the parking lot a few days prior. Hopefully, she broke it! He deserved that and more! *What in the world was he after?* It had been so many years since she leveled his business and drove him into obscurity. Or so she thought. Like a bad penny, he just popped up out of nowhere.

Thank goodness she had Selena and other trustworthy people around her to insulate her from the crazies—most of the time.

She headed into the study, where Selena was busy on the computer booking Casey's flight to Miami.

"Do you want me to arrange a meeting with Spaulding Caine while you're there?" Selena asked.

"Yes. That would be great. If he's in town."

"I'll check," Selena said. Then she added, "I have laid out your outfits for the trip." A task that she was very good at. She had a keen sense of style for outfitting Casey in a trendy but credible way.

"Oh, and I found that nail color you were looking for," Selena said. "I reached out to the manufacturer, and they sent an entire box of it, along with some other nail products." She pointed to the delivery.

"Great! I'll try it," Casey said, reaching for one of the small, black-capped bottles. The lacquer inside was a slate gray. "Come with me, and we'll cover some to-dos."

Selena followed her into the enormous bathroom and took a seat on the edge of the sunk-in giant tub. Casey pulled up to the vanity that looked like it belonged in a high-end salon. The lights alone could guide down a small plane.

Casey twisted off the cap and applied the nail polish carefully to each stubby nail. She never had long talons. She found them vulgar and matronly. Neat, short nails suited her just fine.

"I'm only trying this out to report back to my listeners. Apparently, this stuff is vegan. Who knew!"

Selena smiled and watched as Casey painted herself into two to three minutes of digital paralysis. Then, she made a bold and calculating move.

"Oh, text Ryder back. I can see that he's messaged you three times." Selena could view Casey's phone screen from her vantage point.

Casey hedged, first reaching for the phone, and then thinking twice. "Oh, I'm a bit incapacitated here. Can you—?"

"Of course!" Selena jumped up and reached for Casey's phone. "It needs your passcode."

Without a thought, Casey said, "It's J-O-R-D-Y—my first agent's name."

Selena smiled and met Casey's eyes with a holding glance. "That is so sweet!" She punched in the digits and opened Casey's text screen. "Do you want me to type anything for you?"

"No," Casey said. "I'll hit the dictate feature."

Selena placed the phone back in front of Casey. "I'll give you some privacy. I'll get back to packing. Just let me know when you're ready to tackle that list."

Amber moved into the master bedroom, smiling to herself. Lucas might have underestimated her. Slow and steady wins the race. She had cracked Casey's phone code and would now only have to figure out what vulnerability could be found in her now-accessible digital world.

CHAPTER 51

Amber waited for the opportune time to unleash her inner Veronica Mars. She had the chops, for sure, and knew that there were far more challenging roles she could play. She needed only to prove it to Lucas, and then—Hollywood. Amber had to find the perfect dirt on Casey that would appease Lucas and unlock her big break. If she had her druthers, she would *be* Casey Singer—but a better version. The girl was a hot mess.

Amber's second break came two days later in the early morning, just before Casey's protein drink. "I'm going for a swim," Casey said, coming off a call with a potential podcast guest. "When I get back, we'll go over the itinerary for Miami and the first look at the script revisions for *Starbreaker*."

"Sure!" Amber said. "I'm just about done packing your things for the remote shows."

Amber waited until she heard Casey descend from the staircase and close the gate leading to the pool below. From the bedroom window, she could see Casey unfurl her towel and drop her beach bag next to a chaise lounge. Then she dove gracefully into the sparkling water.

Amber wasted no time. She knew that Casey's phone would

be charging on the counter in the kitchen next to her house keys in a ceramic bowl. She hurried downstairs and carefully lifted the smartphone. She went to work, punching in the passcode. The screen sprang to life, and Amber bit her lip. *Where to start? Notifications? Texts? Photos?* She swiped quickly through it all, finally landing on the camera roll. Among several videos of just Casey, one stood out, and she quickly tapped on the play button. There, in living color, was Casey and a man having sex on a couch with abandon!

Amber watched intently in order to get a better view of Casey's impassioned mystery man. The room was dark, and it was difficult to see much more than his backside—naked and thrusting away on top of Casey, who was getting it on with zeal. The sound was spotty, but it clearly was the soundtrack of ecstasy—with some random jazz singer crooning in the background.

Amber manipulated the screen to enlarge the shot of Casey flipping over on top of him, legs astride, and riding him like a rodeo cowboy. From the angle, and much to her delight, she had a full view of his enraptured face. *Who is this?* she wondered. *Was it anything?* Sex tapes were a snooze these days, and you could hardly see anything in the dim light.

Who knew if it was usable? Damned if she knew who the hottie was that Casey was boinking, but she sent the video clip to Lucas anyway with a few deft strokes and then returned the phone to the counter.

Amber's phone buzzed from her purse in the hall not five minutes later with a text from Lucas: *Holy shit, Amber! You did it!*

Lucas would waste no time in capitalizing on his good fortune. It was as if the heavens opened, and Casey had delivered the perfect bomb to derail her perfect insignificant life and take her down. Retribution was sweet, especially in a world where a post, text, or tweet could instantly wreak havoc on the interweb. Hell, he could break the internet with this! Not counting what a few well-placed calls to his contacts in the media could produce—he would single-handedly cancel Casey Singer from pop culture. He was back, all right.

And it felt fucking great!

CHAPTER 52

APRIL 2022

Before Casey knew it, she was on a flight to Miami with the *Starbreaker* script open on the tray table, trying to balance a glass of cheap airline wine in her left hand while making notes on the script with her other. The quiet teenager next to her in first class was a blessing. He was fast asleep before the plane even took off.

The network expense account spared little when carting their show hosts around in style. Getting their commodities to the show location was all that mattered to the powers that be. Period.

Casey felt unusually exhausted. In fact, she had not felt quite like herself for a while. Was she pushing herself too much? No doubt! She juggled everything as if she were Superwoman. She was good at what she did, and she had the extra help, thanks to Selena, but at nearly thirty-five years old—her still-smoking-hot body was definitely talking to her. She needed more rest than she could afford these past months. And it would not get any easier once she started shooting Alto Vuoria's film.

She touched down at Miami International and was instantly hit with the heavy humidity that was so distinctive. She thought about Spaulding, her agent, and the unfortunate news that on this go-around, they could not meet up. He was far away on the sparkling Caribbean seas, bobbing on his fishing boat. Nice life! He kept a respectable distance from his clients unless there was a reason to communicate.

She was happy to catch her car quickly, waiting outside baggage. All she craved was a room service burger, a bath, and five-diamond resort sheets on a heavenly bed.

THE NEXT MORNING found Casey sleeping in until the bright sunlight behind the blackout curtains had baked the room temperature to over eighty degrees. She stretched and yawned, finally checking her phone. It was ten thirty. She could not remember the last time she slept that late.

Must've needed it! she thought, padding her way to the bathroom.

She would have two full days before the show's broadcast. She turned on the shower jets, wondering if the other gals had made it in and if they were on the same floor.

She had decided to have breakfast in the resort restaurant. It had a stunning view of the beach. She could claim a magnificent table and take her time, reading over the show notes to switch gears for the coming week. Broadcasting the talk show in sunny Miami was definitely going to bring a punch to daytime TV. Casey recognized many of the production crew getting up from one of the larger tables on their way to production meetings and visits to the set to oversee the design. It was going to be epic, all right!

Casey had just bitten into a slice of avocado toast when she heard her name being squealed from across the outdoor patio.

"*Cas-ey!*" La Costa was bounding up in her flowing caftan, sunhat, and large square shades. Hannah was in tow behind her, covered liberally in sunscreen and wearing linen pants and a sleeveless blouse.

"Hi, Ladies!" Casey smiled, and the three exchanged

perfectly timed air kisses that preserved lipstick and powdered cheeks.

"Isn't this gorgeous?" Hannah said. "Is it okay if we join you?"

Casey pointed to the chairs across from her. "Of course. When did you get in?"

"Late yesterday afternoon. We were both on the same flight. We've been drinking mimosas since then!" La Costa said, signaling to the server. "I'll have a Bloody Mary. Hannah, what are you having, dear?"

"Just ice water for me. Oh—with lemon."

Casey was on her second cup of coffee. "I don't know what's the matter with me. I am so sluggish!"

La Costa looked around at the sea and the sand. "This is my kind of digs."

"Where's Kathryn?" Casey asked.

"On her way. She's flying in from Rome, if you can believe it. That one is always jet-setting to somewhere," Hannah said, adjusting her floppy hat.

"Big day for us on Monday. I'm just trying to stay out of the crew's way," La Costa said. "Although, maybe we should all take a peek at the set later today."

They all nodded.

"What's on the grand agenda otherwise?" Casey asked.

"I think some shopping at the Design District . . . then, maybe some R&R near the pool. Have you seen this place? It's boujee!" La Costa said, fanning herself with a napkin. "Are you down with that, Dr. Mom?"

Hannah laughed. "Yep. We are tourists for the next two days. That works for me."

Casey was only after the extra downtime to work on bundling a couple of podcasts and getting some rest. "I have a million calls to make, so I won't be joining you guys."

They both frowned.

"Well, I am sure that once Kathryn gets here, she will find you and pull you out of that hotel room, so be ready!"

Casey signed the tab and scooped up her laptop and colorful Dior tote. "I will catch up with you guys later!"

"*Ciao, Bella!*" La Costa said to the wind.

CHAPTER 53

Roe Evans closed the door to his home office and rubbed his eyes. It was nearly ten p.m., and it was an especially hard day, ending with a battle with Jane to calm her after dinner. She was on a spring custody visitation with her father. A teenager now, she was prone to occasional fits and furies that lived somewhere in her brain that manifested in bursts of discontent. Neither Celeste nor Jane's nurse, Cornelia, could soothe her, even with a bath. Roe had to stroke her arms and legs until she settled down. His presence and touch usually did the trick. Then he would read to her from her favorite princess storybooks until she finally nodded off.

He drew a deep breath and regarded the stack of unopened mail on his desk. Work was the last thing he wanted to tackle on the long, arduous day. What he really wanted was to enjoy a splash of bourbon and thirty minutes of Netflix surfing.

"Are you coming to bed?" Celeste asked from the doorway. She was already in her nightgown.

He rallied for her benefit. "Yes, I will be up soon. I just want to go through some of this mail."

He was ever the conscientious husband and worker.

"Okay," she said sweetly. "Don't take too long."

The door bumped closed, and he reached, curiously, for a large envelope peeking out from the stack. The address was handwritten hurriedly, and there was no return address.

When he spilled the blurry but revealing photographs—screenshots taken from a video—onto his desk, his heart caught in his chest.

A single sheet of letterhead from Lucas Morgan's sham agency read, *"What's this worth to you?"*

CASEY'S PHONE chimed just as she returned to the blasting cool air of her suite. She retrieved her phone from her tote, expecting it to be Shelly. The two hadn't talked in weeks, and she had been on Casey's mind.

It was Lucas! Attached was a video that showed it all. She and Roe entangled in each other, wildly making love! The clip only lasted forty-five seconds, long enough for her to get an eyeful—and then lose her lunch, literally.

She barely made it to the toilet before she vomited.

Then, doubling over, she held her head in disbelief.

CHAPTER 54

The rest of the day was a blur. Casey barely made it through a group dinner with her castmates at a local posh restaurant that served four-star Cuban cuisine. She could barely stomach a thing and settled for soda water and plain bread. The dinner was followed by an Uber to Miami's legendary nightclub, *Story*, with its neon-lit dance floor and multiple bars serving minty Mojitos, frothy Daiquiris, and the famous Miami Vice cocktail.

The place was a collection of Gen Zers, Millennials, and party-hearty locals packed in a pulsating Vegas-style nightclub.

Kathryn paid off one of the floor managers to secure a small table away from the throbbing speakers.

They all fell into place on the garish curved couch, just as they would on the show set.

"Look at us! We can't help ourselves—we have our habits!" Hannah said above the blaring music.

A thin, tattooed girl in skimpy shorts and a cut-off T-shirt appeared to take their drink orders. Casey stuck with soda water and prayed for a quick night. This wasn't the ladies' scene, especially not Hannah's, and Casey was certain that thirty minutes of the hot neon local color was all she could stand.

La Costa was in her glory. She loved a big dance floor and any opportunity to let loose. "I'm going out there!"

"Who would think to find us here?" Kathryn said, smoothing the silk belt on her Valentino jumpsuit.

Just as she said this, a few members of the show crew spotted them. "Hey! It's the girls! Do you all mind if we join you?"

Casey smiled but nodded uneasily.

For the next half hour, she had not looked at her phone, but the suspense was killing her. Finally, she peeked. Still, not another word from Lucas. *What was he planning? What did this mean, him sending her that video?* Obviously, the other shoe was about to drop. Suddenly, she felt warm and dizzy. She just needed to get out of there.

"Hannah—I'll share an Uber back to the hotel with you if you'd like."

"Sure, Casey. I think I've had enough Miami for one night. See you all in the morning!" She climbed over the collection of laps and legs and joined Casey, who was leaving.

"See you all in the morning," Casey said, giving a wave.

Hannah was quiet in the back of the Uber, but Casey knew better than to mistake her silence for ignorance.

"You okay?" she said, touching Casey's arm.

"Yeah, just tired, I guess. It's been a hectic few months, and now this remote show . . . it's all caught up to me, I guess," Casey said, although her intuition knew that Hannah was rarely wrong and had great radar for bullshit.

That Casey never left a party first—ever— might have been a tip-off.

"Okay," Hannah said. "You let me know if you ever need to talk, okay?

Casey nodded, giving a half-smile. Then she said, "Do you mind if we stop off at a Quick Mart? I'd like to get something for this headache."

She was in and out of the all-night convenience store with a brown paper bag tucked into her purse. She had checked her texts at the counter in the blaring white fluorescent lights.

Lucas had sent another. More footage of the video—this time, with both Casey's and Roe's faces exposed. He simply attached three flame emojis. He was baiting her.

Hannah was dozing off when Casey got back into the car.

"To the resort, please," Casey said to the driver.

She stared out of the window, her thoughts racing.

What should she do? Should she contact Roe? What would she say? Would Lucas really use this against her? Would he ruin all of their lives? Could he?

ONCE BACK IN HER ROOM, Casey paced. She couldn't sleep. She thought about texting Lucas, but then decided against it. At four a.m. Central Time, she phoned Shelly.

"Hello? Casey, it's the middle of the night. Everything okay?"

"Shel, I'm in trouble. Oh—and I think I'm pregnant."

CHAPTER 55

The stick showed two pink lines. Casey left it on the bathroom floor where she dropped it.

"*Chica*, what are you saying?"

"I took a test. It's positive. I feel like shit, Shelly. My breasts are swollen; I can't take the smell of food. I'm nauseated. Plus—there's more."

"*Jesús María*! Okay, slow down . . . what do you mean by *more*?"

"It's Lucas Morgan—you remember that asshole? He somehow—oh my God! *Selena*!"

"What are you talking about? Casey—I'm going to FaceTime with you. Hang up."

A few seconds later, Shelly's face was bouncing on the tiny screen. Casey cried once she connected with her best friend's soulful eyes.

"Oh, Shelly! I think he conned me! He set me up with an assistant—she was his mole! Selena was the only one who had access to my camera roll!"

"So? What did she see? Did you have nude photos of yourself on there, or what?"

"Worse. Shelly, she found some video footage—the remote

for the camera must have been triggered somehow. Footage of me and Roe Evans, DOING IT!"

"Holy shit! Casey, you slept with Roe?"

Casey lowered her eyes and nodded. "Lucas is going to leak this . . . oh, my God, *Celeste!*"

"No—your CAREER! That is what you should worry about, *Chicka*! Goddamn Lucas Morgan! That bastard!"

Casey was shaking. It sounded worse now that she had said it out loud. "What am I going to do, Shelly? Do I call Roe? Should I respond to Lucas?"

"At this point, you don't know Lucas's game or what he is planning. It's anyone's guess."

Just then, Casey's phone dinged with a text. It was from Lucas, and it read: *I think TMZ will find this newsworthy, don't you?*

Casey collapsed onto the bed and bent over in fits of sobbing.

Shelly begged, "*Chicka*! What is he saying?"

"He's going to ruin me—and Roe and Celeste's marriage. He's going to do it! Oh, God!"

Shelly let her cry it out for a full minute and then said, "Casey, look at me!"

She raised her wet face, mascara running in pools along her cheeks. "What am I going to do?" she sniffled.

"I think you need to head this off at the pass. Do you hear me? If you still can. Has Lucas reached out to Roe with this yet?"

"I don't know," Casey said, wiping her eyes with a wadded tissue. She collected herself. How was this any different from anything else she had to handle? Yes, it was unfortunate that Lucas seemed to hold the cards, but nothing was unnegotiable. "I have to tell Roe," she said. "It involves us both, and he needs to know. We will have to decide how to play this out."

"I don't think that's a good idea. Not yet, anyway." Shelly had moved into the dark living room of her enormous house and had lit a cigarette. "And don't respond to Lucas's threats. He is just feeling you out at this point."

"Right," Casey said.

Shelly paused and then said, "We need a little more time to figure this out. And the baby—you *will* have to tell Roe about that. After all, it's his, right?"

Casey's face was pained. She thought about the torrid weekend in Chicago with Ryder, which summoned a new flood of tears.

"I'm not exactly sure."

CHAPTER 56

The following day, the show began despite a tangle with the union about gaffers, carpenters, and engineers that the on-site producer handled with efficiency. The set was amazing—a delightful artistic blend of modern-day Miami chic and ultra-feminine flare. Behind stanchioned barricades, the crowd was standing room only. There was some seating on the resort patio, but it was limited. The first day's show was a mix of Florida natives, curious tourists, and fans of the spotlighted local musician Rocco Rubio, who was currently topping the charts with his Latin sound. Plans for the Friday finale would feature an appearance by seven-time Grammy award winner, Gloria Estefan.

It was all Casey could do to hold it together. She had sheltered away in the makeup trailer from her castmates as long as she could. They were calling for her to meet and greet with fans and the press. It was her job to put on a smile, and that was what she intended to do. *One thing at a time,* she said to herself as she alighted from the trailer. She was wearing a Sofia Richie Fleura Mini Dress, looking chic. She paired it with the strappy Jimmy Choos that laced up her ankles. The makeup tech had applied a liquid bronzer to her legs that would be prominent in the camera shots. She was ready.

She managed to shoot off some texts a few minutes prior. One to her accountant, Chantelle, with a directive to go to her townhouse and intercept Selena Rapp when she showed up, call a locksmith, and change all the locks. *"Do not give her access to my home!"* Another one to Regina Madison to give her a heads-up. Maybe she could even press charges against the girl. *"Regina, I will be in touch shortly to explain,"* Casey typed.

Then, without hesitation, she shot off a text to "Selena"—or whatever her name was—that simply read: *"You're fired! Tell Lucas to kiss my ass!"*

She knew it would incite him to possibly come on stronger and follow through with his threat. But the likes of him would not bully her!

Casey took a deep breath and headed to the stage set, which was set up on the resort's wide veranda with a stunning view of the ocean in the background. No. Nothing was going to derail her. She had been through worse. Lucas Morgan did not know who he was fucking with!

It didn't take a second text or an email from Lucas Morgan to convince Roe Evans what he needed to do. He didn't sleep a wink all night, and now it was dawn. There was no way that he could let Celeste—or her family—find out the truth. It would be the end of him and everything he held dear.

He had never thought in his life that he would be in this situation. Fate delivered its worst to his door. This was a mess that he could not simply play off in the press. It must never get that far.

Roe slowly opened the middle drawer on his desk. He removed it all the way from the tracks and felt for a key taped to the back edge of the wood. He peeled away the tape and extracted the key. Then, he moved to the sliding closet doors in his study and reached for a plain metal box on the top shelf, next to some old CD boxes, and dusted it off.

He slid the key into the lock and opened the metal tab that released the lid. Inside was a 9mm compact pistol with 16 rounds, with one in the chamber. He lifted it carefully into his Tumi bag and returned the metal strongbox to the shelf.

There was only one solution, he thought.

Then he headed to his car.

Roe made the four-and-a-half-hour drive to East Williamsburg, a dicey but transformative section of Brooklyn. Celeste's family—some of them—were well known for their "unconventional businesses" and covert ways of dealing with everything from running porn scams to politics. Some of Celeste's uncles were said to have thrived in their heyday, providing mafia-run subcontractors on projects in Manhattan to running loans at two hundred percent interest with elaborate online gambling ventures. Celeste's family ran multiple restaurants and cafes in the Bronx that served as shell companies in which to front operations. Roe knew for a fact that one faction of her family regularly ran South American cocaine covertly shipped in frozen food from a functioning warehouse. He hated that he knew. He had never dreamed that he would be entangled with the likes of such powerful and sinister relatives. But yet, here he was, and grateful that such men knew how to deal with the likes of Lucas Morgan.

He slid a crumpled piece of paper from deep in his wallet and checked the address written on the back. Louie Benedetti's promise was scribbled on the back of a carpet company's business card—one free favor—no questions asked. Louie was Celeste's second cousin, once removed, so technically, he was still family. And family protected family. It was just the way it was. Roe had met Louie only twice—once on his and Celeste's wedding day, and prior to that, at Roe's bachelor party the week before the wedding, when he was whisked away by a cohort of

D'Angelo's and Benedetti's on a private jet to Vegas and a twenty-four-hour rampage of cigars, craps tables, and high-dollar strippers. It had been clear right then that the family he was about to be welcomed into was not to be fucked with—that, and that as far as they were concerned, it would be a flat-out insult not to accept their generosity, ever.

He took the refurbished elevator to the fifth floor. The doors opened onto a deserted factory, dark and vast.

Instantly, he wondered what he was doing.

Saving his marriage, that's what! He felt for the Glock, now pressing into his abdomen, tucked snugly in the waistband of his Jockeys.

The sound of expensive Italian shoes hitting the cement floor echoed in the cavernous and empty sweatshop.

"Ah! *Mio cugino!* I see you found the place. *Bueno!* Come and let's have a talk. *Yes?*"

CHAPTER 57

Day two of the remote broadcast found Casey in better spirits, although she got little sleep. It would be a miracle if the makeup tech could transform her into her usual fresh-faced self.

She had avoided her castmates by ordering breakfast in her room—some dry toast, a dollop of avocado, and some crisp bacon. That and black coffee seemed to enliven her.

There was still no further word from Lucas. Yet.

Later, when her phone did ding while she was sitting in the makeup chair, her heart nearly jumped out of her chest.

"Hi, *Chicka*, how are you feeling this morning?" It was Shelly.

Casey put her on speaker. She instantly felt better hearing her best friend's voice. "I'm here with the makeup tech, about to do the show. Everything is okay. We are really killing it!"

"Oh, that's good to hear," Shelly said, sounding distracted. Then the trailer door opened. It was the intern pointing up at Casey. Shelly stepped onto the flimsy stairs and looked right at Casey. "Surprise, *Chicka*! I'm here!"

"Holy shit!" Casey jumped up from the chair, much to the technician's annoyance. She fell into Shelly's arms and squeezed her matronly frame. "What!? You're really here!"

"Yes, how could I not come when—"

She stopped herself cold. People were milling around within earshot, and the makeup tech was eager to finish Casey's lashes.

"We can catch up after the show," Casey said. "Sit here." She pointed to a small stool next to the vanity. "I will text the floor manager to set up a chair for you close to the set. Oh my God, girlfriend! I can't believe that you flew all the way here."

"Arrived last night. I'm staying at a pretty little air B&B. You can join me. I thought you might like some cozy privacy from all of this. It has double beds and a Jacuzzi."

Casey smiled. *How lucky was she that she had the best friend in the world?*

She didn't know what she had ever done to deserve Shelly.

AFTER THE FADEOUT and exuberant applause, Casey disengaged from her wireless microphone and transmitter. The cast stayed a few minutes more to interact with the audience. A young girl, about seven years old, held up a glossy 8x10 of Casey with a Sharpie for her to sign it.

"What is your name?" Casey asked, smiling.

"I'm Valeria! I think you look like a princess!" she said, all fits and giggles. Her mother was standing behind her, proudly smiling.

"*You* look like a princess!" Casey said. "Thank you for coming to the show."

Casey saw her young self in the girl's eyes.

Suddenly, the girl threw her arms around Casey's waist and said, "I love you!"

The gesture was sweet and unexpected. Casey felt uneasy at first, and then a flood of joy overcame her.

The girl's mother laughed apologetically.

"Oh, thank you so much!" Casey said, making a heart with her bent fingers and gesturing a pulsating heartbeat into the air.

The little girl walked away, waving and clutching the photo to her chest.

"Well, you've got a new fan base, I see," Kathryn said, coming up behind Casey. "They're getting younger all the time! We've got a meeting to attend, *Hollywood*. And then I know one beach chair that is waiting for me just outside of my suite."

"Go on in without me," Casey said. "I have to tend to something first."

"Don't hold us up," Kathryn said, going ahead, careful of the cords and cables on the sand and cement leading to the larger trailer that was serving as command central.

Casey searched the crowd for Shelly. She spotted her talking with Hannah.

She was surprised to see the two together. "I see that you two met—finally! Hannah, this is my best friend in the world, Shelly Escamilla."

Hannah laughed. "So she tells me. You two go back a long way, don't you?"

Casey beamed. If Hannah had found it odd that the two were visiting on a work set, she didn't show it.

"How long will you be visiting?" Hannah asked casually.

"I am here as long as Casey needs me!" Shelly said.

Hannah looked puzzled.

Casey touched Shelly's arm. "Uh, I have some projects that I thought Shelly could help me with—we're brainstorming in her bungalow."

"Right," Shelly said. "Girl, any opportunity I can take advantage of to get away from the three men in my house back in Chicago—I'm *there*! Plus, Casey pays me in chardonnay!"

The three laughed.

"See you inside," Hannah said, gesturing to the trailer.

Once she was out of earshot, Casey turned to Shelly. "Thank you for not letting on that I am in crisis mode!"

"I meant it, *Chicka*. For the duration, I am yours. You and I are going back to LA. We will figure this thing out. No way am I going to leave your side. I *got* you."

Now it was time for Casey to release her inner fan girl. "Well, I just love you."

"I love you too, *Chicka*. I'm texting you the address to the bungalow."

Casey blew an air kiss and disappeared into the trailer.

CHAPTER 58

ouie Benedetti's office was sparse, save for a few ancient file cabinets, two swivel chairs, and an immense mahogany desk that had seen better days. There were no windows, and a stack of dead landline Cisco phones were stacked in the corner on the floor. Everything looked like it had been bought from a bankruptcy auction. Three Mac computers were lined up on a credenza to his right, and one large screen was the only item on his desk, glowing in the half-light.

It was a shithole, for sure, but it was efficient for his needs, Roe supposed.

The empty carpet factory contained not a soul and no carpets to speak of.

Louie opened a heavy drawer and extracted two Cubans, offering one to Roe.

"Here you go, just like we smoked at your party! Here—let me light it." The slightly built Sicilian had to struggle to reach over the massive desk with his Cartier lighter. Soon the room was filled with oaky smoke, delivering rich notes of leather and coffee in the air.

"I take it you need a favor?" Louie said, examining his stogie and basking in the power play.

Roe sat forward in the rickety chair. "I am in trouble."

"Money?" Louie asked flatly.

"No."

Louie raised a bushy silver eyebrow.

Roe hedged, then finally spoke. "Someone . . . is trying to frame me. It's just that—"

"I don't need to know." He stopped Roe cold. "Rule number one. Don't tell me. It's enough that you came to me. I can figure things out enough. Believe me. And I don't wanna."

Roe lowered his head. The shame burned stronger than the lit cigar.

"Look, is this *coglione* threatening you?"

Roe nodded.

"Celeste?"

"Our *marriage*," Roe whispered. "He is trying to blackmail me."

"*Cazzo!*" He slammed the desk hard. "Okay, what is it you want me to do?"

"I want you to make it go away. That's it. Make it go away." Roe was trembling at his own words. He looked like he was going to cry.

Louie nodded slowly as if Roe had just ordered a Persian rug for his rec room. He slid a piece of paper across the desk. "Name and address of this dick-faced piece of shit."

Roe used his own pen, a gift from Celeste on their wedding day. The irony was not lost on him as he scrawled Lucas Morgan's name and address on the piece of paper.

"How soon do you need this done?"

"The sooner, the better," Roe said. "I can't thank you enough, Louie. I—"

"I am not doing this for you. I am doing it for the family. Do you understand? And when I say, 'one time and one time only,'—that is the dead truth."

Roe's voice was small. "I understand."

Louie jumped to his feet and extended a beefy hand. "It is as good as done. Go home. Oh—and from here on out, keep your goddamn *cazzo* where it belongs, *capiche*?"

CHAPTER 59

The third text from Lucas came just as Casey emerged from the shower.

Shelly ran into the bathroom with the phone. "What does it say?"

Casey's hair was still dripping wet when she swiped the screen. "He wants to talk. He says that my silence shows that I don't care if he shares this with the world."

"Fucking bastard!"

"I don't know, Shelly . . . I have an obligation to Roe here, don't I? This is far more damning to him than to me. He has much more at stake."

Then came another text—this time, Lucas included a photo of the envelope along with the pics that he had sent to Roe.

"Oh my God! He knows! Lucas says that he already sent him some still shots!"

Shelly grabbed a pillow and punched it as hard as she could. "Shit! Now you have to contact Roe, *Chicka*. You are both being harassed. We can get Regina on this, and—"

Just then, another text came through. It was a photo of a second envelope, like the one sent to Roe—and it was addressed to *Celeste Evans*!

Casey's hands were shaking as she dialed Roe's number. *"Please pick up . . . please pick up,"* she pleaded. The call went right to voicemail. When she heard his greeting, she could hardly speak.

Shelly grabbed the phone and disconnected it.

"He will call you back when he sees the missed call message. Leave nothing incriminating on his voicemail."

Casey nodded. She looked defeated and exhausted. Lucky for her, Shelly was thinking clearly.

"We'll figure it out, *Chicka,*" Shelly said, rifling through a stack of meal delivery menus. "Can I buy you dinner? You're eating for two, my love."

Casey fell back onto the bed and grabbed one pillow. Placing it over her face, she screamed into it.

Roe drove the four and a half hours back to New Hampshire with Louie's calm, intimidating eyes still burrowing through him. He had turned off his phone so he could think. He could not shake the disgust that he carried on having to call in a favor from one of Celeste's wise-guy relatives in order to save his ass. What were Louie's people going to do to Lucas? Scare him? Shake him down? Break his legs? Is that what those people do when they agree to "fix things"? He wasn't sure. All he knew was that to avoid being in hot water; he would have to have an excuse for being gone for the entire day.

He walked into the quiet house after ten. Jane was fast asleep, and Celeste, he presumed, was reading a book in bed, eyeing the clock. The day's mail was sitting untouched on his desk. Cornelia often fetched it for him before her walk in the afternoons after lunch.

He regarded the pile of bills and junk offers casually. He placed his Tumi bag that held the revolver in the back of the den closet. Then he turned to head upstairs.

In an instant, he saw it. One envelope exactly like the one that Lucas had sent to him—addressed to *Celeste!*

He yanked it from the pile, opened the closet door, and shoved it into the Tumi bag.

Then he sat at his desk and held his head in his hands.

He could wait this out. Louie was on it. By this time tomorrow, it could all be over.

But, he wondered.

Could he survive the guilt?

CHAPTER 60
FOUR DAYS LATER

The flight back to LA found Casey scouring the socials to make sure that Lucas had not leaked the video. Shelly was stowed away in coach, but at least she and Casey were on the same flight. The show had been a success that Bumpy Friedman and the boys could celebrate with big fat bonuses at the end of the year when the sponsor buys and accolades rained down. It would be well deserved. The crew was amazing, and the place went absolutely insane with the final performance of Gloria Estefan bringing down the house.

Barry Paige was keen on keeping the momentum going and had planned on raising the bar in the coming episodes in which he planned on featuring more political banter mixed with the gossip and coffee talk that was the show's mainstay.

This new content would also bolster the not-so-distant fall numbers. "*The Gab* would not be outdone," said pale-faced Barry Paige, "by another network." No, when it came to shameless ad placement plugs and generous jumbo charity checks coming out of nowhere, no one was going to outdo them. Such was the post-show discussion in the cramped trailer to prepare the cast and crew for the best fall sweeps ever. And with award season looming just five months away, no one could afford to get lazy.

Casey closed her eyes. She, for one, would not live or die by the rating numbers. She could not get home fast enough. She wanted to make sure that Selena had not ripped her off or trashed her place. The thought of an imposter minion from Lucas having access to her world made her feel more nauseated than the morning sickness. It was all-consuming.

I should have known . . . I should not have been so trusting, she berated herself.

Casey had called Regina Madison from the bungalow on day three of the show and discussed damage control.

"I don't know if you should try to get out in front of this," Regina said. "Has Lucas asked for anything? A bribe? What does he want?"

"He wants to hurt me because I ruined his business. I crossed him royally, and now he wants *blood.*"

Regina sighed. "Send me the video. I will get back to you."

Casey did so, and Regina replied simply with a shrug emoji. *"This is very grainy. I don't think he can prove your identity in this clip,"* she texted. *"But the man is definitely Roe Evans."*

Which was precisely the problem.

When they got back to LA, Casey and Shelly met with Chantelle, her accountant, on the cement stoop in front of the townhouse.

"All the locks have been changed, and here are the new keys. They are all marked. Don't worry—your books are fine. I don't see any fraudulent activity. I'm off to a SoulCycle class."

"That's a relief!" Casey said, opening the front door and waving her off. "Thanks, Chantelle."

She was happy to be home.

Shelly bounded in with the luggage and offered to make tea.

"Now what do we do?" Casey asked, several minutes later, burrowing into the couch cushions and clutching her favorite mug, steaming with ginger tea.

"We wait, *Chicka*. We wait."

Lucas Morgan did not like waiting, but every sign—the firing of Amber—and Casey's message telling him to *kiss her ass* only meant that he had gotten to her.

As for Roe Evans, the news neatly delivered to both him and his unsuspecting wife should have caused shit to hit the fan by now. If it were just extortion that he was after, he would have waited to inform Mrs. Evans of her husband's indiscretion. Instead, Evans remained silent, so he had no choice but to send the second envelope. One by one, the pieces would fall . . . the Camelot that was Casey Singer's brand and world would crumble.

And it was *her* he vowed to bury under the stones.

Roe Evans left early that morning. He was so restless; he could hardly stand it. He told Celeste that he was meeting with a music client who was only in for the day.

He took the Tumi bag containing the pistol and the envelope addressed to Celeste, tossed it into the backseat of his Land Rover, and headed down to Boston. He figured the drive would clear his head.

There had been no further word from Lucas Morgan, and the deafening silence unnerved him.

What if it was done? How would he know? Would that just be it?

He found himself in a trance, even as he made his way through the labyrinth of tunnels off of I-90 that eventually seemed to magically deposit him on Jersey Street—in front of Fenway.

There was nothing more magnificent than an empty major league ballpark, especially this one. It was all there. His team, his heroes, enshrined in bronze bigger-than-life statues outside the park entrances and the rippling flags encircling the towering brick walls. It was even older than Wrigley Field in Chicago by a couple of years, but the two landmarks equally spoke to his soul like no church ever could.

It was holy ground.

So, he slipped the attendant at the turnstile a fifty to get him in to join the next scheduled tour. Within the hour, he was inside and staring at the Big Green Monster, smelling the fragrance of a freshly sodded field, and blinking at the bluest sky he had ever seen. He took a seat away from the small crowd of tourists and just took it all in.

Suddenly, his phone buzzed in his pocket. It was Casey—surely she knew about the video by now. Lucas was the master of the game, and she and he were pawns in it, for sure. But considering the past forty-eight hours, he knew he could not implicate her any more than she was.

That was why he didn't answer.

CHAPTER 61

"The first thing we are going to do is to get you at least two days off from next week's show to give you time to see a doctor and to deal with this whole blackmail *mishegoss*. Go ahead, text Bumpy's Irish lass, and tell her you have the flu."

"I don't know how understanding the network is going to be if I keep taking time off like this."

"Don't worry. You killed it there in Miami, and the other three can hold their own with a replacement, as you would do for them."

Shelly handed Casey her phone and stared her down. "Do it, *Chicka!*"

Casey hedged and then settled for a text. "I'll add some weight to it and tell Aubrey that I think I have COVID. That ought to shut down any objections."

"Right! And it will buy us some more time, as they assume you are getting tested. Then, you will inform them you do not have COVID, just a bad flu."

"It's done!" Casey said, putting down the phone.

"Next," Shelly said, "we are getting you to a doctor. Who's your OBGYN?"

"Dr. Kaye on Rodeo Drive."

"Ha! Of course, *Bonita*, leave it to you to have a Beverly Hills doctor!"

"She's the best," Casey said, returning to her full diva persona. "She's the OBGYN to the private parts of the stars."

Shelly belly-laughed and then hugged her. "Okay, let's get that hoo-ha checked out, Mama!"

THE EARLY-MORNING APPOINTMENT was granted on Monday thanks to a favor from Dr. Kaye's receptionist, Tara, who was a fan of the show. It would cost Casey an autographed glossy headshot and a shout-out for the women's health practice on the podcast, but it was worth it. Dr. Courtney Kaye was the best there was, and Casey would never settle for anything less.

The exam ensued after pleasantries, and Casey lay, nervous and exposed in a scratchy cotton gown, legs spreadeagle in the rubber stirrups, feeling the heat of the OptiSpec light on her vagina. Dr. Kaye was poking uncomfortably at her cervix and pressing down on her uterus.

"Okay, my dear. From what I can tell, you are exhibiting all the signs. Let's get that bloodwork back, and then we'll take it from there." She tossed the speculum into the sink. "In the meantime, let me know if you have any unusual bleeding or pain."

She helped Casey sit up and snapped off her gloves.

A nurse gathered the paper table covering and handed Casey a hot cloth.

Then, Dr. Kaye, with her caring tiger eyes and expensive pumps, pushed back on her stool and smiled sweetly.

"I hope this is good news for you, Casey. Were you trying?"

Casey pulled the abrasive fabric up around her and crossed her arms. "No, I wasn't. Not exactly." Her voice drifted off as she felt the pang of sixteen years prior, in college, when she found herself pregnant by a reckless jaunt with Professor Jackson Lovejoy—and the devastating agony of an abortion. The stain and shame never quite faded with time.

"Well, I will be in touch then, as soon as the results are in," she said, clicking the mouse on the computer screen and batting over-the-top lash extensions.

"Thank you," Casey said meekly. She was eighteen all over again. But this time, there would be no mistakes or regrets. This was either Ryder's or Roe's baby. The chances of determining the exact date of conception would be anyone's guess, since she had sex with them a little over one week apart.

"Oh," Casey added, "I'm going to need a COVID test result for my employer."

"Let's get that done," she said. "I'll have the nurse pop in with the swab."

"Thanks," Casey said. She slid down from the table and got dressed.

THE FARM-CHIC RESTAURANT on Beverly Drive offered the perfect anecdote for a taxing morning. Casey was all-in for a bison burger stacked mile-high with Bibb lettuce, tomatoes, and garlic aioli sauce. Plus, she had a distinct craving for their famous shoestring fries.

"Can you ask the chef to drizzle some chili sauce on the fries?" Casey asked.

The server nodded and disappeared.

"Oh, I remember the cravings!" Shelly said, sipping her ice water. "They get worse, I promise."

"I'm just happy that I can stomach food again. I have been so insatiable these days."

Shelly gave a little laugh that made her earrings swing. "It's a sign that you truly are stowing away a little bun in the oven, my darling."

"We will see," Casey said. "I think it will hit me when Dr. Kaye delivers the official results." She checked her phone for the hundredth time. "How long does it take to get blood work results back?"

"As long as it takes, *Chicka.*"

Suddenly, a commotion at the bar stirred, and the bartender turned up the volume on a newscast, breaking into the local programming.

From where they were sitting, Casey could see Lucas Morgan's photo on the screen.

"What in *the world?*"

BUMPY WAS LESS-THAN-HAPPY when he heard the news.

"COVID! *Hell no—!*"

"Aye, she is not even sure if it is. Just getting the test today." Aubrey delivered the news from her desk when Bumpy passed by on his way to a meeting.

"When did she notify us?"

"She sent a text over the weekend. I've been up to ninety all day—so busy! I just saw it."

"Call in a replacement. Get that anchor from the early-morning show from the third floor. What's her name? Marla? Or Mora? Follow up with Casey regarding the test results. Shit! This is all we need! And put out a memo right now—mask-wearing for everyone on the set and in the office until further notice!"

He bounded down the hall, fuming. He could not afford to replace the *entire* cast if the virus was on the loose. Every week it was a different strain. Everyone who had been within six feet of her would need to be tested. And that was a lot of staff—not to mention the public at the meet and greets she took part in during their stay in Miami.

He would table the news until he was sure. He popped a square of Nicorette gum into his mouth. Then, as decreed, he fumbled for the crumpled facemask from his suit pocket and strapped it on. He wasn't about to take any chances.

His body ached in all the usual places, and his head was throbbing.

It was a Monday, all right!

CHAPTER 62

Casey's phone dinged—a slew of media notifications scrolled across her screen. One read: *Talent agent Lucas Morgan, formerly of the Lucas Morgan Agency, found dead in his Los Angeles apartment.*

"What?" Casey was incredulous.

Shelly grabbed her phone and began scrolling the internet for more information on the news story. She caught the server as he whizzed by. "Excuse me! We'll be taking our order to go!"

Moments later, the two pulled up to the townhouse, and a reporter was already snooping around to see if he could get a statement from Casey. He boldly approached the car and asked, "Weren't you a client of Lucas Morgan at one time, Ms. Singer? What is your reaction?"

She and Shelly ran from the attached garage into the kitchen entrance, lowering the electronic door in his face.

"Vultures!" Shelly hissed as she deposited the take-out bags onto the counter. "Let's turn on the TV."

Casey was in shock. She sat in the center of the couch and raised the volume on the cable news channel. There was a live shot of one anchor standing in front of Lucas's apartment building with a small crowd forming behind the yellow police tape. *"We do not have all the details, but forty-four-year-old Lucas Morgan, formerly of the Lucas Morgan Agency here in LA, was found dead this morning. His apartment was not broken into, and it appears that he might have let his attacker in. There was no robbery—just a struggle. The coroner is not saying much more than that Morgan died from a bullet wound. No motive is apparent at this time as to why this occurred."*

Shelly took the remote and searched the other local stations for more information. It was the same story on each of them—an attack on Lucas Morgan. No motive. No suspects. Channel four was using the phrases, *" . . . Killed at point-blank"* . . . and *"No suspects or motive."*

Casey blinked. "Shelly, you don't suppose . . .?"

Shelly took a deep breath. "That this is not a random murder? I'm with you there, *Chicka*."

The thought was too unbelievable for Casey to comprehend. "Wait. No—this is not a Netflix movie. We will not assume that anyone would have *wanted* him dead."

By *anyone,* she meant Roe Evans. The idea of it was just too absurd.

"I think," Shelly said, taking Casey's hand, "that Lucas got what he had coming. He has pissed off more than one person in his life—he just finally met the one who could retaliate."

Casey nodded. The shock had not fully set in.

"Maybe I can find out more," Shelly said, reaching for her phone.

Casey stared at the image on TV of the gawkers assembling on the sidewalk in front of Lucas's apartment.

She hoped Shelly was right. Many people probably wanted him dead. The question was, who would have had the means to do it?

Shelly closed the blinds and rechecked the locks. "You should stay out of sight, and don't open the door," she said. "I'm calling my contact here in town." A beat passed, and then she spoke into the phone. "Gregg, my friend! It's Shelly Escamilla. Yes, it's been a while. I'm calling about the Lucas Morgan murder. What do you know?"

ROE SAT in the lavish and high-style lobby of the Liberty Hotel on Charles Street. The structure was once the town jail dating back to 1851, where it housed some of Boston's most notorious criminals. With the passing of time, the blessing of restoration, and the talents of famed architects, the structure was eventually refurbished into a stunning boutique hotel. It would serve as the perfect respite for Roe to think, thanks to the massive amount of business loyalty points gained from Marriott. That, and an interest in not yet going home, brought him to the barstool in the center of all the action.

He ordered a draft beer for a change. It came in a tall, frosted glass. He looked up at the massive TV screen suspended above the top-shelf liquor and nearly fell off the low-backed stool.

The sound was muted, but the caption read: *A high-profile murder in downtown Los Angeles has officials calling the incident a mob-like hit. The deceased—Lucas Morgan, formerly of the Lucas Morgan Talent Agency—was found dead execution-style.*

Roe's pulse quickened. He felt dizzy. He checked his phone. One text loomed unanswered. He still had his phone on silent, never having reverted it back from earlier in the day. It was from Louie Benedetti. He tapped the screen with his thumb. The green word bubble contained only two words: *E finito.*

Lucas Morgan is dead? Who said anything about killing anyone!?

Roe was sweating. He could see that the newscast was on to other national stories, so he scrolled frantically through the newsfeeds on his phone for more details. "*Former talent agent Lucas Morgan . . . Dead on the scene . . . One bullet to the head . . . Found in his kitchen by his live-in model/actress girlfriend. No suspects at present.*"

He peeled a twenty from his wallet, deposited it on the bar, and headed for the valet.

It was time to go home.

CHAPTER 63

"Where is Her Little Highness?" Kathryn asked, removing the lid from her latte.

La Costa gave a good-hearted laugh. "Did she not make it back from Miami?"

"Out. COVID scare. Which brings me to the first order of business," Barry Paige said, dividing the room into sections. "All on-air talent on my left, Conference Room three, all floor crew, Conference Room four. Control room and floaters—Conference Room five. We have nurses on hand to administer rapid COVID tests for all of you!"

"Gee! Lucky us!" Kathryn said, sneering. "We have Casey to thank for this?"

Hannah rallied, "Well, better safe than sorry!" Secretly, she *was* worried—remembering how she shared a car with Casey back in Miami. *How wise was that?*

No one could afford to get sick, that was for sure.

"She did look ashy," La Costa said, moving through the hall with her castmates. "Maybe it was just food poisoning or something. Maybe some bad seafood."

"Well, they said a *possible scare*. What does that mean, for Christ's sake!" Kathryn was livid. They still needed to go over the changes in the show schedule that this would cause. "Who are they getting to fill in for Casey? I hope it's not that airhead from *Sunrise at Seven!*"

Just then, Barry Paige popped into the open doorway. "You've got Marla Yee with you today, Ladies. I know you can handle it!"

"Great!" La Costa said, returning her swab stick to the attendant. "Good. That one hardly talks. More airtime for us!"

Casey watched the playback of the show with a judging eye. She recorded every day's episode to assess her performance and to chart the audience's reactions. The perfectionism in her could not resist it, although seeing herself on air made her extremely self-conscious. She fast-forwarded through the intro to see who her replacement was for the day. It was Marla from the early-morning newscast, looking like a statue with her porcelain skin and jet-black hair. She was around the same age as her, but she looked like a TV anchor—a talking head just like Bethany Peterson Hall from the early days of broadcasting. They were a dime a dozen, this type of woman. She would be good for about fifteen seconds of polite banter, and then Kathryn would run roughshod over her and steer the show in order to see that the camera stayed on the core team. *Would she even be missed?* That was the question.

What did it matter, anyway? Everything in her life was about to change—everything! What did all this mean for her? She would need to reevaluate all of it. Lucas was dead, and with him, the secret of her affair with Roe would be buried, releasing him from any implication.

Shelly returned from her call and sat on the edge of the linen-upholstered armchair. She placed her hand on Casey's leg. "It was a hit, for sure. It seems that Lucas had finally pissed off the wrong guy, pure and simple. He was a con and a pathetic excuse for a human. He can't touch you, or Roe, or anyone else ever again."

Shelly spoke to Casey as if she were a child.

"*Chica*, relax. It's over. Lucas Morgan is gone, and he can't do anything now to hurt you."

Casey nodded, and then a realization crossed her pained face. "What about the girl? *Selena*—she's still out there!"

Shelly patted Casey's hand and sighed. "I'm way ahead of you there. I've got little Miss Amber Herrera's name and her former address. I'll be paying her a brief visit."

SHELLY WAITED over three hours for the girl to show up. It was nearly dusk, and Shelly had been sitting in Casey's SUV in Huntington Beach, conducting surveillance like a seasoned pro. Her back was stiff from sitting still, cramped behind the steering wheel. She had eaten through two full-size Twix Bars and a can of mixed nuts. Her water bottle was nearly empty, and she needed to pee.

Finally, she saw her. A tall, thin girl with dark hair pulled off her face in a ponytail protruding from a cap. She had on a midriff top and jeans shredded at the knees. She was carrying a knockoff Prada backpack and was walking toward the house.

Shelly emerged from the car. The girl caught sight of her. She instantly recognized the Audi and started up the stairs.

"Amber!" Shelly called. "Wait! Please, I want to help you!"

The girl shot her a nasty glance. "No comment!" she said, heading for the door.

"I am not with the press . . . Amber, I have a message from Casey. She will not get you in trouble."

Amber stopped and turned toward Shelly.

"Please, can we just talk? *Podemos hablar? Latina* to *Latina*?"

Amber paused. "Not here," she finally said. "This is my parents' house."

"I'll talk anywhere you'd like," Shelly said.

"The Corner Diner on Slater Avenue. In an hour."

"Okay," Shelly said. "I'll be there."

At precisely six p.m., Amber showed up, scanning the tables for Shelly.

She was sitting near the window in the back, just off the restrooms. Shelly waved, and the girl sidled into the booth across from her.

"Thank you for coming," Shelly said.

Amber was all business. "You said that you have a message for me from Casey?"

The server appeared and deposited two ice waters in plastic tumblers on the table. "Hi, Ladies—what can I get you?"

Shelly paused and then said, "Two coffees," which sent the waitress on her way.

Amber shifted uncomfortably.

"I know you must be very upset about all that has transpired."

Amber showed no emotion. She looked like she still might be in shock, but appeared not to be taking any chances.

"I am not a cop. I am Casey's friend, and I intend to undo some of the damage that you have contributed to, namely concerning her brand and her life."

Amber looked confused. "Undo?"

"Yes, what you did was unlawful—and immoral. I suspect Lucas pulled you into his web and that you are unsuspecting in all of this. Have you spoken to the police yet?"

Amber shook her head. "Just when I gave the report. I found him—" Her voice caught in her throat, and she struggled to fight the tears.

Shelly produced a fresh tissue from her Chanel tote.

"—on the floor, bleeding." Amber dabbed around her fake lashes and blew her nose into the tissue. She went on, spilling her secrets as if with relief. "I didn't know him all that well. Just that he hired me to 'pretend' to be a personal assistant—you know, as a gig. Casey paid me, and I gave the money to Lucas. He promised to get me a read for a film. That was the agreement."

Shelly looked at Amber with compassion. *Bastard! He deserved what he got, all right!*

"So, am I in trouble?" Amber sniffed.

"It depends," Shelly said as the two steaming cups of coffee appeared with a saucer of creamers between them. She waited a beat and then leaned in. "What you did was impersonate someone who did not exist in order to have access to Casey Singer and her world. You would have to be *loca* not to realize how that, in itself, is a crime."

"I just want it all to go away. You know . . . I didn't mean to hurt Casey. At least now the sex tape will not be shown to the world, right?"

Sex tape? She thinks all she found was a sex tape of Casey? That was all that Shelly needed to hear. The girl was no threat to Casey or to Roe Evans.

"It's important that you never speak of this to anyone, okay? Casey will not press charges if you just disappear. Go back to your *familia* and maybe go to school . . . get a job—a proper job—and stay out of Hollywood. If this ordeal has taught you anything, it should be to avoid the likes of goons like Lucas Morgan."

Amber looked relieved and nodded her head. "*Si*. I will, ma'am. I will. Oh, *gracias a Dios!*"

"Don't thank God for this one, *Mi amiga*—thank Casey Singer."

CHAPTER 64

Casey tried to keep busy. To keep her mind off all the different directions it was pulling her—*Lucas . . . her test results . . . Roe.* She was sitting in her home office with Shelly, working her way through a mountain of emails and text messages.

"I can book both our flights for mid-week," Casey said. "We'll get you back to Chicago, and I'll head back to work before Marla Yee takes my job."

"No chance of that," Shelly said. "And no worries about Amber Herrera—she's going off the grid and won't be a problem."

"Who?" Casey said, half-listening.

"Your Selena Rapp," Shelly said.

"Oh, don't remind me!" Just the name of that girl sent Casey reeling. "Thanks for everything, Shelly," she said, swiping a stray blonde strand that had fallen from her messy bun. "I don't know what I'd do without you."

"Let's not test that theory!" Shelly said, cross-legged on the plush couch. "Are any of those messages from Roe?"

Casey shook her head.

There was no word. Nothing since the day she left Roe's apartment in London.

Suddenly, Casey's phone rang.

"Hello, Dr. Kaye!" Casey said, standing up from the chair.

Shelly unfolded her limbs and hoisted herself onto her stocking feet.

"I understand. Okay, yes. Thank you. I will do that. See you then."

When she hung up, Shelly touched her arm. "*And . . .?*"

"Yep. I'm pregnant," Casey said, strangely calm.

Shelly squealed and wrapped her friend in a bear hug. "*Mira,* this is a blessing, *Chicka.* A big one! It changes everything."

That is precisely what Casey thought—but exactly *how*?

ROE REMAINED THE DILIGENT, loving father and husband, just as he always had. He continued to dote on Celeste with flowers and gifts and showered Jane with loving hugs and bedtime stories. He made it a point to be home more than ever. He reduced his meeting schedule to just one late night a week, ate dinner with the family regularly, and was home all weekend, tending to house repairs. He mowed the lawn and even cleaned out the shed to build Celeste a greenhouse.

Most notably, he avoided his study.

The Tumi briefcase remained forgotten, shoved into the deepest recesses of the closet. The Glock returned to the strongbox, and the key affixed to the back of his office middle drawer, like a videotape that had been rewound to reverse time.

He made love to his wife in the dark and then folded himself into her warmth, telling himself that he was still the man he was before.

In other words, he lied.

Later that week, a large package arrived for Celeste postmarked from Italy. She ripped the tape off and opened the box. It contained a fragile object tightly wound in bubble wrap. "What in the world—?"

She curiously unveiled the mysterious figure—a figurine of a woman holding a docile dove. It was milky porcelain and was signed at the base by the artist. A note was included. "It's from my cousin, Louie Benedetti. He says that he owed us a proper wedding gift. An artist from his father's village commissioned it for us. How sweet is that? I'm going to find the perfect place for it," Celeste said, beaming.

Roe regarded the statue as a sign, a signal to him that there were no more "favors" indeed to be had by Louie Benedetti—that, and the fact that it would serve as a tangible reminder of their transaction—forever.

Message received.

CHAPTER 65
ONE MONTH LATER

Casey needed to see it for herself. She *needed* to know for sure that Lucas Morgan was dead.

"The memorial service is tomorrow afternoon, according to the online obituary," Casey told Shelly on her speakerphone as she packed up her office post-show.

"Why the long wait? He's been dead for weeks," Shelly's response was valid.

"I googled the details. I guess they had to wait for a distant cousin to arrive to finalize the arrangements. I wonder if anyone at all will show up to view his sorry ashes."

"Oh, I'm sure they will—the pretty people like to feel a part of the drama. He was once a well-respected agent. It's a sure bet that the rat bastard will draw a 'thirsty' crowd. It's a pity that he bought it the way he did. But that's not *your* problem, *Chicka*. Or your fault. He did it to himself." Shelly was somewhere at an ice rink in the northern suburbs. Both of her boys were in the hockey league, one as a center and the other as a left-winger. Practice time was Shelly's golden opportunity to catch up on calls. Being the consummate hockey mom that she was, she was adept at multitasking.

"I guess you're right," Casey said, reaching for her wool coat.

The New York winter was brutal. She was about to catch an Uber to the airport. She was eager to leave for the weekend without the interrogation from her castmates on why she had consistently declined meeting them for group lunches and industry parties as of late. She was exhausted.

"When do you start shooting the *Starbreaker* film? Does the production company know about your *situation*? HUSTLE! GET IT! SHOOT!" Shelly yelled into the phone. "Sorry about that!"

Casey laughed. "So this is how you work out your aggression! I love it!"

"You should see my pom-pom hat. It is serious! All the hockey moms have them. I'll knit you one, too, if you'd like."

Casey laughed. "Yeah, I might need one where I'll be going. The shooting has been delayed, thankfully. It starts next month here in LA. I'll be four months along by then. I don't know if I can conceal this pregnancy for the entire length of the project. I suppose I'll have to level with Alto and the team."

"And Bumpy Friedman? When are you planning on dropping *that* bombshell?" Shelly asked.

"I don't know. I haven't thought it all through just yet. We will be airing reruns over the summer." Casey said. "So that will buy me some time. It's still all so surreal."

Hurrying for the lobby, Casey was a revolving door away from the cool winds of Manhattan and an airplane to sunny LA when Kathryn Delacorte suddenly stopped her.

"Share a car with me to LaGuardia?" Kathryn asked, donning her Prada trench coat and gloves. She was pulling a Louie Vuitton soft duffle on wheels.

"I've got to go, Shelly," Casey said into the phone. "Talk later!"

"Bye, *Chicka!*" Shelly said, and then signed off.

"Sure. Why not?" Casey said to Kathryn.

"Good. We can catch up on things on the way!"

The two slid into the waiting car. The heater was on, and the leather seats were warm. A sprinkle of rain was spitting down from an overcast sky. The tumult and rhythm of the city never really appealed to Casey. It was far more Kathryn's scene.

"You're not staying in town over the weekend?" Casey asked.

Kathryn smiled. "Got an event in Dallas that I have to attend. It never ends . . . and it never gets easier all this back-and-forth traveling."

"Tell me about it!" Casey sighed. Of the four, she was always the first one out the door on a Friday.

"How are things with the podcast?" Kathryn asked, although Casey was sure that she couldn't give a hoot about it.

Instead, she chose to bring up the movie project. "Pretty good. Oh—and I film the *Starbreaker* project at the end of next month, in Canada."

"How nice for you!" Kathryn patronized. Again, not all that interested. Finally, she hit the nerve. "Have you seen the latest on your friend Roe Evans?"

Casey's heart skipped.

Kathryn held out her phone so that Casey could see the post. "Looks like trouble in paradise." It was a photograph on one of the socials of Roe and Celeste leaving a restaurant after a "strained argument" in public.

Casey glanced and waved it off.

"You dodged a bullet with that one," Kathryn said with a placid tone. "The last thing in the world you would need is to be anyone's trophy *anything*!"

Casey nodded, watching the headlights stream by through the rain-streaked window.

Once on the plane, Casey turned off her phone and placed her hands over her midsection. It was all she could do to believe that there, inside her, was life itself. No matter what happened now . . . she would be responsible for a tiny life—a whole *person*! The idea of it all both frightened and excited her. *What if she couldn't be a great mom like Shelly? What if the baby never knew its father?*

Hell, she didn't even know who the father was, and in a world of confusion, smoke and mirrors, and delusion, she only knew *one* thing for sure. She knew she could not withhold that truth from her child.

She turned on her phone and shot a text to Ryder—*I need to see you ASAP.*

Casey saw the return text from Ryder once the plane touched down: *I'm in LA through mid-week and then gone for a project in Dubai.*

Perfect! Casey texted back. *I just need about an hour of your time —and a blood sample.*

CHAPTER 66

Casey pulled the Audi onto the grass behind a long line of cars snaking along the cement pavement. A cluster of people had assembled at the open graveside in the distance. It looked like a respectable turnout. Mostly young girls and a spattering of middle-aged industry dinosaurs in dark suits, looking uncomfortable in the midday sun. Holy Cross Cemetery was in Culver City, and offered Lucas a Catholic mass and modified interment, thanks to a relative who was able to pull strings with the archdiocese.

There was no casket, just a simple urn with the ashes, which would be buried in the gaping ground.

Casey slipped in the back, grateful that she had opted for flats in the mushy grass. She wore a plain wrap dress, a hat, and oversized sunglasses.

Lucas Morgan was gone.

Buried with Lucas's ashes would be the secret of her affair with the newly married Roe and the bitter contempt that Lucas had for her.

Good riddance! she whispered as the crowd dispersed to head back to their cars and their lives.

She looked around and saw Selena—*Amber*—out of the

corner of her eye, heading with three other girls toward a sun-faded Nissan. A familiar instinct welled within her to confront the girl, to say her piece. But she thought better of it and left well enough alone.

What good would it do? The girl was capable of a lot more than Lucas led her to believe. But she would have to find that out for herself.

Casey walked back to her car and drove out through the gates.

R\ YDER WAS WAITING in the physician's office when Casey bounded in, out of breath. She had made the four-mile drive in record time, despite the traffic.

"Hi!" she said, giving Ryder a little kiss on the cheek. "I hope you haven't been waiting long."

He looked like a deer in the headlights. "Casey, why am I meeting with you here? I had to check the address twice." Then he lowered his voice. "Please don't tell me you have some sort of disease or something."

"Not exactly," Casey said. She gave her name to the receptionist and soon, she and Ryder were ushered in, down a hallway, and into an exam room.

The door closed, and Casey blurted, "It's like this. I'm pregnant, Ryder, and the baby might—or might not—be yours."

"What?" His cheeks turned red, and he raked his hand through his perfect hair, which was now shoulder-length because of a role he was prepping for.

Casey remained calm. "I'm not asking anything from you except for your willingness to submit to a paternity test. We both give a blood sample, and then they look at the genetics, and—"

"And then what?"

"We will know if we even have an issue."

"So, you're saying you had sex with me—*and another dude*? Like, back-to-back? When was that?"

"Chicago."

"Right. Chicago—and then you had sex with someone else?" he said, now unable to stand still.

"Yes. I am sorry to be putting you in this position, Ryder. Really. But we can have the answer soon. My doctor is going to fast-track this for us."

"How long?"

"A day or two."

"Shit, Casey . . . I don't know about this. It's just a lot to process right here. Holy *fuck!*"

"Listen, as I said, I am not looking for anything from you. Nothing. But I have to sort things out, and I can only do it if I know the truth. Whatever it is."

He sat on one of the two small plastic chairs and blew into his cupped hands. He was sporting two new tattoos on his exposed forearms and was dripping in silver chains around his neck. His high tops were tapping on the laminate flooring. "Okay, Case. I'll do it. I'll take the test. *Jesus!*"

The door opened, and a pretty nurse in scrubs took a seat at the desk. "One paternity test today?"

Casey nodded. "Yes, please."

CHAPTER 67

Roe had grown tired of the secrets and the strained conversations with Celeste that only resulted in bitter arguing. She had questioned him on every front, realizing that something had changed; a switch had gone off inside of him and taken the light that was Roe away from her and their family.

He was at a loss for what to do. To make it right. Could he? Was there a way?

The trouble was, although he'd had no contact with Casey since the night they spent together in his London apartment, he could not stop thinking of her. *Had she known about Lucas Morgan's little blackmail scheme? Was she trying to protect his reputation? His marriage?*

And now, even with the fact that Lucas was gone, hadn't the worst of the damage happened anyway?

He was adrift on a raft on an ocean that he could not see his way out of. He had been helpless to a desire that only grew more intense with time, and in an instant of fear and shame, he panicked.

So what if he told Celeste the truth? It could not undo the worst that had been done, but it could strangely free him in a way that nothing else could. He could only offer his confession —and hope for forgiveness. As for Louie and his goons, they were just as culpable—even more so by taking matters into their own hands. That secret, most likely, would go to his grave.

And what they would decide to do as a result was of no matter to him. At least he would be free.

He walked into the bedroom. Celeste was sitting, propped up against the headboard, reading a historical Cold War romance. He knew it was her guilty pleasure. *How ironic was that?*

"What?" she said in reply to his wordless gaze.

"We have to talk. There is something I have to tell you."

"Let me buy you lunch," Casey said as she and Ryder exited the shiny medical building out onto the sidewalk. "I know a great little place that has the world's best tacos!"

He followed her SUV to La Cienega Park on Gregory Way. They walked a short distance to the food truck that was parked nearby. Tito's Taco Bus was a little-known gem in the neighbor- hood. It originated from somewhere in the city, but could always be counted on to service the Beverly Hills elite, looking for the authenticity and charm of the colorfully painted truck and its amazing tamales and roasted peppers wafting from the grill vents.

"Trust me, you're going to love it," Casey said.

"You had me at Taco Bus," Ryder said, attempting humor, although there was nothing funny about a pregnancy scare.

Casey knew it was a lot for him. She could only hope that they both would get the outcome they hoped for.

After they ordered, they each carried their paper taco trays and found an open bench with a view of the baseball diamond. A few families were milling around, and some people were walking their dogs or pushing strollers. Casey noticed Ryder seemed distracted by all of it.

"I can't get enough of this hot sauce!" Casey said, ripping

into a packet with her teeth. "And I never liked it before. Weird, huh?"

Ryder was half-listening. He barely touched the steaming street tacos in front of him.

Casey changed the subject. "Tell me about this project in Dubai. What is it?"

"An epic production. It's a crime thriller with a twist—the lead is a woman. She's part human, part Artificial Intelligence. She's a real badass. I would be her love interest. Actually, there is more than one of her, which is the twist. It's like a futuristic-Matrix-Superhero-Shape-Shifter kind of thing.

"Sounds amazing! Who's playing her?"

"Would you believe Suranne Jones? Well, that's the rumor."

"How awesome is that? She *is* a superhero, for sure. And gorgeous!"

"It all depends if everything looks right on the screen tests and for the promos. That is what they base it all on. You know?"

"Ryder, you are a great actor—the camera loves you. You are the perfect match for this AI Bot. You're versatile and hot—a bad boy with a devastating smile and killer abs. Plus, you do all of your own stunts! I mean, come on!"

Ryder wagged his head. She was really pouring it on.

"It's only bigger roles and more broken hearts in your wake, Ryder. I'm sure of it," Casey said with sincerity.

The truth of the matter was that she meant it. He was a hot commodity, and when paired with the right leads and box office gold scripts—he could write his ticket to anywhere.

"What about you, Case? What does this mean for you now? Is the role of motherhood going to gel with your game plan?"

She dabbed her lips with a flimsy brown napkin.

"It was not in my game plan. No. But I can't say what I want to do. You know?"

He nodded. "Well, I'm here for you, Case. Whatever you decide to do."

She smiled. How was it they always found each other up

against a wall? It was as if they were twin flames—cursed to the core and somehow attached at the hip.

They finished their lunch and then hugged like two star-crossed lovers in a summer-run play.

"I'll call you as soon as I hear," Casey said.

"I'm here until mid-week. I'm staying with my buddy in Riverside." He waved and headed to his rented convertible, leaving her standing there, on a tiny patch of grass, alone.

CHAPTER 68
JUNE 2022

Roe loaded his car with just the needed provisions. Hiking boots, wool socks, moisture-wicking cargo pants and shirts, rain jackets, hiking poles, and mosquito repellent. He included a few essentials to soothe his blistered soul. A catalogue of music albums, an old record player, a generator, and four blank journals—one for each month he planned on living off the grid.

He would ditch his phone, computer, and all connections to the outside world. Where he was going, there would be no chance of him colliding with his recent disappointments and failures. The divorce papers were signed, and a thousand apologies would never be enough to erase the pain he caused Celeste and her family. He couldn't even think about Casey or the fact that he was ghosting her so completely.

What could not be dealt with in England or LA would be given to the cool arctic winds of Alaska and the eighteen hours of daylight to keep the nightmare that was once his wretched life at bay. He had to admit that only time and distance would ever hope to heal what was broken inside him.

As he pulled away, he prayed for peace, forgiveness, and a way out of the mess he had made of his life.

. . .

THE CALL CAME when Casey least expected it. She was heading to the set of *Starbreaker*, which was currently filming on an independent sound stage in Valencia. She had made the trip lost in blissful reverie as she ran over her lines on the fifty-minute drive along I-5 to the studio. It was seven a.m., and she was in full character mode when her phone buzzed from the dash.

"Miss Singer?" It was her OBGYN.

"Hi, Doc. Great timing. I'm on my way to work."

"I have the results for you regarding the paternity test. We've just mailed you the paperwork. Do you want to know the result of Mr. McKinley's sample?"

Casey paused and then braced herself. "Yes. I would like to know."

"Very well, then. The results show there is no probability that he is the father."

"Not the father?" Casey said, void of any emotion.

"That's correct. Ryder McKinley is not the father of your baby."

A short silence followed, and Casey audibly sighed. "Thank you, Dr. Kaye. I will be in for my next checkup in a few weeks. I will see you then."

"You are most welcome. I am sorry if this is not the news you wanted to hear. Take care, Casey. I'll see you then."

"Thanks so much, Dr. Kaye." The line went dead, and Casey took a moment to process the reality that it was *Roe's* baby she was carrying. A ripple of excitement shot through her, surprising in its intensity. Then, just as instantly, it was followed by a sad, empty reality—there would be no hope of her child having a father in the picture.

Roe Evans was nowhere to be found. He hadn't responded to any of her calls since the Lucas/Amber sex tape scandal erupted in both their lives. It was harder on him, for sure, she had reasoned. Still, four long, silent months had passed since she had last spoken to Roe—or seen him, not since Bristol on that one fated night when they gave themselves to each other. A night it was now glaringly evident had changed her life forever.

She would need to level with Bumpy Friedman and her cast mates, as it would soon become increasingly harder to conceal the pregnancy on the set of *The Gab*. Surprisingly, it hadn't been an issue for Alto when she told him on the first day of filming *Starbreaker*. He took the news good-naturedly and said he would make arrangements for the filming of her scenes to be wrapped up in the next few months—out of sequence and at a higher budget. He wanted her for the part of Oren, and that superseded any extra complications.

"Okay, *chérie*," he had said, with a nicotine smile beneath his silver goatee. "We'll use a stand-in for the body shots along with your stunt double. You are not the first starlet who was knocked up on the job. We will work around it, yes?"

She didn't know if she felt grateful or degraded. It was a harsh business, for sure. She knew one thing for certain, though; nothing stopped the moving cogs of a picture's production or promotion. It was simply the unwritten rule and stark reality of the business. People were interchangeable. It was as simple as that. It was all smoke and mirrors anyway, right?

Casey arrived on the lot and hurried to her trailer, past a flurry of technicians, assistants, production designers, and other crewmembers. Closing the door to the chaos, she plopped her designer bag onto the stool and flipped on the switch to the makeup bureau. She stood there, staring, in the unforgiving million-watt lights at the image looking back at her, fresh-faced and stripped down to her plainest, raw self. She had to ask, *Is this what I really want? Is this still the dream?*

Tears filled her eyes, and she began to sob with an abandon she had not allowed herself to release since her parents' deaths on that cold day in a Chicago church so many years ago. What was it? Fear? Relief? The rush of raging hormones?

She looked at the face in the mirror. Gone was the girl she once was.

The only thing she knew for sure was that the role she was about to play, as a single mom to this child—Roe Evans's child—was the only one that mattered. It was not about the next conquest or the elusive brass ring.

With Roe's precipitous disappearance after the highly publicized divorce from Celeste, his impending and perplexing silence, and the circumstances at hand, she had to accept the fact that her life—which was about to take a new direction—would never include him.

To Casey's surprise, as she pulled herself together and got ready for the makeup artist and stylist to arrive, a sense of pure joy and calm overcame her, and, remarkably, that not-so-alluring spotlight she had been chasing for so long was beginning to sputter and flicker in the distance as a deeper passion now burned inside of her.

She reached for her phone, wiping the tears away from her cheeks with the back of her hand. She scrolled for her last text to Ryder and typed: *Paternity test negative. You are off the hook!* She added a smiley face and the fishhook emoji. She imagined his relief, and it did make her happy to free him of any obligation moving forward. It would be a one-woman show from here on out, and she was up for it.

She decided that she would text Shelly later when they could talk. There would be so much to sort out. She had no plans further than the present.

And that was okay because *this* Casey Singer was going to love something more than she loved herself.

CHAPTER 69
TWO WEEKS LATER

Casey emerged from the bathroom stall and was surprised to find Hannah Courtland- Murphy cross-armed and laser-focused on her, like a mother hen.

"So, how far along are you?"

Casey broke her gaze and reached for the soap dispenser. "What are you talking about?"

Hannah turned to meet Casey's reflection in the mirror. "Sweetheart, it's evident to anyone with eyeballs that you have put on weight, spend more time in the restroom than Bumpy with his IBS, and you've been ditching Happy Hour for weeks. What gives?"

Casey turned and leaned back on the sink. "Is it that obvious?"

Hannah nodded and then removed her electric-blue frames. "Ever since Miami. I see you, Casey Singer."

Casey's rigid frown transformed into a timid smile. "About four months now."

"I knew it!" Hannah beamed. She embraced Casey in a warm, matronly hug that smelled like Chanel.

Casey let happy tears well in her eyes. It felt good to tell another person besides Shelly. It was really happening. "I have to tell Bumpy . . . any support on that front would be appreciated," Casey said, facing the sink.

Hannah smiled. "You got it! This calls for a girls-only rap session. What time should I be at your place?"

LATER THAT EVENING, the door buzzed, and Casey, in comfy leggings and an oversized sweatshirt bought from a street vendor at a production of *Hamilton*, answered the door. "Hi! I threw some Hot Pockets in the oven."

Hannah beamed. She was carrying a brown shopping bag from the pricey grocery store up the street. "Great! They will go great with the Pinot—only you can't have any. I bought some sparkling water for you."

"You didn't have to do that," Casey said, beginning to close the door. Just then, a stiletto appeared as Kathryn boldly pushed the door open, followed by La Costa, also stiletto-clad and carrying a homemade pie covered in foil.

"Watch the Louboutins, sister!" Kathryn said. "We hear that there is a new mama-to-be!"

"*What the—?*" Casey said, startled.

"We are *all* here!" La Costa said, holding up the rear. "Did you think this news would not affect us all? We are a TV family. Sit down—we've got this."

A few minutes later, Casey's spacious loft living room was transformed into a veritable buffet of charcuterie delights of assorted hams, sausages, terrines, pâtés, aged cheeses, and gluten-free crackers. Grapes and olives rounded out the spread, along with the Hot Pockets. Corks were popped, and pinot, rosé, and sparkling water were poured into a mixed assortment of juice glasses procured from above the kitchen sink.

"How is it that you don't have any proper wine glasses?" Kathryn said disapprovingly.

Casey shrugged. "I've dropped and broken more than I can count. I guess I never got around to replacing them."

Hannah and La Costa exchanged a knowing glance.

"I put the pie in your fridge, honey. You can enjoy it when the cravings hit," La Costa said, smiling.

"I appreciate this, really, but you didn't have to do all of this. I was planning on telling you all . . . eventually."

"Like when, Miss Thing? When you were nine months along?" La Costa chortled.

The reality being they were all evidently upset that she had withheld the truth from their little cohort.

"Well, we all know now, and the important thing is to discuss how you are going to tell Bumpy. Have you given it any thought?" Hannah asked, stacking a tiny wedge of Brie onto a salt-free cracker.

Casey blinked. "Yes, I've thought about it. I just have to find the right time. With fall sweeps coming and the Emmys around the corner . . ."

"Set up the meeting with him for early next week. Just do it. I will accompany you if you'd like," Hannah said, ever the calming voice of reason. "You do not want to let this get too far away from you. Timing is everything."

"That's right," La Costa chimed in. "I think he would appreciate *not* reading about it in the rags."

They all nodded.

Casey hated that she would need to once again parade her personal business out in front of the world, but there would be no avoiding it. She was a master of spinning any situation to suit her. In this case, however, she was highly sensitive about how her pregnancy would be perceived by the viewers and her fans. Up to this point, it had been her little secret, and something that she did not have to share with anyone. She was just getting used to the reality of it herself. Soon that would all change.

"Not to pry," La Costa said, leaning in for the scoop. "What does Ryder think about all of this?"

"Huh? Well, nothing, seeing as he's not the father." Casey's words silenced the room like a needle scratching across a seventies LP. Then, she stood and started for the kitchen with her empty plate.

The women were struck agog. All except for Kathryn, who slowly refilled her glass with the blush wine and then stood to follow Casey. A sharp glance at the others rendered them glued to the couch.

"So, this baby is not your ex-husband's?" Kathryn said to the point, trapping Casey in her kitchen, now out of earshot of the others.

"No, it's not," Casey said brightly. "Do you think anyone would like some coffee? I can make a pot."

Kathryn leaned back against the granite counter, eyeing Casey and allowing the uncomfortable silence to linger.

Casey finally huffed and crossed her arms. "I'm not ready to reveal who the father is at this point, so don't even ask."

Kathryn said nothing, but her knowing eyes interrogated Casey as if she had been branded with a Scarlet A across her chest.

"Of course, that's your prerogative," Kathryn said flatly. "I am certain that you have your reasons, dear." Then, she turned and slowly started back into the living room.

Casey could *see* Kathryn's wheels turning behind that botoxed forehead of hers and imagined that she would eventually find a way to the truth. *What would it matter?* This was *her* child and *her* secret.

If there was anything sacred in this dysfunctional coven of women she was somehow mythically and explicitly linked to, it was that fact.

CHAPTER 70

YAKUTAT, ALASKA

The remote village of Yakutat, an isolated stretch of land connecting the Inside Passage to the rest of Alaska, was Roe's new home. He had found the location in an article in *Forbes* that outlined the best places to "get off the grid." It had been perfect timing because that was precisely what he wanted to do. He had arranged for a rented cabin on the northern side of the Inside Passage, with a population of just under six hundred people. The area was rife with wildlife fjords and tidewater glaciers and boasted the largest rainforest in the world. It was as remote as he could get, with the only way out being daily jet service from Anchorage or passage via the Alaska Marine Highway ferry that only ran a few times during the summer.

It was the perfect place for him to pen his memoir, reconnect with himself, and soothe his broken soul. And—the most difficult of all—to get over her. No social media. No cell phone. No computers. He would live in a bubble of beauty, seawater, and hiking trails, far from any reminders of Casey Singer. It was his belief that he had somehow ruined both their lives by wanting the impossible—by wanting it all.

From what he had last heard, she was free from her own mistakes and ready to soar to great heights.

Somehow, the universe had tricked him. Cast him as a fool in the charade that was his life. Like a tortured Greek protagonist, he was blown by fate to a disastrous end. Ruinous and predictable only by the fancies of the gods.

He would commit himself to solitude and thus bear the burdens of his sins—even if it killed him.

CHAPTER 71

NEW YORK CITY

"Don't fidget," Hannah said, placing her hand on Casey's crossed leg that was bouncing in tandem with her racing heart. "Why don't you try EMT—the emotional freedom technique?"

"The what?" Casey had heard of it but never tried the method. "It is a bit woo-woo, isn't it?"

"I've used it and find it calming in certain situations. Give it a try." Hannah took Casey's hand and made it into a fist. Then she pointed to the area just below her pinky finger. "There. Tap it there like this," she said, tapping rhythmically on her own hand.

"How does it work?" Casey began tapping away, feeling a bit foolish.

"You're focusing on one of your hot zones, like acupuncture. It helps to restore balance to your body's energy. And say this mantra while you are tapping: *'Even though I have this fear/problem, I deeply and completely accept myself.'*"

"Do I have to say that aloud?"

"Yes. Do it. I promise it works."

Casey kept tapping. "I feel ridiculous, really, Hannah. Do you charge your clients for this advice?"

"Don't knock it until you've tried it."

"Tried what?" Bumpy said, walking briskly into the room and over to his desk. He was holding a file folder in one hand and a can of Diet Coke in the other.

"Oh, we're just discussing New Age remedies for anxiety," Hannah said.

Bumpy grunted. "I just take a pill for that. So, tell me . . . to what do I owe the pleasure? You two have me in suspense. I don't like surprises."

Hannah cleared her throat. "Right. Well then, Casey here has something to tell you."

She glanced at Casey, who was still tapping away and breathing measuredly.

"Bumpy, there is just no easy way to say this. I'm expecting."

"Expecting what?" He looked like a lost ball in high weeds.

"A *baby*. She is going to have a baby," Hannah said, connecting the dots for him. "She's due in November."

He lifted a bushy silver brow and then produced a slow, wide grin that creased his forehead and summoned a chuckle. "Well, Casey, that's some news!"

"I am very happy about it, for sure. Unexpected as it was . . . but here I am!"

Hannah gave Casey a little sideways hug and stood up. "I'm going to leave you two to discuss things." Then, she looked Casey squarely in the eyes. "We are all so happy for you, dear."

She slipped out, leaving Casey alone on the enormous leather couch.

Bumpy nodded pensively, taking in the news. Finally, he spoke. "I suppose we can work this in. Hell, we'll have to. I am sure that the viewers will eat it up. It'll be reality TV at its best, right?"

Casey relaxed. She was happy to see that he was on board. Then came the question, pitched like a bomb.

"Will you and Ryder have joint custody?"

There was no other way to circumvent the truth. No amount of tapping would change a thing.

She paused, and then finally blurted, not giving him room for a retort, "Ryder is not the father. I choose not to name the father. And further, I will be raising this child on my own."

"Oh, I see." Bumpy's smile flattened into a thin line. He leaned back in his chair and scratched his bristly chin. "Well, that is ambitious."

Casey softened. The man who was like a father figure to her held the power to uplift or destroy her. It mattered what Bumpy thought more than she would admit. More often than not, he was the wisest person she knew. She *needed* his blessing.

"We'll work it in, and you will work it out, Casey. I know you will. I believe in you."

He stood up, and this time, she rushed to him for a hug, catching him by surprise. He embraced her and, giving her a little pat on the back, sent her on her way.

This can work, Casey thought as she hit the elevator button. *Everything is going to be all right*. The car arrived, and the doors popped open on cue. It was a sign for sure that she was on the right track.

BUMPY SHOVED the file folder into a drawer, sat back in his well-worn chair, and closed his eyes. He was tired. The truth was there, right in front of him, no matter how he tried to deny it. The job was a circus. A never-ending race for the next conquest, the next big thing. He was beginning to grow weary of it all. Casey's news would have rattled him in the past, but not now.

It was a different time, for sure. Things were changing faster than he cared to admit. Viewers were fickle, and attention spans were getting shorter by the minute. He was old-school, and everyone knew that dinosaurs didn't pull off the wins with ease forever. The station was poised to win another coveted trophy just a few months from then, but what about next year? And the year after that? What would the future hold? Damned if he knew. He ran on instinct, and that was all he had. He was tired, and the pain in his gut was a daily reminder that the wear and tear was taking its toll. Sure, his bum heart was still holding up, but for how long? He felt like there was a ticking time bomb somewhere, taunting him.

He sighed and stood up, acknowledging the aching in his knees and crick in his back as a testament to his sacrifices; to doing the job. *If you aren't careful,* he heard a voice inside himself softly whisper, *you might miss out on what is left and ahead for you.* He smiled to himself, feeling his angel wife, Hylda's, prediction from above. Then he grabbed his hat, sighed, and flipped off the light.

CHAPTER 72
THREE MONTHS LATER

Casey had never looked more beautiful. She had let her hair grow past her shoulders, and her stylist had added some highlighted extensions that wound up to an elegant updo with long, wispy bangs. She was stunning as a honey ash-blonde, which was her natural color.

Her stylist was leaning over to apply the butterfly lashes. "Lady Gaga, eat your heart out!" she said, pressing down the glue.

Casey's phone buzzed with a text: *Good luck tonight, Chicka! You deserve this! Wish I could be there. We will be watching!*

The doorbell rang, and Casey quickly excused herself to answer it.

A delivery of a high-style arrangement of spray roses, hyacinth, and Oriental lilies in a clear, beveled vase was presented to her at the front door. The note read: *YOU'VE GOT THIS!* It was signed *Ryder X O.* She placed the arrangement on the marble vanity near the sink.

It was a sweet gesture, indeed. She was so lucky to have his support in spite of everything that had ensued in the past several months. Ryder was a champion of her decision to pull back on chasing movie roles to focus on the talk show and preparing for motherhood. He knew better than anyone how much the business could take without giving back. It was a hard lesson for her to have learned, but she finally had peace with her decision and had never been surer about the future.

It was going to be about all of them tonight—the cast and crew of *The Gab*, coming together for their seventh nomination, and hopefully win—in their day-part category. The coveted Emmy would only be further affirmation that she was in the right place, contributing in a way that meant success for everyone.

Casey's dress was hanging on the bathroom door. It was a stunning sapphire blue, just like her eyes. Kathryn had commissioned an up-and-coming designer from her trove, Estelle Gallagher, to create a gorgeous, dropped-sleeve sweetheart-neck maternity gown in a tight-fitting jersey fabric that would cling to her body like a glove. It had a sexy slit up the front and a flowing train that was perfection.

The car would be there in one hour. She touched her swollen belly beneath her satin bathrobe. She was a ripe seven months along. Casey did not mind at all that she had no escort for the event. It didn't matter.

She wouldn't be alone. She had this little one inside her.

CASEY'S UBER ARRIVED at the red carpet in a frenzy of flashbulbs and paparazzi, hungry to get a glimpse of any celebrity as they emerged from their cars.

Casey caught sight of Hannah arriving solo at the same time and was happy to connect. She called out to her, "Hannah! Over here!"

Hannah beamed widely. "Casey! Oh, don't you look simply radiant?"

The two locked arms and began heading toward the theater entrance, stopping at the press wall to give the waiting photographers what they wanted. Collectively, they all bid for their attention, calling to them from all sides. The two posed side by side and then separately, standing on the marks on the carpet that afforded the best angles and views.

A stunning gold-and-diamond choker encircled Casey's neck, shooting rays of light in all directions. She also wore an asymmetric set of earrings, one moon-shaped ear cuff and the other, a drop chain earring with a diamond starburst and matching studs. All were from APM Monaco, a company that makes high-quality, affordable gems that look like the real thing. Truth being, they were high-quality imitations, but if the gems were good enough for the likes of Rihanna, then they were good enough for her. She looked like a rock star.

Casey's skin was beautiful and bright. And her smile, a thousand-watt wonder.

"Let's see the bump!" someone yelled.

Casey turned, placing her hand beneath her belly proudly. There was nothing left to the imagination in that dress.

She beamed, having never felt such joy and utter contentment. She was in her element and had never shined brighter.

THERE WAS no red carpet or paparazzi where Roe Evans resided. No television or internet to suck him back into the real world.

As the days ticked slowly by, his only contact in Yukutat were the locals, who lived off the occasional tourists who came to hike, surf, and kayak. He'd fished, slept, and written letters to Jane and had them sent via air post from Anchorage.

He now sported a beard and had let his hair grow long on his neck. He'd cooked for himself and cut wood to stoke his fireplace. He'd taken long, thoughtful walks. He'd basked in the sun while it shone and listened for an inner voice to guide him. He was broken, and it seemed that the only way he could make his way back was to lie low. To disappear. To detox and rebuild his tortured self. And that is precisely what he did.

Music had been his salvation. He'd played CDs on a battery-operated boom box. He'd gone through his collection twice over, from start to finish—Stevie Wonder, the Beatles, the great Sinatra, and Michael Jackson, the Rolling Stones, Springsteen, and Zeppelin. He'd found himself again and again in the music, which was always his passion and had been his life's work.

But still, somehow, everything always brought him back to *her*. To Casey Singer and her exciting spirit and mesmerizing eyes that drew him in and held him hostage unto himself. He simply could not erase her from his soul. She had gotten in and possessed him. She was all light and all matter of insanity; she was a thrill ride and his refuge—at the same time. He could not, it seemed, exist on this earth without her.

Finally, after three soulful months, he decided to stop running and knew it was time to face what he could no longer fight.

It was time to go to her.

CHAPTER 73

"La Costa's here!" Hannah said, checking her phone.

The two found their way to the reception area, where La Costa stood with her husband, Henry.

"We're one less in the row of seats," La Costa said with a serious face. "Bumpy will not be coming. Aubrey says that he wasn't feeling good."

"Oh, that's too bad," Hannah said sadly as they filed into the massive theater. "This is his night if it's any of ours.

"Bet you're happy to sit down," Hannah said to Casey with a wink when they reached the aisle for their seats, referring to the *Sex in the City* Manolo Blahniks that were surely punishing her swollen feet.

Kathryn would be fashionably late, more likely just in time to soak in the lights and attention out on the red carpet.

Finally, she walked in and descended the aisle with an escort that none of them had ever seen before. He was tall and a good twenty years younger than Kathryn. Casey surmised that this had to be her latest boy toy. But to bring him to the Emmys! Even for Kathryn, that was in poor taste.

They all stood up from the red velvet seats and exchanged pleasantries and air kisses.

The room was abuzz with celebrities of every ilk, from television, movies, and the music industry. Everybody watched TV—and now more than ever, programming had to be better to compete with the streaming conglomerates.

The empty seat for Bumpy was painfully obvious. Within a few minutes, however, LeMaster appeared, looking dapper in his after-five attire and extra pomade in his gleaming silver hair.

"Bumpy suggested that I come in his place. Happy to stand in for him. Win or lose, Ladies, you are all winners in my book," he said, climbing over La Costa's taffeta dress and taking a seat next to Henry.

Sweet of him to say, Casey thought. But there was nothing wrong with winning. After all, wasn't that the idea?

Within a few minutes, the house lights went down, and the orchestra struck up the intro to the broadcast. Cameras swept the crowd, and a buoyant host—an androgynous comic from the edgy nightclub circuit—took the stage.

Later, when the award for the best daytime talk show was announced, La Costa gripped Casey's hand on one side and Hannah's on the other. Kathryn sat stoically as the nominees were read off.

Finally, the beautiful veteran soap star said the tagline, and everyone moved forward in their seats.

"And the Emmy goes to . . . *The Gab!*" A round of applause thundered, and the music swelled—the opening theme track to the show.

One by one, the cast took in the moment, bathing in the lights, the jubilation, the attention.

They all thrived on it, maybe in different ways, but they did.

They each made their way to the stage, careful of the hems, the heels, and the slick stairs.

Casey beamed with her hands beneath her belly, proudly showing her bump to the world.

Hannah did the honors. "I will accept this award on behalf of the team who makes *The Gab* possible, every day. And I would like to give a shout-out to our producer, Bumpy Friedman. Bumpy, you have to get better!" She held up the Emmy and said, "Nothing is more important than family, friends, good health, and faith. That is what will get anybody through anything." Thunderous applause followed as the countdown clock was ticking.

She paused a beat and then thanked her cast mates, without whom there would be no show because, somehow, they had found the perfect combination. "Thank you to Kathryn Delacorte, Casey Singer, and La Costa Reed. We are here for you every weekday at eleven, and we love you! Thank you!"

Bumpy watched from the comfort of his couch. They did it—again! What an accomplishment! He popped open an imported beer to celebrate. He hated the fuss and pretentiousness of it all. It was good, though, to revel in the glory.

His phone was pinging with accolades and "attaboys" from everyone and anyone in the business. He had written his ticket, for sure. Perhaps reaching the final summit in his career. And all for what? His beloved Hylda was in heaven, and he ached in places that no man should, all the way to his heart.

Another statue. Another season in the books, and always someone closing in behind you to beat you and knock you off the mountain.

No, he was done. He was sure that for him, this would be the last victory. New blood was what was needed now. He lifted his beer and took a generous swig.

His resignation would be on Conrad's desk in the morning.

CHAPTER 74
LAS VEGAS, NEVADA

Detective Ruby Heart had the name of a stripper, the mouth of a sailor, and a to-the-groin kick that could annihilate a bastard's princely delicates in two seconds flat. She was just blessed that way.

A native of the town, Ruby had grown up in Las Vegas and had walked the filthy streets surrounding the unholy circus and heathen-laden casinos, bars, and clubs along the Strip since childhood. She knew them well, often having to retrieve her father from a smoke-shrouded poker table filled with strangers smoking cigarettes and ogling her as she pulled him from the temptress of the dice and cards in many pointless attempts to keep him from blowing the rent money. She was only fourteen.

It was her father who named her Ruby. He loved the way that it sounded with their last name, Heart, with its esteemed Eastern Irish ancestry dating back to the kingdom of Brega, which, he was certain, amounted to some sort of dynasty or royal lineage. Regardless, it was easy to be teased when you had a name like Ruby Heart, and she became quickly adept at dodging bullies at school and degenerates who preyed on young, pretty girls who, when riding their bikes to the park or the corner quick mart, had to dodge their taunts and unctuous whistles.

Perverts were everywhere, and Ruby quickly learned at an early age that men were only interested in what they could score, and that included money, sex, and power. What they couldn't win, they would take. This, too, she knew all too well.

After high school, she studied criminal law at the University of Nevada on an academic scholarship, which was a reprieve from Sin City, where she holed up in a dorm, sharing space with a fierce, take-back-the-night Dyke. Sully was the real deal and helped educate Ruby in women's liberation movements that would shape her world views and inform her life's work. Ruby graduated Magna Cum laude with a 4.0 GPA and the prospect of a job on the police force back home. She had a Black Belt in Brazilian Jiu-Jitsu, which she started practicing in junior high and had mastered to perfection.

Ruby joined the Las Vegas Metropolitan Police Department and quickly climbed up the ranks from police officer to patrol officer to detective. After nearly seven years on the force working the filthy streets of the Strip, she applied for candidacy with the FBI, passed the rigorous enrollment, and became a field agent. She was quickly promoted to a senior special agent, for which she found her true calling in criminal investigation.

And since she despised criminals—especially bastard lowlifes who breached national security in the process—she excelled in putting them away. Ruby was an effective and respected agent, even if she often employed unorthodox methods in the process of closing her cases.

After the retirement of her supervisor, she began taking on cases that more personally interested her, namely in criminal profiling.

She was highly proficient in nailing the assailants, which garnered her more cases in this arena. This involved being on call 24/7 for work that could take her anywhere in the world. She often kept a duffle bag with a change of clothes—warm weather and cold weather options—at the ready for any situation that might arise. This was ideal, since Ruby traveled light as a rule and did not like to stay in one place too long. Remarkably, she could transform her look to serve any situation with little fuss.

Senior Special Agent Ruby Heart was born to do the job.

So, when she got the lead on a con in Mexico who went by the name of Jake Trainer, who was working a "male escort service," stealing from his clients, embezzling money from high-profile celebrities, and committing cyber-crimes via the internet, she was more than game to take him down, and maybe catch some rays in the process.

CHAPTER 75
NEW YORK CITY

"*Hello, all my gorgeous beauties! What's poppin'!*" Casey said into the desktop microphone set up in the empty conference room on the eleventh floor of Global Studios, where she recorded her podcasts when she was in town. The victory from the previous week of the show's seventh shiny Emmy was more than a trophy on the shelf. It was a testament to the talents of the wonderful cast, crew, and management that brought the fab four—the ladies of *The Gab*—into the hearts and households of America every weekday.

The news of Bumpy's retirement had not yet gone public. Even Aubrey, his assistant, would be kept in the dark. Willard Conrad, Bumpy's boss, had convinced him to stay on until the end of the year, and that was fine with him. He hated goddamn goodbyes more than anything. The less the talent and staff knew, the better as far as he was concerned.

The celebration of the Emmy win was still buzzing in the halls of Global Studios and added that extra credence to every-thing, including Casey's value in the eyes of her agent, Spaulding Caine. There were plans to create a spin-off of her podcast, sanctioned by the network, directly linking it to the show and expanding out to the audio-listening audience who wanted the banter to continue after *The Gab* signed off daily.

The new podcast would be called *After the Show* and would feature all four women conversing in tandem with a stellar lineup of guest interviews each week. Casey would be the lead host on the project, which was already garnering high-dollar affiliate media buys. It would be ideal work for once the baby arrived, as Casey's TV host appearances would be reduced to limit travel. Handily, she would be able to record the podcast segments from her LA home and not miss a beat.

Plans were also in the works for booking "revolving" guest hosts to fill in intermittently for Casey on *The Gab*, which would mollify the millennial set and appease the rating gods in the process.

Things were changing, for sure.

Casey was a natural at inspiring her listeners. *"Let's keep the tea spillin'. I'll tell you what—here's the best-kept secret that any of you could incorporate into your own life. I am here with my incredible TV co-host and friend, Dr. Hannah Courtland Murphy, and she is going to discuss the key to unlocking your happiness and tamping down that anxiety with something called EMT, my princesses . . . and here's a hint, it does not involve kissing any frogs!"*

Roe smiled. He turned up the volume on the dashboard and listened. It was like *religion* to hear her voice! He had only been in D.C. for two days, having been back from his three-month sabbatical in the arctic tundra on a strict cleanse of all things internet and social media.

He had packed up ten days prior and taken the ferry to Skagway, where he hitched a ride with a trucker making the long trip along Alaska's interior to Fairbanks, where he stayed for a week in a rented lodge.

There, he shaved off his beard, got a haircut, and shed his flannel shirts and work boots for a quick re-entry into society in a Polo shirt, jeans, and Nikes. He booked a flight to Washington, D.C., where he had stored his share of the belongings after the divorce several months prior. He retrieved the Lincoln Navigator from vehicle storage and powered up his smartphone with the adapter on the dashboard. He hit an ATM for cash and would reactivate his credit cards once he had a full working signal on his phone.

He was making the four-hour drive to Manhattan, hoping to catch Casey before she headed back to the West Coast for the weekend. He refrained for the first few hours from looking at the deluge of texts and voicemails that were beginning to populate and ping on his waking phone, filling his feeds and inboxes to over-capacity. He just wasn't ready to pollute his detoxified state of mind by looking at any of it. Not yet.

Hearing Casey's voice on the podcast over his car speakers made his heart leap because she was his *muse* and reason for living. It was all that he needed. He knew it with all his being. His head was clear, and his heart was ready.

Finally, he was just thirty minutes from the big city, and his pulse was racing.

But knowing that fate rarely waited for anyone, he had to ask. *Could there still be a chance? Had she met someone after her divorce from Ryder? Was she free and uncoupled? Did she still have a place in her heart for him?*

He had been—and still was—cut off from any news of her life, and the world.

He pressed the pedal with full conviction.

There was no better time than the present to find out.

CHAPTER 76

It was just after five p.m. when Roe pulled up to the Global Network building and parked the Navigator at the curb in a restricted zone. He paid no heed to the directive and hurried toward the building, through the revolving glass doors, and into the massive lobby.

He was instantly thrust back into the hustle and tumult of the corporate world as waves of zombie-like executives rushed past him, extracted from their cubicles out into the polluted city air with their busy lives and agendas.

He approached the large security guard sitting behind the podium desk. "Good evening. I would like to see Casey Singer, please."

He did not need to check. "Ms. Singer is gone, sir. She's left for the airport. I called for her transport. Would you like to leave a message?"

Roe's smile dropped. Too late. It had been a risk at best to think that he would be able to catch her. "No, thank you. I will try back again."

Just then, he looked over and saw Kathryn Delacorte alighting from an open elevator. She was fumbling with her gloves and walked briskly past him.

"Excuse me!" He followed quickly at her clicking heels. "Ms. Delacorte!"

Kathryn turned and, recognizing him, stopped cold.

He proffered, "I'm Roe Evans, formerly of Epic Media. I've spoken to your editorial team in the past."

She extended her hand. "I know who you are, Mr. Evans. What can I do for you? I was just about to fetch a cab."

"I was hoping to catch Casey before she left for the weekend. I understand that I missed her?"

"Yes, she left this afternoon. She's on a flight to LA by now."

He nodded. "Bad timing on my part, for sure." He then asked, "Are you in need of a ride? I'd be happy to give you a lift."

Kathryn smiled at the irony of what was unfolding. *Why not?* she thought. *This ought to be interesting.*

"Well, if it's no trouble, Roe. I am not far—Lexington and 3rd."

"Great. I'm parked just out in front."

The two settled into the leather seats, and Roe blasted the heater. "Feels like winter is making an early appearance," he said, easing into traffic.

Kathryn could see that Roe was more nervous than he was letting on. She could smell it. *What is his game?* She couched her words. "So you and Casey go way back?"

"Yes. We are old friends. I nearly ran over her, actually—in Chicago when she was just starting out in the business. We've stayed in touch over the years. It's a funny story, really."

"I see." Kathryn did not want the details of their "meet cute." She was most interested in what was bringing him back into Casey's life. She shot some lukewarm sympathy his way. "Sorry to hear about your quick and public divorce."

"Thank you. I have done a lot of work on myself in order to—"

"So, what are your intentions, exactly?" she asked, right to the point. "Why exactly are you here, Roe? Why are you looking for Casey *now*?"

"I have been trying to reach her recently, but she doesn't answer my calls."

"Then, there you are. She is very busy with everything . . . what with the baby coming and all."

"*Baby?*" Roe hit the brakes to avoid the back end of a Tesla. "Is *Casey*—"

"Wow, have you been living under a rock?"

"Sort of. I've not touched the internet or social media in three months. I've been off the grid—literally. I've just gotten back."

Kathryn had her suspicions all along. There was more to these two than met the eye. And now, she was put in a precarious position. The poor bastard had no clue, and she was quickly connecting the dots. "Well, that's the reality. She is just starting her maternity leave. She won't return to the studio in person until after the new year."

Roe was dumbstruck.

"You really should do some scrolling and see what you missed—if you can even believe what people post out there. A lot of it is smoke and mirrors, but this *is* happening. She's due in less than two months."

Roe's wheels were turning. "I really need to reach out to her. Kathryn, can you give me her LA address? There's something I want to send her."

They were nearly at her corner, and Kathryn's inclination was to let him fend for himself on this one. But then she felt a strong pull at her conscience to do otherwise. *What could it hurt? Casey is a big girl and capable of sorting this out herself.*

Kathryn grabbed his phone tethered to the console and swiped into his contacts. She retrieved her phone from her Birkin and tapped Casey's address into his, and hit *Save*.

It was done. "Good luck to you, Roe."

He pulled to the curb and nodded. "Thank you, Kathryn. I owe you one."

She lifted the handle and opened the heavy door. Once out, she turned around and leaned in, offering one last piece of advice for free as her Chanel earrings dangled. "You need to know that Casey has changed. She's truly happy now. Take that for what it's worth."

Then, she slammed the door and headed into the evening breeze toward her building.

Roe sat in silence as he watched her disappear through the glass doors.

CHAPTER 77

LOS ANGELES, CALIFORNIA

"Where are you planning on putting the crib?" Shelly asked.

"Perpendicular to that wall," Casey said, gesturing with her hands. "It's away from the window and provides 'support' of the wall behind the baby's head."

"Really?"

"Yeah, I have this woman, Genesis, an expert in Chinese *feng shui*, helping me to arrange things so that everything will be in balance. This room is good because it faces the back of the house, away from the noise, and has a window with a calming view of nature."

Shelly looked puzzled. "Where does one find a *feng shui* expert?"

"She was a referral from my yoga instructor," Casey said, rearranging her messy bun.

It was early morning, and the sunlight was coming in from the east. They had just had breakfast, and Casey was in her floppy overalls, ripe as a melon. She was sipping herbal tea, and Shelly was already on her second cup of Dark Roast.

"Genesis says that the natural light is key as it creates a

constant flow or cycle for the baby to adapt to," Casey said assuredly.

"I see," Shelly said, folding her hands in prayer and doing a little bow. "Sounds like you are going to be parting with hard-earned money in order to do what we could accomplish in a day with Pinterest and a catalogue from Wayfair!"

They both laughed. Sure, it was a bit unconventional, but Casey was not taking any chances.

"Oh, no worries. We get to do some old-fashioned work, for sure. We are going to paint this whole room—shades of pastels and soft white to reduce stimulation. It's all about balance and harmony."

"Great! That's what I'm here for. You've got me for the whole week to help you get things ready. If we're going to paint, that's my jam! You, dear, need to stay far away from the fumes."

"I really appreciate you being here, Shelly," Casey said with blue-eyed sincerity.

"Where else would I be? Besides, my guys can fend for themselves for seven days. I don't want to even think about dirty socks, math homework, carpool lanes—or stinky farts!"

"Well then, you'd better keep a distance from me, girlfriend, 'cause I am throwing air biscuits like nobody's business these days!"

Shelly roared. Then, the two hugged, wiping happy tears from their eyes.

"Can you believe it?" Casey said. "I'm going to be a mom!"

Shelly gave her a one-armed squeeze. They stood silently in the empty room. It was hard to believe that very soon, Casey would be bringing a new human—a precious little person—into the world.

"You've got this, *Chicka*," Shelly said softly.

"Well, let's get started, then," Casey said, throwing her arms into the air. "I'll get the color swatches!"

CHAPTER 78

The painting of the nursery was completed by the end of the week. Casey settled on a warm cocoa and soft coral motif with an aim to provide a clean, calming energy in the room that would soothe her little one.

Casey and Shelly removed the ceiling fan, which Genesis warned disrupted energy, and hung sheer, airy curtains on the window to let in "possibilities" with the rising sun.

They had visited a boutique in Beverly Hills that provided mindfully designed furniture free of sharp edges and accents that could be perceived as "bad energy daggers" if pointed anywhere at or near the crib.

Shelly had learned a lot about how the Hollywood elite conducted their version of baby-proofing a home. It was as extensive and pricey as installing a home gym or meditation room.

"I'm going to dip out and get a Caramel Macchiato before we get started on the stenciling. Do you want a hot tea?"

"I'd love one!" Casey said. "And thanks for making the run. Those stairs are a killer these days. I'll be here measuring the stencils." She had settled on tiny graphic butterflies and caterpillars to border the walls just beneath the molding.

"And I'll get the mail on my way back," Shelly said cheerily as she headed downstairs.

Thirty minutes later, she was back with an armful of mail, the hot beverages in a cardboard carrying tray, and a bulky package tucked under her arm.

Shelly tossed the stack of mail on the kitchen counter and bounded up the carpeted stairs to the nursery with the Starbucks tray in one hand and the package in the other.

"Hey, *Chicka*. There is a package here for you. It's from *Roe Evans*."

Casey looked up from the floor. She was sitting on her heels, cutting away at a sprightly image of an insect. "What? No. I don't want anything from him. Toss it . . . throw it away. Return to sender."

"Aren't you at least a little bit curious?"

"No. Wait—where did he send it from?"

Shelly squinted at the print. "The return address is in Washington, D.C."

"Burn it. Lose it. I don't care. Just get it out of here."

There she was. The sweet, calm, Zen-inspired mother-to-be was still presiding in the body of the former ball-buster, Casey Singer. Old habits do die hard!

"Do you want me to open it at least? I can tell you what it is. It feels like a book."

"Oh, great! He wants to force some sort of self-help nonsense on me. Hell to the no! Toss it!"

"But, *Chicka*—"

"Listen to me, Shelly; I do not want any negative vibes coming in here and stirring up bad energy. I will not subject my baby to that."

"May I remind you that it is *his* baby you are carrying?"

Silence.

Too far.

Casey huffed, threw down the paper bugs she was cutting out, and looked at Shelly dead-on.

"You did not just say that to me, did you, *Girlfriend*?"

Shelly froze. It was a low blow, meant to hit Casey squarely in the reality level of her aura—wherever *that* resided. Yes, she'd said it. The truth was the truth, and she was not going to sugar-coat anything just to spare her friend's feelings. Shelly was a straight shooter. It was high time for the Tarot Tower to come down. Casey had to face the facts. She couldn't hide the truth forever.

"Look, *Chicka*, I know you are dealing with a lot; raging hormones, uncertainty . . . Lord knows, indigestion, bloating, and probably hemorrhoids, but don't be a dick to this guy. That should not be the play here. You can't control everything."

Casey was fighting a surge of tears. She stood up ungracefully and said, "Don't follow me!" She disappeared into her room and slammed the door.

Well, great, Shelly thought. She knew her dear friend was a handful, but nothing tested her more than fear, and Casey was afraid.

Shelly looked at the package and felt around the edges. It was some sort of book for certain. She decided to take it down to the kitchen and leave it on the counter with the rest of the mail. She went back upstairs and decided that she would pick up where Casey left off with the stencils and let her have her space.

"*Jesús María!* This one's a handful!" Shelly said to herself as she cut around the paper bugs.

CHAPTER 79

Dinner was a bit stilted, with Shelly struggling to make small talk as Casey picked at her vegetables and only managed to eat half of her baked chicken breast.

"C'mon, *Chicka*. You always loved my cream sauce. It's the one made with Campbell's Soup. What gives? Are you going to stay mad at me forever?"

Casey sighed and pushed away her plate. "I'm just not feeling very hungry, I guess. There is too much going on. It's getting closer to the birth, and I am beginning to freak out about everything not being perfect."

"It doesn't have to be perfect. That baby is going to come into this world, and your loving heart is going to be the only thing that they will need. Period."

Casey pulled a face and then gave Shelly a half-hearted smile. "I know that. I can't stay mad at you—ever!"

"Right?" Shelly said, laughing. "It's a curse!"

"But I mean it about that package. I don't care to know what that's all about. It took me so long to get my head straight about things and to put all those feelings behind me. I don't have the capacity to deal with any more drama."

Shelly patted her hand before reaching for Casey's plate.

"You're going to be a parent. Trust me; there is going to be a lot more drama, Mama!"

Casey gathered up the water glasses and utensils. "I'll wash, you dry."

"No, *Chicka*. You go relax in the living room. I'm on cleanup duty. Go!"

Casey did not have to be told twice. Having her BFF there was more than a treat. It was truly a blessing because they didn't make friends like Shelly anymore. What would she do without her?

Casey fell asleep halfway into the re-watching binge-fest of the first season of *Girls* on Netflix. Shelly had never seen the series, and Casey had saved the indoctrination for their "Girls Week" visit.

"You'd better head upstairs, sleepyhead. We can pick up where we left off tomorrow. Let's get you to bed."

Minutes later, Casey had brushed her teeth and changed into her PJ bottoms and Taylor Swift concert T-shirt that barely covered her very ripe belly. She yawned and waved at Shelly from the top of the stairs. "Good night. See you in the morning."

"Night, *Chicka!*"

Shelly was in the kitchen, eyeing the mystery package from the stack of mail on the counter. *What harm could there be in her taking a peek? Casey definitely didn't want anything to do with it.* In her mind, it was fair game.

The suspense got the better of her, so she poured herself another glass of Malbec and carried the small manila envelope with her to the couch. She checked the stairs for any sign of Casey and then tore open the top end of the bubble envelope and turned it over. Out spilled a small, leather-bound journal. *So it's not a book, exactly!* She flipped through several pages and spot-read the contents. It was all penned in Roe's handwriting, presumably.

It didn't take long to realize that nearly every entry from mid-June through to September contained his thoughts and feelings about Casey. In fact, every page reflected his longing and undeniable love for her. *Wow! This puppy definitely has it bad!*

Shelly settled in, turned the journal to page one, and began to read it front to back.

Three hours and two hundred ninety-one pages later, she realized the truth.

Roe really had loved Casey all along, *and he had never stopped!*

CHAPTER 80

The next morning, Shelly kept the conversation light when Casey emerged from her room, looking like a grizzly bear that had just awakened from hibernation.

"Well, good morning, you! What's say we get you showered and dressed and head out to the farmer's market in Huntington Beach? We can grab breakfast there at one of those trendy food tents."

Casey yawned. "Sure. Oh, and there's a baby boutique I want to check out in Newport Beach later too, if we have time."

"Done and done! I'll bet we can get some great shots for the socials near the water. I'm sure that your adoring fans would love to see how you are faring."

"Who needs a publicist when I have you, right?" Casey said. "I am sure that no one wants to see how fat I am. I am as big as a double-wide!"

"Well, maybe not a *double*-wide." Shelly laughed.

Casey disappeared back upstairs, and soon the sound of running water confirmed that she was in the shower. Shelly retrieved Roe's journal from the counter and placed it into her cloth tote bag. She would have to get Casey in the right mood to broach the subject—if *she didn't cause a scene and bite her head off for reading it.*

Being Casey Singer's bestie had its risks.

Shelly made the sign of the cross and topped off her travel cup with another splash of dark blend.

ONE HOUR LATER, the two pulled up in Casey's sporty Audi to the large, sprawling park near the harbor, with rows of pop-up tents and food carts that housed merchants hawking their wares every Saturday morning.

"I'm starving," Casey said. "The omelet guy is over there."

They carried their paper plates loaded with steaming eggs, delectable hash browns, and multigrain muffins to one of the picnic tables with a great view of the boats. It was a bit brisk for October, but being able to be outside in the fresh marina air was a treat for Shelly.

"You get to do this every weekend?" Shelly asked.

"Yep, but not as much as you'd think. I do love it here, though. I always feel so peaceful watching all the people and the seagulls and the ocean. Lucky us, right?"

Shelly nodded. Then, she blurted out what had been churning in her for the past few hours and was burning a hole in her designer tote bag. "He loves you, Casey."

"Huh? Who loves me?" Casey said with a half-chuckle.

"Roe Evans."

"What?"

"Don't be mad. Please, Casey . . . listen to me. I opened the envelope—"

Casey stopped chewing and shot her a perplexed look.

"I know—it was wrong of me to snoop, but I figured that one of us had to see this through. And Casey . . . it was a *journal.* Roe's diary." She opened the flap of her tote bag and produced the leather-bound book.

Casey turned her gaze to the ocean. She did not look at it, but she didn't ask Shelly to stop talking.

"So, I read it. You know, his words. Written over the past three months when he was there in Alaska, which, let me tell you—does not sound like a Club Med vacation in the least!"

"*And?*" Casey was clearly impatient.

"And it was all there. His love for you is undeniable. He loves you, Casey, and that is clear as Arctic ice. He's reaching out to you to prove to you where his head is. You have to read it for yourself. If I didn't tell you, I'd never forgive myself—and you would never know this or have proof that it's true."

Casey was silent now, taking it all in. Her face softened.

"I don't know what it all means, *Chicka*, but this man loves you. And I believe that deep down inside, you love him too. It's fate, you know. You're carrying his baby. Doesn't that count for something?"

Casey sighed. "I can't get hurt again. Shelly, I appreciate what you did here, and I know that you love a happy ending . . . but I have made up my mind. I am going to raise this child by myself, and we are going to be just fine."

Shelly turned her face into the wind. She drew in a cleansing breath. "Okay, *Chicka*. It's your choice, of course. I am sorry if I overstepped—again. I just love you, that's all. No matter what. I got you."

"I love you too. I appreciate what you are trying to do. It's just not going to happen, okay?"

"Okay . . . " Shelly said, her voice trailing off.

"Good. Let's go check out the heirloom tomatoes before they are all gone!"

Hours later, the two arrived back at Casey's townhome, loaded down with parcels of produce and a few shopping bags from the boutique in Newport Beach.

"I'm going to take these things into the nursery," Casey said.

"Sure, I'll put the food away. Think about what you want to do for dinner. Anything you want." It was Shelly's last night in LA. She would be heading back to the Midwest in the morning.

"I was thinking we could order in—catch some more Netflix?" Casey said from the landing.

"Sounds perfect!" Shelly said. She quickly grabbed the manila envelope from the counter. She was going to toss it in the trash but instantly thought better of it. She scrutinized the address. *Why on earth would Roe be living in D.C.? What would be his next move?*

Then, absentmindedly, she turned the opened envelope over, and a note slipped out.

Shelly held her breath as she slowly unfolded it, watching the stairs for Casey to appear at any minute.

How did she miss it? It must have been tucked in the bubble wrap beneath the journal. It read: *Meet me at our bench in the park, just like the night we attended the presidential gala in Washington, D.C. Next Friday at five p.m. If you are there, I will know you forgive me, and I will be the happiest man on earth. Casey, I love you. ~ Roe.*

"Holy shit!" Shelly said aloud. She tucked the folded paper into the last page of the journal. Then thrust it back into her tote bag. *Damn you, Roe Evans!*

CHAPTER 81

Shelly left Casey with a kiss and a hug at the airport curb at LAX.

"You didn't have to drive me," she said, pulling her wheeled suitcase close and plopping her large designer purse on top of it.

"No worries. It's the least I could do for you. Thanks, Shelly. The nursery looks amazing. I could not have done it without you."

The two hugged once more, and then Shelly disappeared through the sliding glass doors toward the check-in line.

Casey waved, watching her go.

Minutes later, when Casey was just about to pull onto the Interstate, her phone pinged with a message. It was a text from Shelly: *I left a little something for you in my room. Please don't hate me!* There was a smiley face emoji with a coy smirk.

"Oh, Shelly, what did you do?" Casey said aloud, shooting back a thumbs-up emoji and then tossing her phone into her Gucci.

. . .

AN HOUR AND A HALF LATER, Casey arrived home, exhausted. She had picked up some Ramen noodles and spring rolls on the way home, which she would save for dinner later, along with another Netflix binge-fest. She remembered Shelly's message and made her way into the spare room where Shelly had slept. The sheets were stripped from the bed, and a new set had been expertly placed to perfection on the bed, along with the accent pillows and shams.

Casey looked over at the bureau, and there it was—Roe's journal! Shelly just did not know when to quit. There was also a note in Shelly's handwriting set on top of it. It read: *Decide for yourself, Chicka. All you have to do is read this. And be sure to see the note from Roe. It's tucked into the final page. Love you, my Bonita. ~ Shelly.*

Casey took the journal into her hands and ran her fingers over the rugged weatherworn cover. *How many times Roe must have touched this,* she thought. She held it a minute more, feeling his energy on the bound pages.

No. She could not bring herself to read it.

Not fifteen minutes later, she traipsed back upstairs and retrieved the journal. She carried it downstairs and placed it on the coffee table. She chided herself for being so afraid of what it contained. What Roe wanted her to know. Had she not survived every trial in her life up until now and came out intact? Then, what could it hurt to take a look?

CASEY STAYED up well into the night, reading the pages that Roe had written. A box of Kleenex and cartons of half-eaten Chinese food littered the coffee table and counter. Casey was a mess as the tears kept flowing.

What she read was far more poignant than the most perfect love story. All the things that she had wondered about them, about them being together, came to life in the hopes and dreams of Roe Evans, expressed in ink.

It was always there throughout all those years that they had been in and out of each other's lives. Mostly out. He had never forgotten her.

And he had never stopped loving her.

She held the note that he had written in her trembling hands. Shelly had placed it on the last page, and she read the words asking her to meet him at "their" bench at Lafayette Square Park in Washington, D.C., that coming Friday at five p.m. It was their special place from the night so many years ago when they attended the president's benefit dinner. The time when they stole away to the tranquil gardens and serene beauty of the landmark park in the city's center. It was their own little haven where they had claimed a park bench near the statue of Andrew Jackson and laughed and flirted like teenagers. It was there that they kicked off their shoes to feel the cool grass and shared a frozen yogurt in their black-tie attire. It was there, under a cloudless night sky, that Roe kissed her deeply and with a passion that hurled them into a spiral of unending depths of longing.

Now, he was asking her to meet him there like a scene from a romantic movie, like something that could only be contrived in Hollywood.

She wondered if she would have the courage to show up, knowing that doing so would change the trajectory of her life forever—a life that she had envisioned in the past many months as one in which *she* called the shots.

What would it be like to fall into his arms and surrender to love once and for all? Now that she knew his true heart? That was a question she could not answer. All she could do was sit there, caressing the journal with one hand and wiping away the tears with the other.

She dozed off and surrendered to her tortured dreams.

CHAPTER 82

As the sun began to rise and the birds chirped their morning songs, Casey opened her eyes and felt clarity and peace like she had never known. She sat up and, seeing the journal there next to her pillow, she smiled. Then, she felt the baby kick, and a sense of hesitation broke her reverie. *What if this is not what Roe had in mind?* Sure, he wanted her, but the *former* version of Casey Singer. The party girl who lived for the moment and kept everyone guessing. What if a new family was not on his agenda?

She realized no matter what might happen; she would need to see it through. She had to meet him and let destiny determine the rest.

THE FOLLOWING WEEK WAS A BLUR. She had to prepare to head back East, even though her travel plans had previously been halted due to the advanced stage of her pregnancy. She communicated with Shelly nearly on an hourly basis with text messages and long, rambling phone calls.

"Do you think I'm doing the right thing?" she asked Shelly for the hundredth time while packing.

"Yes, *Chicka*. But I have never known you to second-guess yourself. This is proof that you have grown. You are putting someone else's needs in front of your own. You know in your heart that Roe deserves to know the truth about this baby, regardless of what happens. Both of your futures ride on it."

"That's what scares me. What if it's just all too much for him?"

"Let Roe be the one to decide that. You might be surprised."

FINALLY, the day arrived. Casey had booked the flight to Washington, D.C., packed a small suitcase, and left her return ticket open-ended. She was all in. Heart and soul.

She stepped off the plane, feeling a mix of excitement and nervousness. A bracing breeze encircled her, whipping up a million memories in the musky-sweet smell of fallen leaves that only the East Coast could invoke. She hadn't stopped thinking of what would happen when she and Roe met at their bench. Either way, it would be all right. She could accept the outcome, whatever fate delivered. She was terrified, but she was ready.

CHAPTER 83
LAS VEGAS, NEVADA

Tailing Jake Trainer had been easy enough, thanks to a hotel worker who blew the whistle on his little covert operation. Trainer lived on the resort and "made the rounds" with every fresh crop of tourists who would arrive on the weekly cycles. He passed himself off as an eccentric loner who made his way with an online consulting business conducted from his bungalow. Most people bought it. In truth, he was targeting wealthy women, and when he was not servicing them, he was stealing from their beach totes to the tune of hundreds of thousands of dollars.

The informant was a server in the bar. He had a beef with Trainer, who was a shit tipper and preyed on the female clientele like they were bear meat. The older, the better. This raised red flags for months before the informant finally decided to call in his suspicion that Trainer was pimping himself out and possibly bilking the guests.

"I have a grandmother, for *Christ's sake*! This guy is relentless—does it openly here at the bar," the server said on the recorded call. "I don't want to be involved."

Ruby had played the voicemail message several times to

assess the validity of the lead. The informant was a young Latino with a slight lisp. She wondered if it was worth her time.

Finally, she decided to do a little digging and hit pay dirt. She conducted a thorough background check on Jake Trainer and came up with a litany of petty transgressions, not least of all, high-profile theft, along with personal connections that included two former felons with a history of arrest and jail time. There was also a recent and very detailed allegation against him from the resort of identity theft made by an Australian business-woman who was traveling alone in Mexico and was eager to press charges. *Bingo!* Catching scumbags was *always* worth her time!

By now, she had already invested hundreds of hours tracking Jake Trainer's internet whereabouts via his IP address and his general phone activity, but she would need a warrant to do more. It was time to go in and catch him in the act. She contacted the resort manager and made the arrangements. She would employ another agent who would fit the role of a mark, and together, they would set up the sting. It would be easy.

She approached her colleague's desk with a wink, smiling wryly. "You ready to 'Thelma and Louise' it and catch this witless prick, Glenda? I got us a hot warrant and two tickets to Mexico!"

CHAPTER 84
WASHINGTON, D.C.

Roe had been waiting for what felt like hours at the bench in the brisk wind, his nerves getting the best of him. What if she didn't show? What if she didn't even read the journal, or worse, read it and had no feelings for him in the least? Was he too vain to realize that she had moved on? Over the past week, he had thrown himself into her social media and was fully caught up on the very public details—Casey and Ryder McKinley were amicably divorced, Casey was still doing the talk show while "considering" various acting roles with a new hot-shot agent, and she was seven months pregnant. That was the biggest shock of all when Kathryn had relayed that truth bomb.

As he stared out at the sprawling park, everything seemed to be happening in slow motion. He closed his eyes and remembered the way Casey's smile lit up his world, and how the sound of her laughter filled his heart with joy. He had never stopped thinking of her; never stopped loving her, even after all these years. Nothing else mattered now except knowing if she loved him back.

When he heard footsteps approaching, he turned around and saw Casey walking toward him. He could hardly believe his eyes. She was even more beautiful than he remembered. She was simply glowing. She wore a long floral dress, suede ankle boots, and a denim jacket. Her hair glistened gold in the fading sunlight, long and swirling at her shoulders. And, when she smiled, he felt his heart leap in his chest.

They stood for an awkward beat, staring at one another. Nothing else existed but the two of them.

"Casey," he said, his voice trembling with emotion. "I can't believe you are here. You look amazing."

"You too," she replied, tears brimming in her eyes. "I just—"

Before she could finish her sentence, Roe swept her into his arms, lifting her off the ground and spinning around in a fit of unbridled joy. "You, Casey Singer, are my heart. My everything!" he exclaimed, gently setting her on the ground, being mindful of the baby bump pressing into his midsection. Then, taking her face into his hands, he kissed her gently, savoring the taste of her lips against his. She kissed him back, pulling him in closer. They held each other, oblivious to the world around them.

Roe took a deep breath, inhaling her like a sweet perfume. She did not pull away.

He remembered every moment they'd had together; fragments of time flashing across his mind, making it seem like nothing else that had transpired outside their stolen minutes mattered. He had wondered if he had imagined everything.

There was no doubt in his mind that he was right where he was supposed to be. In her arms, and she, in his.

The two sat down on the bench, clinging to each other, oblivious to the sun setting on the busy park. Roe struggled to find the right words. There was so much to say, so much to ask. But for now, they just sat quietly, taking it all in.

"I've made mistakes, Casey. God knows I have," he finally said, his eyes soft and hopeful. "I have been selfish, and I have been unreliable. I have made you wait. For that, I am so sorry."

Casey turned to look at him, her eyes piercing and genuine.

"I forgive you, Roe. The truth is, I've always loved you. And I never stopped."

With tears in his eyes, Roe slid off the bench onto one knee. Pulling a ring box from his pocket, his eyes fixed on Casey, he whispered, "I love you, Casey Singer. Will you do me the honor of becoming my wife?"

Casey gasped, tears streaming down her face. Then, she swallowed hard and regarded him with fearless vulnerability. "Roe, isn't there something you might want to ask me first?"

He knew what she meant, and it didn't matter. "I don't care if you are carrying Ryder's baby. It makes no difference to me. I love you, and I will love your baby like it's my own."

Casey was stunned, and then she burst into laughter and fresh tears. "That's good, because it is your own. The baby is ours! And yes, Roe, yes, I will marry you!"

They both wept as he slipped the beautiful marquee-cut diamond onto her trembling finger.

As the sun set in a blaze of oranges and pinks, they sat together on the bench, lost in the moment. Roe held Casey in his arms, his heart bursting with joy. Finally, after all these years, he had everything he had ever wanted. She was the missing piece in his life, the one who had always been meant to be his. And now, with their child growing inside her, nothing else mattered except the two of them and the life they were creating together.

She placed her hand on his cheek, and he could feel the warmth of her touch right to his soul.

He leaned in and whispered in her ear, "You are my heart, Casey Singer. I will always love you, until the end of time."

She smiled up at him, and he could see the love in her eyes.

For the first time in as long as he could remember, Roe Evans had everything he'd ever wanted. He knew that he had finally found his home, his sanctuary. He was ready to face whatever life threw their way.

And together, they would conquer the world.

CHAPTER 85
MEXICO

Jake Trainer was oblivious to the female detective eyeing him from the third table.

The place was humming with tourists in resort wear and cover-ups, mulling around like a giddy crowd that had just boarded a cruise ship.

He looked dapper in white linen pants and a matching shirt, rolled up at the sleeves, buttons left open to advertise the manly chest that rippled beneath the gauzy fabric. He reeked of expensive cologne, sported a flashy watch, and his hair was slicked back. His five-o'clock shadow looked perfect on his tan face. He grinned at a middle-aged woman seated two stools away as he caressed a sweaty *cerveza* with provocative strokes of his thumb and forefinger.

She was a plant. But he was too dumb-shit to realize it.

"Like a fly to the web," Ruby Heart said under her breath. She was sitting inconspicuously at a table across from them.

The woman smiled at Jake, drawing him in.

"Hi!" he said over the chatter and the music, Jimmy Buffet streaming from the speakers.

She waved coyly and took a sip of her margarita.

"Are you here by yourself?" he asked, leaning toward her.

"I'm here with my husband. He's playing golf right now."

Jake moved the two stools over to deposit himself next to her. "Oh? So, you're from out of town?"

"East Jersey," she said with the bonafide accent to sell it.

Then he waited. Giving her a look at his biceps as he stretched and yawned like a baboon, he said, "Yeah, sure is hot here. I'm just in for a convention. My name is Ray."

That was it—the code word for his little island business. If the woman told him that her name was Molly, then the connection would be made. "What is your name?"

"I'm Molly," she said shyly.

Bingo! Another fish on the hook! His valet connection at the resort was earning his commission for a healthy stream of referrals. Now, all that was left was to negotiate the terms of the deal. "What are we looking for, Ms. Molly? One hour or two?"

"I think one hour will be fine," she said.

"Seven hundred in American," he said, sizing up her breasts already with his beady eyes.

"Okay. Do you have a room?"

He slid a duplicate key card across the bar over to her glass. "Bungalow 5A."

She palmed the card and smiled. "In about twenty minutes?"

He grinned and tossed a few crumpled bills onto the bar. "I'll be over there now, waiting."

Ruby chuckled. "Yeah, asshole. We'll be waiting too!"

NOT THIRTY MINUTES LATER, **once the transaction of funds had been passed, Ruby and two other cops broke through the lock and entered the room with guns pointed at him. Jake was butt-naked on the bed and in shock as Ms. Molly turned all Ninja-Warrior on his ass and** *Wooted!*

From the doorway, pulling out her badge, Ruby regarded his quickly deflated hard-on with a half-smile. "Gotcha, asshole!"

CHAPTER 86

DECEMBER 2022

Shelly walked into the room, slowly turning toward the silhouette of her beautiful friend standing in the large picture window overlooking the courtyard. It was winter, but an array of blossoms were in bloom—a magnificent collection of white roses, hydrangeas, and gardenias in her stunning bouquet on the coffee table.

Casey's veil fell in a soft cascade along her bare back to the top of her waist, and the train of her sleek, ivory satin wedding gown hugged her curves like a movie star icon.

"*Mi amore!*" Shelly said in awe. "It's time!"

Casey turned and smiled, holding back the tears that spoke more plainly than she ever could. She was breathtaking and beautiful. The shimmering fabric skimmed over her very flat tummy that four solid weeks in the gym had helped her to reclaim—that and breastfeeding.

Shelly leaned in, wrapping Casey's bare shoulders with a faux fur shrug. Then, she sweetly kissed the air on either side of Casey's cheeks.

"Don't you cry, *Chicka* . . . or I will start."

Casey smiled. "Where is he?"

"Right outside the door. Hannah is holding him. That way, I

can stand by your side and watch you marry the man of your heart and your dreams, *Chicka*."

Casey squeezed Shelly's hand.

"Can I just say that the day you called to tell me it was Roe's baby that you were carrying, I had hoped that this little one would be a blessing to you either way, regardless of the circumstances. And *mi bonita*, he turned out to be so much more than that."

Casey nodded, her emotions welling in her shining eyes.

Shelly went on. "You stood up to the challenge, and you did not throw it away or run from it. Casey, you are an amazing young woman who has found her purpose. Finally, I know . . . and seeing you here today, so happy and so complete, is the greatest gift. You realize that, don't you, *Chicka*?"

Casey blinked, fighting another flood of tears. "I do, and it has made every struggle up to this point worth every minute. I was always moving toward the prize."

"Let's go get your prince!" Shelly said.

THE TWO WALKED out onto the stone pavement. A small crowd of close friends and colleagues wearing coats and scarves were seated in white wooden chairs arranged on the lawn. A Chicago outdoor wedding in early December would be no bride's choice, but it was home to Casey, and the weather did not matter. She remembered the day she entered the Cathedral, cold and alone on a gray winter's day so many years ago. It was time to return to the promise of rebirth and renewal. And she knew that her parents were watching over it all.

La Costa beamed from behind a large church hat that matched her navy dress, and Kathryn Delacorte looked stoic and elegant in a siren-red Versace dress and simple pearls enveloped in a full-length white mink fur coat with a matching hat. She had given Casey her "something old"—an exquisite set of vintage diamond earrings that glistened in the sunlight. La Costa had lent Casey her Bible, which the reverend would use for the nuptials. A blue sapphire pendant—the only piece of jewelry that she had from her mother—was tucked into the bodice of her gown. Shelly saw to it and had sewn the treasure herself into the satin. And Hannah was holding the "something new"—Casey's one-month-old son—in her arms.

Everyone turned at the sight of Casey and Shelly, ready for the walk that would change Casey's life forever.

Shelly took her best friend's hand and kissed it. Then she whispered, "Your dad is looking down on you today, *Chicka*. He is so proud!" Casey trembled as she walked tall and purposeful toward the reverend, who was standing beneath an arch, shrouded in white roses. A gust of brisk wind kicked up the veil that danced across Casey's face. She touched the cheek of her son, swaddled in blankets, suckling on his fist in Hannah's arms, and then she walked past Ryder, who smiled and nodded as she passed, on her way to the front, where Roe Evans was standing, waiting to make her his wife.

EPILOGUE
FOUR YEARS LATER

"*That's it for today, my lovelies! Catch you again next week. In the meantime, stay beautiful, and when in doubt—Blonde Up!*" Casey signed off her podcast with the deep satisfaction she felt by truly resonating with her millennial listeners, balancing life, success, and parenthood. One million downloads and counting told her so.

Who would think she would still be going strong with the talk show and living the life of her dreams in a historical colonial just outside of New York City? It suited her just fine. The main thing being it was much closer to the network—and to London for frequent trips to see Roe's daughter, Jane.

Casey was a sensation all right—she was unstoppable, the kind that flew coast to coast to make public appearances, promote her new skincare line, Pretty Sensation, and tackle the current issues of the day on the talk show as well as on her acclaimed podcast. She did this while still fulfilling her favorite role of all, motherhood. They were a family, and being a mom and Roe's adoring wife was what mattered most. She had never been happier.

The only difference was that now, she didn't always do it in heels.

Roe called to her from the deck, "Hey, are ya coming down? I have a little man here who wants to show you what he dug up in the yard!"

Casey ran out barefooted in the grass and scooped her giggling son into her arms. "Roland, you'd better not be getting into my garden! I'm a real pioneer-woman, trying to plant 'taters!"

Roe flipped the burgers on the grill and grinned. "Hey, have I ever told you about the time I survived on canned tuna and moldy bread for two solid weeks in the Yukon?"

Casey rolled her eyes. "Yes, dear. Oh, remember that Regina Madison is stopping by with her daughter, Gael. She and Roland are going to have a play date."

"Okay, sweetheart." He gave her a little kiss on the cheek.

"I think she has something she wants to discuss with me—she mentioned it in her text."

"Well, if it's work-related, shouldn't she run it by your handsome manager?"

Casey wrapped her arms around him from behind. "Of course, dear. We know who runs the show in *this* family!"

Roe's phone buzzed. He closed the grill's lid and said, "Five more minutes on these," and then disappeared into the house.

He checked the screen.

It was Celeste, and it was the fifth call since the day before. He was reluctant to answer it, but he thought better of ignoring it when an accompanying text from her got his attention: *I was recently digging up bones with my dear cousin Louie over one too many Chiantis.* She included the skull emoji, followed by the glass of wine emoji, and a winky face.

His heart skidded—full stop.

He waited an eternity as he watched the word bubble dance on the tiny screen, stop, and then finally deliver the simple text like a bomb: *There are no secrets in this family, dear heart, that cannot be unearthed—and I know where yours are buried!*

ABOUT THE AUTHOR

Jamie Collins writes larger than life fiction about the fast-track world of media and entertainment. As a former model/actress, she infuses her stories with Hollywood grit, sizzle and heat reminiscent of the great women's fiction writers (Collins, Sheldon, and Goldsmith) of decades past on which she cut her writing chops reading and emulating their iconic styles.

Collins brings a fresh, modern-day take on the throwback pocket novel tomes that defined an era of extravagance and excess in exchange for a world where women are more powerful, smart, and driven than ever. Collins's stilettos have been everywhere from nightclubs in Japan, to the Playboy mansion, to dinner with a Sinatra. Her aim is to delight and entertain readers of women's fiction everywhere.

Look for the other books in Jamie Collins' **"Secrets and Stilettos"** series—a behind the scenes look at the competitive, glamorous, and often exploitive world of media and entertainment, available everywhere.

If you enjoyed this book please be sure to take a moment to leave a review where you bought it to help let other readers know about this author and the fun, sexy **"Secrets & Stilettos"** series!

Follow Jamie Collins on Twitter:
https://twitter.com/@novelgirl3

Visit Jamie Collins on Facebook:
https://www.facebook.com/JamieCollinsAuthor

Check out Jamie Collins' feed on Instagram:
https://www.instagram.com/jamie.collins3

Head over to Jamie's website for contact and other information
at: **www.jamiecollinsauthor.com**

ALSO BY JAMIE COLLINS

Sign up for the author's New Releases mailing list and get a FREE copy of the series novelette, *Sign On!* (The Casting of the Ladies of The Gab -- Secrets and Stilettos Prequel)

Head to Jamie Collins' website for links to the next books in the series:

www.jamiecollinsauthor.com